The Aftermath

Tamera Lynn Kraft

Ladies of Oberlin Series, Book 3

www.MtZionRidgePress.com

Mt Zion Ridge Press LLC
295 Gum Springs Rd, NW
Georgetown, TN 37366

https://www.mtzionridgepress.com

ISBN 13: 978-1-962862-56-1
Published in the United States of America
Publication Date: January 15, 2025

Copyright: © 2025 Tamera Lynn Kraft

Editor-In-Chief: Michelle Levigne
Executive Editor: Tamera Lynn Kraft

Cover art design by Tamera Lynn Kraft
Cover Art Copyright by Mt Zion Ridge Press LLC © 2025

All rights reserved. No portion of this book may be reproduced or transmitted in any form or by any electronic or mechanical means, including photocopying, recording or by any information retrieval and storage system without permission of the publisher.
Ebooks, audiobooks, and print books are *not* transferrable, either in whole or in part. As the purchaser or otherwise *lawful* recipient of this book, you have the right to enjoy the novel on your own computer or other device. Further distribution, copying, sharing, gifting or uploading is illegal and violates United States Copyright laws.
Pirating of books is illegal. Criminal Copyright Infringement, *including* infringement without monetary gain, may be investigated by the Federal Bureau of Investigation and is punishable by up to five years in federal prison and a fine of up to $250,000.
Names, characters and incidents depicted in this book are products of the author's imagination, or are used in a fictitious situation. Any resemblances to actual events, locations, organizations, incidents or persons – living or dead – are coincidental and beyond the intent of the author.

Scripture quotations from The Authorized (King James) Version. Rights in the Authorized Version in the United Kingdom are vested in the Crown. Reproduced by permission of the Crown's patentee, Cambridge University Press

Dedication:

I dedicate this book to my godly husband who changed his life when he surrendered it to the Lord. I also dedicate it to my partner and friend, Michelle Levigne, who wouldn't leave me alone until I wrote this story.

I also want to thank the Wellington Spirit of '76 Museum and its project manager, Scott Markel for all of his help.

Author Notes:

Wellington, Ohio is a real place and many of the events and places in this story are real, but the characters and a few of the events and places are fictional. Wellington was in the center of the temperance and suffrage movements when crime and alcoholism became rampant after the cheese factories opened and men from all over moved there for work.

Prologue

November 1863
Chattanooga, Tennessee

Nate Teagan woke in worse pain than he'd ever known. A blanket had been pulled up to his neck, and he lay on the floor next to the fireplace in a cabin that had been turned into an infirmary for wounded soldiers. At the moment, he was the only one there. Even though the fire was blazing, he still shivered from the cold. He let out a groan, but in a way, the pain in his right leg was comforting. He had been afraid they would amputate.

The Ohio Seventh Regiment doctor knelt beside him and gave him a spoon full of horrible tasting medicine. As soon as Nate swallowed it, the doctor darted outside before he could call out to him. A moan rose in his throat. It hurt so bad. He gritted his teeth and tried to focus. He closed his eyes for a moment.

When he opened them again, his wife, Betsy, was holding his hand. She looked as beautiful as the day he left her. He shook his head and looked away. It couldn't be her. She was still in Cleveland, Ohio where he'd said goodbye when he enlisted. That was when she had told him if he left, she'd never be his wife again.

"Am I dreaming?"

"Nate." Betsy squeezed his hand, her blue eyes shining with a glint he'd never seen before.

"You can't be here. Did they give me too much morphine?"

She shrugged. "You're not hallucinating. I joined the Army Nursing Corp"

"But you couldn't... how did you get here?"

Betsy smoothed out her skirt. She wasn't wearing her normal fancy dress with a large, hooped skirt. Instead, she wore a blue nurse's uniform with a white apron and bonnet. "The train, silly. I took the train from Cleveland to Columbus to Indiana, to Louisville, to Nashville, to Dayton. Then I had to walk the rest of the way if you can imagine that. Anyway, I finally made it."

"But it's too dangerous for you to be here."

The dimple on her cheek deepened. "I go where you go. You're not going to shut me out ever again."

Nate bit his lip as another wave of pain shot up his leg. He took a few shallow breaths before he could continue. "Why would you do something so foolish as joining the nursing corp? You could be hurt or killed."

"Horsefeathers. Anyone would think you aren't happy to see me. I told you before, I'm stronger than you think I am."

He let out a heavy sigh. His wife had to be the most exasperating woman he'd ever known. "You shouldn't have come."

"Drink this. It will help with the pain." She gave him some powder in a cup of water and held it up to his lips. "It will start to work in about fifteen minutes, but before you fall asleep again, I need to tell you something. Dr. Patella gave me permission to be the one."

He lifted an eyebrow.

She kissed him long and deeply, the way he'd dreamed about so many times. "You're alive and you're going to be all right. That's all that matters." She paused and grabbed hold of his hand. "They had to amputate."

"No, they couldn't have. It's still there. I feel the pain." He pulled his hand away from her, pushed the covers aside, and stared at the bandaged stump where his leg used to be.

A muted scream came from deep inside as his whole body quaked. "You let them do this! You let them take my leg? How could you?"

"Hush now," Betsy said in a calming voice, almost like she would use with a wounded animal. "It's not the end of the world. I'll nurse you back to health in no time."

"I'm not going to get better," he said through gritted teeth. "Do you think I'm going to magically grow my leg back, and we'll live happily ever after? You need to grow up."

She pressed her lips together and looked down. "I have grown up." She said it so quietly he could barely hear.

A strange look he'd never seen covered her face as she glared at him. She seemed more confident, as if she could conquer the world. "Looks to me like you're the one who needs to grow up. So, life didn't go as we planned. None of this took God by surprise. You're my husband and losing a leg doesn't change that. I told you in that letter, you're stuck with me no matter what." Her gestures became more animated, even her curls bounced. "Did you think I'd stand by you when I thought you were a deserter and a traitor and make it through all that nursing training, traipsing halfway across the country and enemy lines trying to find you, just to leave because you're feeling sorry for yourself?" She jabbed him in the chest. "I'm. Not. Going. Anywhere."

A knot formed in his stomach. "It won't last. You didn't stay when I wanted to rescue slaves or when I decided to go to war."

Her chin trembled.

Nate needed to finish it no matter how much it hurt her — and him. It was better she left him now than wait until things got too tough for her.

"Let's face it, Sweetheart. I married a rich little princess whose daddy let her do whatever she wanted. You're not equipped to handle a man who can't even walk. Why don't you go back to your daddy where you belong? He'll take you back when he finds out I'm out of the picture."

Betsy dabbed the tears off her face, but she didn't look away. "The only way I'm leaving is if you throw me out. That will be rather difficult with only one leg."

Nate opened his mouth to say something, but no words came. Lethargy overtook him. He turned toward the fireplace, afraid that when he woke, she'd be gone.

Chapter One

Wellington, Ohio, 10 miles south of Oberlin
March 1, 1870

Betsy woke to screams again. She shook her husband, Nate, until he quieted. His forehead wet with perspiration, he trembled under her touch.

She pulled him close. "Shhh, there, there. Everything's all right."

These nightmares were a frequent occurrence happening at least once a week. Hopefully, this time, it wouldn't disturb the children.

"I'm sorry. I..." He lay there a few moments, his sky-blue eyes wide with fear, until his breath grew more even. He let out a sigh and looked at the wind-up alarm clock setting on the bed table. "Might as well get up."

She shivered and scooted to the side of the bed. The chill convinced her it had snowed during the night. After lighting the lantern, she wrapped her robe around herself. "I'll start a fire going in the stove and make some breakfast. You have a big day today." The vents coming from the stove would heat the bedrooms before the children awoke.

He grabbed hold of the iron bedframe to pull himself to a sitting position and out from under their down comforter. With one of his legs missing, this was the easiest way to get up in the morning. He heaved himself up with the crutches leaning against the wall, hobbled to the matching blue flowered basin and pitcher sitting on a small round table in the corner of the room, and washed up. Pulling his trousers off the hook by the door, he sat in the wooden chair and began dressing by first pulling on a clean sock large enough to fit over his stump. Betsy had knitted it for him because she couldn't find a sock large enough to protect it from chafing. Then he grabbed his trousers with one leg pinned up so it wouldn't get in the way of the crutches.

"Aren't you going to wear your leg today?" She pointed to the wood and leather artificial leg leaning against the wall next to the chair. The war department had supplied one to every soldier who lost a leg during the war, every Union soldier. At first, he was grateful for the leg and had almost been to the point where he didn't need his crutches, but he hadn't worn it in a year.

He let out a heavy sigh. "It rubs me raw. I get around better with crutches."

"Dr. Clark said you can't start and stop like this, or it won't do any good."

"What's wrong? Embarrassed to be seen with a one-legged cripple?"

She bit the inside of her cheek to hold back the words she wanted to say. His hurtful words came more often lately, but she tried to remind herself, he didn't really mean it. He had been devastated by the loss of his leg. If she were patient and loving, someday he'd be able to move on from it.

After pouring water in the basin on their washstand, she finally trusted herself enough to speak without a sarcastic tone in her voice. "I'm only thinking of you. Besides, you'll want to look your best at the job interview with Mr. Hayes."

Nate grabbed the artificial leg. "You're right. I'll wear the blasted thing."

Betsy raised an eyebrow.

He plopped in the chair and groaned. "I know. I shouldn't use that language, but you don't know how hard it is to be a cripple."

She might not know what it was like to be a cripple, but she sure knew what it was like to be the wife of a man who couldn't get over the war... or his injury. He spent most of his time feeling sorry for himself. He still attended church, but frequently used language not fit to speak and, many times, would find comfort in a whiskey bottle. She disapproved but nagging him about it always made things worse.

She bit her lower lip and washed up in the basin.

He'd always wanted to be a lawyer so he could help those who were treated unjustly, but now he seemed to have no interest in it. When she told him about Mr. Hayes wanting to hire another lawyer, she was afraid he wouldn't apply, but he shined to the idea. He even set up this appointment and asked his boss to allow him to take the day off. Maybe working as a lawyer would give him a sense of purpose that he'd lost.

He might even stop visiting the saloon.

She laid her undergarments and gold dress out on the bed. "After I get dressed, I'll fix breakfast. How about some eggs, bacon, and biscuits?"

"You don't have to. Toast will be fine."

"Not on your big day. You need a hearty meal."

Nate fastened the leg strap, and unpinned the trouser leg, then paused before slipping on his trousers. He swiped his hand across the back of his neck. "I want this so bad, Betsy." His voice cracked. "I need... I need to feel like I'm doing something useful, something important."

Lord, please let him get this job. It wasn't the first time she'd asked God to grant this request. He couldn't take another disappointment. "It's going to be fine. You're an Oberlin College graduate and a war hero. Now that you have your law license, Mr. Hayes would be foolish not to hire you."

"Foolish, huh?" Nate flashed the grin that made her heart thump in her chest, the dimpled smile she hadn't seen in a long time. "I can always count on you to look on the bright side." He kissed her on the cheek.

"There's no other way to look at it." Betsy dressed quickly. She'd always used to dress in the latest fashion, even for everyday wear, but since she'd become a housewife with two young children, a day dress was more practical. She did sew small bustles into the back of her skirts. No need to be too drab. She also sewed the skirts wide enough to expand when she was in the family way.

The new blue satin dress she'd stitched a few months ago with a large bustle in the back was saved for church and special occasions. It had lace on the sleeves, and white braiding around the edge of the high neckline with a bonnet to match. It was vain and impractical and wouldn't leave much room to grow when she had another baby, but she loved it. She'd found the pattern for the fashionable dress in *Godey's Lady's Magazine* she'd bought at Baldwin General Store.

Nate gave his permission to buy the material and notions, and she'd spent weeks making it. She'd even had enough left over to sew a church dress for Naomi. She'd change into that outfit before he got home to celebrate his new position as a lawyer. At least she hoped it would be a celebration.

She tied on her brown linen apron that protected her gold dress from getting soiled while she worked. "Since the cheese factory opened two years ago, Wellington is growing faster than ever. At the temperance meeting, Mrs. Hayes said that with the increased population, her husband is always complaining about having more work than he can handle."

Nate buttoned his shirt. "I wish you'd quit going to those."

"You didn't forbid it, and I said I'd think about it if you would stop going to the saloon. You didn't, so I didn't. Besides, I never would have known Mr. Hayes was hiring if I had quit."

He pulled on his vest and buttoned it. "I know. You've told me this before."

Betsy tried to give him a warm smile. "I was just reminding you."

"Once I become the lawyer I was meant to be, I won't ever have to work at that telegraph office again." He slipped on his Sunday black wool morning coat. "Things will be different. I'll stop drinking and I'll be home on time every night like you want. You'll see."

She started toward the kitchen of their two-story house on Clay Street, a few blocks from the telegraph office at the railroad depot where Nate worked. Every day, he walked along the railroad tracks to get there, the fastest route, but with the uneven ground he had to navigate, it still took him over a half hour. They had a horse and wagon, but Nate said it took too long to hitch the horse to the buckboard when they lived that close. "It feels like snow. You should take the wagon today."

"I might." He looked in the small mirror attached to the dressing table and tied his necktie with a four in hand knot. "I wouldn't want to slip in the snow on the way to such an important interview."

Maybe she was worrying too much. Mr. Hayes would hire him. Everything would be better then.

He grabbed his crutches. The thumping they made against the wooden floor followed her past the staircase into the kitchen. The doctor had told him that if he'd wear the leg all the time, he could get rid of the crutches for good, but he didn't listen. He never listened to anyone anymore.

The kitchen wasn't affluent, but it was nice enough. It had an indoor pump and sink, large floor floor-to-ceiling cupboards, and a nice wooden table in the middle of the room. On the sides of the table were benches, and each end had a wooden Shaker chair. The stove put out enough heat to keep the kitchen toasty, and with vents going to every room, it kept the entire house warm, even in the middle of winter. It was so much nicer than trying to keep a fireplace going in every room like she used to do in their home in Cleveland before the war. A door opened to the back yard as well as the door to the front porch, and its greatest feature was a three-by-six-pane window that provided plenty of light during the day. She could look out that window over the indoor pump and basin while the children were playing outside.

She stared out the window now. The sun had not yet begun to rise, and all she could see was darkness. When the moon was full, it would reflect off the snow, but not now. No moon. Clouds obscuring the stars. Always darkest before the dawn. She hoped so.

He took hold of her hand, pulled her from the window, and took her in his arms. "There's nobody in town better educated or more qualified." He kissed her gently then pulled back. "I'll get the job, you'll see. Unless Mr. Hayes has something against cripples."

Her stomach tightened. "I'm sure you will."

~~~~~

That afternoon, Betsy paced her kitchen floor. What was taking her husband so long? The interview should have ended hours ago. Maybe Mr. Hayes was putting Nate right to work. That was why he was late.

She let up a prayer and went to the stove to stir the stew she'd planned for supper. Beef stew with potatoes and carrots was his favorite. No matter the news, a full stomach would make things better. At least, that was what a Godey's article she'd read said. She'd also changed into her blue silk dress in case the news called for a celebration.

Four-year-old Malachi chased his younger sister, Naomi, through the kitchen with giggles filling the air. Both children had her blond curls and Nate's blue eyes and firm chin. Naomi brushed past the bench, and when Malachi grabbed her, the chair at the head of the table fell over.

The Aftermath

"Children!"

Naomi pushed out her lower lip at the scolding.

"Sorry, Mama." Malachi tried to pick up the chair.

Betsy let out a breath. They were only playing. They didn't mean any harm. She tousled Naomi's blond curls and leaned down to hug her son. "Why don't you take your sister outside to play while I cook dinner? You can make a snowman."

Both children grabbed their coats, scarves, mittens, and boots and ran to the door.

Betsy buttoned their coats and helped them put on their scarves, hats, and mittens. "Stay in the backyard where I can call for you. And don't go by the railroad tracks."

"Yes, Mama," Malachi said as the door slammed shut.

She watched out the window into the backyard until she was sure they weren't anywhere near the tracks. Last summer, she had fussed at Nate to build a picket fence on the edge of their property to keep the children from danger, but he didn't see the need. Those tracks worried her, but she couldn't very well keep them from playing outside. Instead, she would remind them every time they were out there and would check on them through the window every few minutes.

She went back to kneading her bread when the door opened again. "What is it this time?" She turned and saw it wasn't her children. Nate was home. As he removed his brown double-breasted overcoat and scarf and hung them on the hook inside the door, his stoic chin and furrowed brow told her all she needed to know.

"He didn't hire you." It was a statement, not a question.

His shoulders slumped, and he pulled off his gloves and tie. "No." He hobbled to the table in the center of the room, propped his crutches on it, and sank onto his chair. He pulled his wide trouser leg up, removing his false leg and throwing it on the floor beside him, then pinned the leg up and folded his arms on the table.

She put her hand on his shoulder. "Why? You were in the top of your class at Oberlin. You have your license. Why wouldn't Mr. Hayes hire you?"

He lifted his head and glared at her. "Why do you think?" He pointed to his missing leg. "That's why."

"Surely not. There must be another reason. What did he say?"

"He said he was sorry, but a man with one leg wouldn't be able to hold the attention of a jury or a judge, let alone persuade them with verbal arguments. He told me a lawyer must have self-assurance about him, and no matter how qualified I am, he can't use me. He offered me a position as his law clerk for half of what I make now. When I refused, he said I have a good job at the telegraph office, and I should be grateful. Grateful?"

He kneaded the back of his neck. "Anyone could be a telegraph operator. All you have to do is learn Morse code." He pointed to his stump. "Maybe it is the right job for me. Even a cripple could do it." He rested his head in his arms, and a sob escaped his lips.

"Horsefeathers." She glanced at the children through the window then sat beside him. "We still have money saved up from both of our salaries during the war, not to mention your inheritance from your father. You could open your own law office and show everyone in town how valuable you are."

Nate grabbed his crutches, stood, and paced a couple of steps toward the door and back, then banged his fist on the table.

She startled. It wasn't like her husband to be physical when he got angry, even if his words had become harsh. After what happened with her sister, even him pounding on the table caused her heart to race. "You'll feel better after you've had something to eat. You'll see the sense in what I'm saying."

"They don't want a cripple. I'm half a man. Why can't you get that through your head and leave me alone?" He grabbed his overcoat and headed for the door.

Betsy ran to it and blocked his exit. "Please, don't go. Supper's almost ready."

He stepped closer to her and put his face within inches of hers. "Get out of my way, woman."

A twinge of fear ran up her spine. She moved away, and he slammed the door as he left. The next time she saw him, he would be drunk. She picked the artificial leg up off the floor and sat at the table, her eyes burning from unshed tears. *Lord, help me.*

Chapter Two

Nate sat at one of a handful tables, each lit only by one candle at each table in the dark saloon made from rough-hewn logs. The small fireplace wasn't enough to keep the chill out of the air, and he blew into his hands to warm them. There were no windows. Only the swinging doors and the glow from the fire let in light, although the shadows they produced made the room murky, especially now that the sun was almost set. Just as well. Men didn't come here to socialize. They came to drink.

Nancy, a scantily dressed barmaid, came over to him. She didn't try to flirt like she did with the other men. She knew from the other times he'd been here he wasn't interested. All he wanted was to get drunk enough to numb the pain of being so worthless.

"Whiskey," he said. "Bring the bottle."

She nodded and went to do his bidding then came back with the whiskey.

Doug Hanson, a big, burly man with an unkempt reddish-brown beard, bushy sideburns, and hair that had not seen a barber for a long time, came over and sat at his table. Probably wanted him to share his bottle. The man worked at the Horr Cheese House, and when he wasn't at work, he was here.

Not like Nate. He limited his visits to the saloon to no more than three times a week, except when something horrific had happened, like today. He always did a hard day's work and supported his family even if the job was not what he wanted. At least he wasn't a total scoundrel. Although he did have to admit the way he acted toward Betsy tonight was shameful, but that was only because he was angry about not getting the job. He wouldn't normally act that way.

"I didn't invite you." Nate poured some whiskey in his glass and gulped it down.

"I heard what happened." Doug reached for the bottle and poured some of Nate's whiskey into his glass. "So, the high and mighty Mr. Hayes sent you on your way."

Apparently, the news was all over the village. "None of your concern." Hayes's secretary no doubt. Everyone knew Millie was the biggest gossip in Wellington, and her husband worked at the cheese factory and was just as eager to share news with the men he worked with.

He pulled the bottle back to his side of the table and poured another drink. This time he kept his hand around it so nobody could grab it.

Doug chuckled. "So, what did your wife say? She get all teary-eyed and nagging when you didn't get the job?"

A lump formed in Nate's throat. She'd been wonderful, and all he did was yell at her and abscond without even touching the dinner she'd made for him. She didn't deserve that. Worse yet, he'd never seen Betsy afraid of him before. The fear in her eyes shook him to the core. "My wife is none of your concern."

"If it were my wife, she'd know better than to sass me, but you and your friend, Marshal Cage," he said the name with disgust in his tone, "treat your women like they wear the pants. Women need to know their place." Doug reached for the bottle again.

Nate pulled it closer, out of the man's reach. "I didn't ask you to sit here or to drink my whiskey. I sure didn't ask for your opinion about my wife or my friend. Now skedaddle or, cripple or not, I'll give you a whooping you won't soon forget."

Doug held his hands out and chuckled again, low and rumbly from within. "Just trying to help." He got up and went back to his usual table.

Nate stroked his beard. An image of Betsy in her blue satin dress haunted him, her eyes damp and lips trembling as he yelled at her. She must have dressed up just for him, and if he wasn't mistaken, he'd smelled beef stew. She'd cooked his favorite meal.

He was a horrible husband. Maybe not as bad as Hanson, but he wasn't what she deserved. She was sensitive to him getting angry and showing it by banging his fist against the table or slamming a door ever since her sister died at the hands of her abusive husband a year ago. Even though he would never lay a hand on her, he knew it bothered her, but he did that very thing anyway. He wanted to kick himself. Instead, he took another drink. Then another.

If he were smart, he'd go home and beg Betsy's forgiveness. Just as well. He was a worthless human being. Betsy ought to take the children and go to live with her folks in Philadelphia. Since he lost his leg, she kept saying she wouldn't leave him, that she meant her marriage vows, but maybe it would be better for her and the children if she did.

If he had the courage, he'd do what was best and leave her, but he loved her too much. He couldn't face living without her.

~~~~~

When Nate had come home drunk in the middle of the night, Betsy pretended she was asleep. He didn't wake her. He just wound up the clock, took off his trousers, and climbed into bed. He didn't even bother to take off his dress shirt or put on his nightshirt. She smelled the liquor on him, and it took forever for her to get back to sleep.

This morning, she slept through the alarm bell, and he didn't wake her. Now that she'd fed the children breakfast and sent them upstairs to play, she sat at the table and prayed.

"God, what am I going to do?"

She tried to see Nate's side of things. He'd had a shock when Mr. Hayes said he couldn't hire him because of his leg. Of course, he was tempted to drink. He was a proud man. That didn't excuse all the other times, but it did explain him being so angry.

A knock sounded on the door. Lavena. A small woman with dark eyes and an olive complexion, she had been one of Betsy's roommates when she attended Oberlin College. They had been best friends ever since, even rooming together in a small apartment in Cleveland when Nate was away during the war. She'd forgotten all about agreeing to watch her friend's daughter today. She opened the door and let Lavena and little Penelope in.

"Thanks for taking care of her." Her friend rushed inside. "*The Wellington Enterprise* is excited about me covering the speech at Oberlin today. I should be home before supper." Lavena paused and gazed at Betsy, a knowing look in her eyes. She removed her dark blue cloak. "Penelope, give Mama a kiss, and go upstairs to play with Naomi and Malachi."

The four-year-old girl, with her mother's olive complexion and big brown eyes, did as she was told.

Lavena turned to Betsy. "Why don't you fix us a cup of tea and tell me what's wrong?"

Dear sweet Lavena. They were nothing alike. Betsy had blond curls and tried to keep up with the latest fashion. All she'd ever wanted in life was to become a wife and a mother. Lavena, on the other hand, liked to dress practically, sometimes even shocking people by wearing pantaloons instead of skirts, and she never wore a corset.

Today, Lavena dressed conservatively with a white blouse and a plain straight skirt with no bustle, navy-blue to match her cloak, the outfit she wore to church and when she was reporting on a story. Her hair was in its usual braid that came out the back of her matching navy-blue bonnet. No feathers, beading or ruffles of any kind.

She'd been involved with the abolition movement and the suffrage movement as well as other movements since graduating and had used her journalism skills to further the causes. She even was a war correspondent traveling with the Ohio Seventh Regiment during the war.

When they were in college, she claimed she would never marry. Instead, she'd pursue a career in journalism and do what she could to further rights for women. That all changed when she'd met and married Nate's regiment captain, Cage Jones, during the war. Her pursuit of a career in journalism never went away, but since Penelope was born, she stopped working a full day every day. *The Wellington Enterprise* gave her assignments from time to time, and Cage, now the marshal of Wellington, not only gave her his blessing but encouraged her. Betsy was happy to watch Penelope at least once or twice a week. She would do anything for her friend, and the children loved having their playmate around.

"So, what is the lecture about today?" Betsy placed a tea kettle onto the stove to heat.

"Dr. Fairchild will be speaking on his view of women having the right to vote. Some of the women at the college have come out against women's suffrage, but I know if the president of Oberlin speaks in favor of it, it will have a lasting effect on the movement. Mr. Guthrie, the publisher of the newspaper, is allowing me to do a front-page article."

Betsy steeped some Lapsang Souchong tea in a porcelain teapot Lavena had given her as a wedding gift. It was her friend's favorite brew. When they'd attended Oberlin College, President Finney encouraged an austere lifestyle including no alcohol, coffee, tea, or tobacco, but Lavena always said that they went too far banning tea, and Betsy had to agree. After the tea was poured, they sat at the table, and Betsy poured out her heartbreak as easily as she'd poured the tea.

"Nate goes to the saloon three or four times a week now. At first, he said the whiskey helped the pain in his leg, so I tried to ignore it."

Lavena raised an eyebrow. "I know some Christians claim it's not a sin to have an occasional drink, but we graduated from Oberlin. You and Nate both never believed drinking alcohol was acceptable before."

"I know, but if I nagged, it would only get worse. I tried to be a good wife and keep it to myself, but now, I never know if he'll be on time for supper or show up hours later, staggering home intoxicated and smelling of liquor. What am I going to do?" Betsy dabbed her eyes with her yellow embroidered handkerchief that matched her skirt.

"I'll tell you what you're not going to do." Lavena poured some tea into her saucer to cool it then drank it. "You're not going to sit here like a shrinking violet and let Nate go to ruin. Aren't you the one who became a nurse and traveled to Chattanooga during the war to make sure your husband was all right?"

"That was different," Betsy said. "When I heard Nate had deserted, I had to find out what was going on. I knew it wasn't true."

"And if he had deserted, if he hadn't been a spy for the Union Army, would you have still fought to save him?"

Betsy shrugged. "I had determined to save my marriage."

"Then you nursed him back to health after he was shot and lost his leg."

Betsy nodded. "So, why are you bringing all this up? That was a long time ago."

"Find the fortitude to help him now like you did back then. I know you have it in you."

She blinked. "What can I do about this? I've begged Nate to stop drinking. I've encouraged him to open a law office. He's not listening to me."

Lavena gave her a half-grin. "You belong to the Wellington Temperance Society, don't you?"

"Yes, Reverend Fowler's wife invited me. We have meetings once a month at the church."

"What do you do at those meetings?"

"We pray, and we discuss how to get more men to sign the pledge to not drink."

Lavena crossed her arms. "That's all?"

Betsy started to take a sip of tea, but it was too hot, so she poured a little into her saucer and sipped it. "What else is there?"

"You need to do more if you want to save Nate and the other men who frequent the saloon. You should have meetings every week. I'm sure there are other women who wish their husbands would stop drinking. Why don't you invite them to the next meeting?"

"I don't know. Nate is already irritated about me being involved with the temperance movement. He would be furious if I stirred things up."

Lavena set her teacup down. "Has he forbidden you?"

"No, but he doesn't like it. I told him I would quit if he'd stop drinking."

"There you have it. You battled for him during the war. Now it's time to battle again. It's time to step up and save your husband from his vices. You know Cage and I will do everything we can to help."

Betsy poured tea into her saucer to cool it. Was it possible? Could she help her husband sober up and be the man of God he was before the war? She shook her head. "No, this isn't a good idea. He doesn't visit the saloon every night. It's not like he's a full-fledged drunk. He says it helps with the pain."

Lavena sipped some tea. "If it was really because of the pain, why doesn't he ask the doctor for something?"

Betsy didn't have an answer for that. As a former nurse, she knew of dozens of new medicines that were effective to curb pain, but many of them were as addictive as whiskey and caused more harm than good. "I'm not going to be one of those women who stand in front of a saloon carrying signs and singing hymns while my husband is inside getting drunk. It would be humiliating. The whole town would know."

Lavena propped her chin on her hands and gazed at her.

"Besides, First Peter says wives should submit to their husbands if they want to win them to the Lord." She wasn't about to become the rebel her friend was. "I'll pray and ask God to bring my husband back to his senses."

"Prayer is a good start, but sometimes God requires more than prayer."

Chapter Three

The more Lavena listened to President Fairchild's speech, the more her pulse raced. The man had lost his wits. That was the only explanation she had for what he was saying. If she hadn't been on assignment to do a story about his speech, she would have walked out. Instead, she continued writing on her notepad, using the shorthand she'd learned, trying to get every word so she could quote him correctly.

When he said the vote would weaken family ties and cause husbands and wives to think only of their individual rights instead of joining together in unity, she wanted to stand up and shout that she and her husband were unified in the belief that women should have the right to vote and that her daughter's future depended on it.

Instead, she pressed her lips together, pushed down the lever to fill her fountain pen with more ink, and furiously scribbled on her paper.

As soon as the speech was over, she strode out of the church, carrying her lap desk where she kept her papers, fountain pens, and ink. She walked around the block to try to calm down. It had snowed the day before and a light dusting covered the grass, so the chill in the air helped with that. She was so heated from what President Fairchild had said that she had sweat beading on her forehead. With her gloved hands, she wiped snow off a bench on the campus grounds, opened her lap desk, and took out the supplies she needed to write out her report on the speech. As angry as she was, she had a job to do. She tried to portray what he said correctly and without commentary.

After she was done, she wrote an editorial saying that she, a former female student, was distressed by how President Fairchild had abandoned the principles of the founders of Oberlin College where men and women earned college degrees together for the furthering of the Kingdom of God. Fairchild had turned away from the good sense of the last president, Father Charles Finney. She smiled at herself as she read it over for mistakes. It was a well-written commentary she hoped would be published in more newspapers than *The Wellington Enterprise*. She'd ask Mr. Guthrie if she could also send it to the *Cleveland Banner* and *Harper's Weekly*. After all, *Harper's Weekly* often published her articles during the war.

She also included two events that would take place for those who supported women's suffrage. The first would be a meeting of the newly formed Women's Suffrage Association at Oberlin First Church on April 29th. Mary Ashton Rice Livermore, a journalist and hero of Lavena's, would be speaking. The second would be a march in Elyria in early May that Lavena planned to take part in.

After finishing the articles and gathering her supplies into her lap desk and fastening it, she prayed. *Lord, let my articles be a beacon of light for this movement, and help Betsy regain the fortitude she once had to fight for her husband.*

The sun had peeked out and warmed her. It would melt the snow if it continued, but she'd been through too many Ohio winters to believe this would last. The snow and the cold would continue a while longer.

She climbed aboard her buggy and headed to the newspaper office in Wellington. She was sure Mr. Guthrie would want a series of articles on the subject since he supported women's suffrage along with many other just causes.

These pieces had to change the minds of men in this nation, maybe even the new Oberlin president. Her daughter was the only child she and Cage would ever have, and she didn't want her to grow up in a society that oppressed women. A knot formed in her stomach as she lifted her eyes toward Heaven. *I'm doing my part.*

~~~~~

Nate waited for Johnny to arrive to deliver the telegrams he'd transcribed. Johnny was Doug Hanson's oldest son. At fourteen, he was short and scrawny enough that he looked more like ten. He'd dropped out of school when he was nine to get work and help his mother buy food for his eight younger brothers and sisters. Until he got the job at the grocery store and delivering telegrams, he used to work at the steam mill, a dangerous job for a child.

Nate was the one who talked Mr. Wilson into hiring him. It was too dangerous for children to work at mills and factories, and they were paid very little. Nate glanced at his stump. If he hadn't been a cripple, he would do something to change the law to keep children out of those factories.

Twice a day, Johnnie would drop by the telegraph shop and pick up any telegrams that needed delivered. He didn't earn much for the deliveries, but with what he earned as a stockboy at Baldwin's General Store, he was able to make more than he was paid at the mill to help his family.

A shiver went through Nate. The telegraph office was a small room with a very small stove and scuttle in the corner that barely kept it warm enough on cold days like today. Behind the counter there was only enough room for a small desk and chair. There was so little space in front of the counter that when the door opened, it hit against it. Barely enough room for a customer to stand behind the counter. With no windows and such a small space, it became stifling at times, and the small lantern barely gave enough light to see. When summer came, it would be so hot that Nate would prop the door open and keep a small basin of water nearby to dampen a cloth and place it behind his neck.

The office was next to the train depot by the railroad tracks near the center of town because most of the telegrams were about train arrivals, departures, and hazards on the tracks. It had to be manned twenty-four hours a day, Monday through Saturday, to forward messages along the line, or there was a danger of calamity on the tracks. At least, trains didn't run through Wellington on Sundays. Nate was one of three operators who worked at different times. In the morning at six, he relieved Sam Shaffer, a scrawny older man with gray hair and glasses. He would leave at two o'clock when James Piper, the operator who relieved him in the afternoon and evening, arrived. As Wellington grew, the office received enough telegrams to need a delivery boy like Johnny.

The real reason Nate was anxious had nothing to do with the boy being a few minutes late or the poor working conditions. He felt horrible about the way he had treated Betsy. When he got home the night before, she was asleep, so he couldn't apologize and make things right. Even if she had been awake, would he have wanted to make amends when he was so staggering drunk? Probably not.

Normally she would rise and make him breakfast before work, even though he left before dawn. It was so considerate of her. She would even rise if she'd been up with one of the children in the middle of the night, but this morning, she had stayed in bed. He doubted she was sleeping. She probably didn't want to face him. He didn't blame her.

When he got home this afternoon, he would make up for everything. He would beg her forgiveness and promise to stop going to the saloon. Even if he had to work at the telegraph office for the rest of his life, it would be worth it to make her happy. Besides, he was a cripple. He was lucky to have a wife like her.

It was almost two before Johnnie came through the door, his eyes downcast and shoulders slumped. He walked in slowly and slightly hunched. "Good day, Mr. Teagan. Do you have anything for me to deliver?"

Nate grabbed the telegrams. "What's wrong, Johnnie?"

"Nothing. Just some stuff at home."

Nate set his hand on Johnnie's shoulder, and the boy winced. "You hurting? What happened?"

"It's nothing. My Pa lost his job at the cheese factory is all. I shouldn't have sassed him."

An ache formed at the back of Nate's throat. It was easy to deduce what Johnnie left out. "So, was he drinking on the job?"

The boy nodded but wouldn't look up.

"He beat you?"

"It was my fault. Pa was yelling at Ma and shaking his fist in her face. Ma started crying, and I got in front of her and told him to leave her alone."

Nate lifted Johnnie's shirt and gasped. This wasn't a normal beating with a switch or a belt. There wasn't one place on his skin that wasn't bruised. Some places were scabbed over where the skin had broken. It looked like the backs of some of the slaves he had rescued before the war. The chill in the office suddenly turned warm. "Did he use a horsewhip on you?"

Johnnie pulled away, but Nate grabbed his wrist. "As soon as my replacement gets here, you're coming with me."

"But... I... I have to get the telegrams delivered."

"Don't worry about that. I'll deliver them."

James, a tall young man barely old enough to grow a beard, entered the office. Nate waved to him and escorted Johnnie outside. He started walking as fast as he could with his crutches.

Johnnie hurried to keep up. "Where are we going?"

Nate didn't answer. He was afraid if he told the boy, he'd resist coming along. They crossed the railroad tracks, went down Railroad Street for a block, and turned on Main Street, passing a dozen businesses, then turned on Dickson and walked a block before reaching the jail and the marshal's office. He entered the building and opened the door to the office. "Go on inside, boy."

Johnnie shuffled in.

Marshal Cage Jones, a rugged, dark-haired man with scars running down his cheek and chin, wore a badge on his chest and sat at his desk pouring over wanted posters. The man had been Nate's closest friend since they served together in the Ohio Seventh Regiment during the war.

When Cage saw Nate, he grinned. "I didn't expect to see you here." He glanced at the boy, and his smile slipped. "What's going on?"

"I have a crime to report."

The marshal stood, walked around his desk, and leaned on the edge. "What happened?"

"This boy was assaulted." Nate motioned to Johnnie to pull up his shirt. The boy blushed but did what he was told.

Cage stood and let out a noisy sigh. "Who did this to you, boy?"

Johnnie didn't speak.

Cage looked at Nate. "Well."

"Doug Hanson."

"Who is Doug Hanson? Where does he live? And why did he beat this kid?"

Nate let out a gusty sigh. "The boy's father."

Cage let out a low whistle.

"It doesn't matter who he is. The man was drunk and started in on his wife. The boy tried to protect her, and Doug did this to him. You need to arrest him."

"I can't arrest him for beating his son. You know that. The law considers it a family matter."

He pounded his fist on the desk. "Cage, he used a horsewhip. I haven't seen a back this tore up since I rescued slaves. I know there isn't a law against it, but isn't there something you can do?"

"I don't know." Cage paced a few steps. "I could charge him with assault, but the town prosecutor, Jake Nelson, would never take it to trial. If I arrested him, I could keep him in jail for a week or two until Mr. Nelson forced me to release him. It might give him pause the next time he decides to beat on his family."

"No!" Johnnie's voice took on a pleading tone. "Please don't. If you do that, he'll take it out on my ma and me when he gets out. Just leave it be."

"Are you sure, boy?" Cage asked. "I don't feel right allowing him to get away with this."

"Pa will calm down. When he gets like this, he'll act sorry for a few days, sometimes a few weeks. It'll be fine."

Cage leaned against the wall and folded his arms. "You could leave home. You're old enough to support yourself. That would get you away from him."

Johnnie pressed his lips together. "I won't leave my ma and younger brothers and sisters to suffer his wrath at home. When I'm there, sometimes, I can calm things down."

"It looks to me like you get in his way and take the brunt of it," Cage said.

"The law needs changed," Nate said. "That man should rot in jail for the way he treats his family." He pressed his lips together. "But I can see why the boy doesn't want you to do anything if nothing will come of it."

Cage pulled on his ear the way he did when he was deep in thought. "I'll talk to the mayor and the town council. Maybe we can change the law. There's been too much of this sort going on with the men from the cheese factories and mills going to the saloons and getting drunk after work. They should outlaw alcohol for good. It would make my job easier."

Nate swallowed hard. He knew Cage's beliefs about alcohol. During the war, he banned any sutlers selling whiskey in camp and would come down hard on any soldier who drank. Until now, Nate had kept his visits to the saloon away from his friend.

Cage continued. "But I can't get them to ban the stuff. For now, maybe I could at least get them to let me arrest these men who beat up their families. I could use your help at the meeting."

"We'll see." Nate headed toward the door before Cage could say any more. He didn't want to go to the meeting. Even though he wanted laws enacted against wife and child abuse, they wouldn't listen to a cripple. "Let's go, Johnnie."

"Where?"

"I'm taking you to my home. My wife will treat those wounds, and while she does, I'll deliver the telegrams."

The boy crossed his arms. "I'm not a charity case. I don't want you doing my job."

"Not charity. Just helping out. You'd do the same for me." He turned to the marshal. "I have a telegram for you. Might be important. Billie Horton is headed this way."

Cage opened it and whistled. "I hope he stays out of Wellington. That scoundrel has robbed banks all over Ohio including Sandusky, Columbus, even Cleveland. When he robbed the bank in Akron, he killed the teller because he was moving too slow putting the money in the bag. Horton is meaner than a meat axe. Thanks."

Nate nodded, opened the door, and motioned for Johnnie to follow him.

Chapter Four

Betsy wiped her hands on her apron. Nate should have been home an hour ago, and she didn't know what to think. Was he angry at her for not getting up to make him breakfast?

She glanced at the children playing with blocks on the floor behind the table, oblivious to the trouble brewing in their home. Did he decide to stop at the saloon again? Maybe last night wasn't enough for him.

The door opened, and she let out a sigh of relief when her husband walked in. A scrawny boy followed him, wearing worn clothes that looked like they came from the church clothing charity box. The trousers were too short and showed his ankles, and the shirt, obviously two sizes too large, hung on his skinny body. Dirty brown hair fell in his eyes. The boy stood with his hands at his sides like he wasn't sure what to do with them.

Malachi and Naomi jumped up and ran to hug Nate. "Daddy, Daddy." Penelope looked up but didn't stop playing. Lavena should be here soon to gather her.

Nate hugged Malachi, picked up his daughter, and buried his head in her shoulder. He let her down and tousled Malachi's curls before stepping over to Betsy and kissing her on the cheek.

She wasn't sure what to make of this. Last night, he was angrier than she'd ever seen him, and he'd scared her. Now he came home and acted like nothing happened. And he brought in this poor boy.

Penelope wandered over to the boy. "Do you want to play blocks with us?"

Nate smiled at the dark-haired girl. "Not now." He turned to Betsy "This boy needs some nursing."

"Of course." She walked over to him and shook his hand. "I'm Mrs. Teagan."

"I'm Johnnie, Johnnie Hanson. I make deliveries for the telegraph office."

"Nice to meet you, Johnnie. I've seen you at Baldwin's General Store stocking shelves. Do you work there too?"

He nodded.

"You're an industrious lad for someone so young."

"I'm fourteen. Indus... trious?"

"It means hard working."

This made Johnnie stand a little straighter. "I try."

She turned to Malachi. "Go get my medical satchel on the shelf in my bedroom."

"I do it," Naomi said.

"Me too," Penelope said.

"You can all go, but hurry." Betsy turned to Johnnie. "What's wrong?"

"Take off your shirt," Nate said.

"But Mr. Teagan. I can't do that in front of a lady." The boy's face turned red.

"Nonsense," she said. "I was a nurse in the war, and I have a boy of my own. I've seen lots of boys and grown men without their shirts on."

Johnnie hesitated a moment then removed his shirt. Betsy gasped at the marks across his back. Many were open sores with black, blue, and purple bruises around them. Other faded wounds and scars were in various states of healing. "Who did this to you?"

"His father." The muscle in Nate's jaw twitched. "He was drunk and tormenting his wife. Johnnie tried to help."

"Fetch some water," she said, "and some clean linens out of the rag basket."

Nate grabbed a bowl on the counter, placed it in the sink, and used the pump to fill it with water. Then he grabbed a few rags from the basket on the shelf next to the counter and carried them to the table.

"Sit," Betsy told Johnnie, and he sat on the bench nearest him.

She took one of the cloths, dipped it in water, and started washing the blood off his back. The boy winced a little but held still. She knew she was hurting him, but he pressed his lips together and refused to utter a sound. By the time she finished washing the wounds, the children had brought her brown leather bag where she kept bandages, various medicine powders, and a jar of a honey and vinegar mixture she used to treat wounds and prevent infection.

Malachi stared at Johnnie's back, and tears welled up in his eyes. "Is he going to be okay?"

"He'll be fine. He just needs a little doctoring." She tried to smile. "Children, go play upstairs."

This seemed to satisfy the children, and they gathered their blocks, went into the hallway, and climbed the stairs with a fair amount of noise.

She rubbed liberal amounts of the mixture onto Johnnie's back then wrapped a cotton dressing over the wounds. Finally, she mixed some laudanum in a cup of water and told Johnnie to drink it, which he did. "The medicine will make you drowsy. You need to go to our bed chamber and lay down for a while."

Johnnie stood. "I can't. I need to make my deliveries."

Nate pointed to the hallway. "Do as she says. I'll deliver the telegrams."

The boy looked like he was going to argue, but it was obvious drowsiness was overtaking him. He headed to the bedroom.

"Can we talk?" Nate tilted his head toward the door.

Betsy nodded, put on her cloak, and followed him outside onto the porch.

~~~~~

Nate stood by the railing. Since the sun had come out, most of the snow had melted, but the steps where they would normally sit were still wet. Smoke from the chimneys of a dozen houses up and down the street rose to the sky and blocked the sun on the horizon. Hopefully the slush from the snow melting wouldn't cause any problem while he made the deliveries.

Betsy stepped beside him and placed her hands on her hips. "Marshal Cage needs to know about this. That man should be arrested, or better yet, horsewhipped like he whipped his son."

"I'm for the horsewhipping." Nate kneaded the back of his neck. "I've already talked to Cage. Beating your own child isn't against the law. There's nothing he can do."

"The law needs changing."

"Cage agrees. He said something about meeting with the city council. It would be great if they could make a law like that to protect women and children. Now, that's a cause you could fight for. Especially with what happened to your sister. Maybe you could talk to Lavena about writing an article about it. This is the kind of crusade she would get behind."

"She might, but what about you? It used to be the kind of crusade you'd fight for. Are you going to the council meeting with Cage?"

Nate stared up at the sky. The sun was completely obscured now. Dark clouds moved in threatening more snow, or worse, icy rain. His wife was right. It did sound like something he would have taken on… before he lost his leg, but he wasn't about to go and be humiliated by those pitying looks. "We'll see."

A burst of wind blew, and she gazed at the looming clouds. "How are you going to deliver those telegrams with a storm brewing?"

"I'll have to hitch up the wagon." A tightness filled his chest, and he let out a slow, pained breath. This wasn't what he came out here to talk to her about. "I'm so sorry I scared you yesterday. I had no call to speak to you like that."

Her arms tightened around her body. "What is wrong with you?" There was a catch in her voice that broke his heart. "When we first met, you were a man of God. You would have gone with me to the temperance meetings, and you would have been the first one at the council meeting demanding a change in domestic laws. You would have never allowed alcohol to touch your lips, let alone treat me or anyone else like you did last night."

He swallowed back the lump in his throat. As much as he wanted to lash out at her, to protest that he was still the same man she married, she was telling the truth. He had changed, and not for the better. "You don't know what it's like to be so useless." His voice grew thick. "I was going to change the world. Now it takes all of my energy to walk to work in the morning. That war destroyed me."

"Horsefeathers." She touched his cheek. "Things might be more difficult, but you're not useless. You could do your part if you would open a law office. You could still fight injustice and advocate for those who have no voice, boys like Johnnie. Even if you don't want to pursue the law, you're a husband and a father to our children, and you do what you need to do to support us. Your problem isn't your missing leg. Your problem is with God."

A flush of heat warmed his face and neck.

She touched his arm. "Until you work that out and get right with Him, you'll never overcome this."

He bit back his angry words and didn't respond to what she said. "Will you forgive me?" He wrapped his arms around her, knowing the effect his closeness had always had on her.

At first, he felt her rebuff. Every muscle in her body tightened in his embrace. Then, she melted into him. "Of course I forgive you, but you need to pull yourself together."

He distracted her with a passionate kiss the way he'd done so many times before when she was angry with him.

After a moment of giving in to the embrace, she pushed away. "I mean it, Nate. If you really are sorry, you'll stop going to the infernal saloon."

He sighed loudly and let go of her. "I need to get these telegrams delivered." He gave her a peck on the cheek and left. He didn't want to give up drinking, and he wasn't ready to make things right with the God who took his leg. Maybe he could cut it down to once or twice a week. That would make her happy.

~~~~~

Betsy stirred the soup she had waiting on the stove for when Nate returned. At least, the storm had held its peace for now, but clouds still darkened the sky. It would be worse now that some of the snow had melted earlier in the afternoon. Now, all that slush would turn to ice.

Almost two hours ago, Nate had shuffled to the barn out back and hitched his dark brown horse to the wagon to make deliveries. When Johnnie woke a few minutes ago, he'd left to go home with instructions from her to come back the next day and let her change the bandages. Hopefully, her husband would be home soon.

A knock sounded on the door. Lavena coming to collect Penelope. Betsy greeted her. "How did it go?"

"I could use a cup of tea about now."

Betsy put a kettle on to boil and got a tin of lavender tea leaves off the shelf. "That bad?" She sat with her friend at the kitchen table.

"Worse. Remember how Father Finney encouraged women students to do whatever God called us to do and always supported our right to vote and to be involved in missions, ministry, and social issues that affect our children and homes every bit as much as being a homemaker?"

"He certainly did. I disagreed at first. I didn't think it was ladylike, but even I came to see the sense in it."

Lavena pressed her lips together. "That's all changed."

The tea kettle boiled, and Betsy poured the tea. "How so?"

"President Fairchild preached against women's suffrage. He said that a Christian woman should know her place and concern herself with her home and her children. Her husband should represent her in society and in the ballot box."

"Horsefeathers," Betsy said. "My man would not represent me when it came to outlawing liquor. God gave women a voice, and it's high time we had our say."

Lavena stared at her with her mouth slightly open. "I've never seen you so passionate about women's suffrage. What happened?"

Betsy shrugged. "I still believe being a wife and mother is the highest calling a woman can have, but husbands have a calling as well, and women voting might wake them up to that." She told Lavena about Johnnie's beating. "Maybe you could do a story about creating a law to protect women and children from their drunken husbands."

"A worthy cause. I'll talk to the publisher about it." Lavena gazed at her with compassion. "A law like that might have saved Helen."

Betsy pressed her lips together and nodded. She took a sip of tea to hold back the lump forming in her throat. "It's too late for my sister, but others might be saved."

"So, what did Nate say."

"He apologized for speaking to me the way he did. I think Mr. Hanson's drunken rage toward his family got through to him. I've been praying for him to see the light. This may be what he needed."

"I hope so for your sake." Lavena didn't sound convinced, and her tone mirrored Betsy's doubts. "What happens if he goes back to drinking? Are you ready to carry signs in front of the saloon?"

"I doubt it. I'll have to pray about that one, but I am going to do something. I'll talk to the temperance society about having meetings once a week and opening them to the public. Maybe we could hand out advertisements letting people know."

"Is that all you're planning to do?"

"I did have an idea of convincing employers to pay more for their employees who are willing to sign the pledge not to drink. I'm sure we could get some of the cheese factory and mill owners to agree. I know the man who owns the tannery would."

"That's a start anyway, but I think you should do more if you really want things to change."

Betsy shrugged. "Like you said, it's a start. She took a sip of tea. "What about you? After that horrible speech by President Fairchild, are you going to do anything about it?"

Lavena's mouth curled into a smirk. "*The Wellington Enterprise* did send me to Oberlin to write an article about the speech. I wrote two. When I delivered them, Mr. Guthrie said I could do a whole series of articles on the common sense of women's suffrage. He said I could send them to the *Cleveland Banner* and *Harper's Ferry* to see if they'd publish them as well. Now that slaves have been freed, and black men are permitted the vote, the next step in securing our rights is for women, no matter the color of their skin, to have the right to vote. Next month, I'm going a suffrage meeting in Oberlin, and at the beginning of May, I'll join the women's suffrage march in Elyria. Of course, I'll write about what happens. Would you be willing to watch Penelope for both events?"

"I'll watch her for the meeting in Oberlin." Betsy said, an idea forming in her mind. "This march is for the future as well as now. If women had the vote, we could outlaw alcohol and abuse and create a better world for our families. Most abusive men get that way because they've been drinking. I'm going with you, and we're bringing the children."

Lavena took a sip of tea. "Even better."

Chapter Five

April 29th, 1870

After attending the women's suffrage meeting in Oberlin, Lavena headed home completely defeated. They lived in a small house on Courtland St. where Cage's office and the jail were located. It only had a kitchen and two bedrooms, but it was large enough for the three of them. She blinked to clear her eyes and reached for her handkerchief. They would never have to worry about needing more room.

When Penelope was born, there were complications, and Lavena almost died. The midwife was able to stop the bleeding, but afterward, when the doctor checked on her, he said she might never be able to have more children. It had been four years since then, and no other pregnancies came along, so it appeared the doctor was correct.

In a way, it surprised her that she was so devastated. Wasn't she the one who always said she'd never get married or have children? But that was before she fell in love with Cage. Since getting married, her maternal instincts had bloomed, and she'd intended to quit her job and raise a passel of offspring. She had decided she might write a story occasionally, but the children would be her focus.

She was thankful for Penelope, but if she couldn't give her husband more children, she was bound do everything she could to create a world where Penelope had the same rights as any man.

Sometimes that seemed as hopeless as having more children. She let out a sigh. The sun had already set. At least she hadn't had to collect Penelope from Betsy's. Since the meeting was so late, Cage had gone to pick her up after he came home for the afternoon. He would be expected back later at night when most of the crime happened. He would have fed their daughter some soup Lavena had left simmering on the stove and tucked Penelope into bed before she got home. He was such a treasure to her.

When she walked in the door, Cage put his arms around her and gave her a kiss on the cheek. Not the passionate greeting he normally gave.

She pulled away from his embrace. "What's wrong?"

He led her to the chairs around the table and sat beside her. "I had a meeting at the town council today. I presented them with a proposal to make laws to protect the innocent of this community. Crime in this village is only getting worse with the warmer weather, and as more cheese factories and mills open and workers make their home here, it increases every year. I do what I can, but I feel like the little boy with his finger in the dyke."

"What laws? Did you talk to them about laws to protect wives and children from abuse?"

"I decided to have a full-frontal attack. I mentioned the abuse, but I also encouraged them to close down the saloons and make this a dry town. And, of course, the danger of having boys as young as eight work at those factories. Many of them are getting hurt when they should be in school."

Lavena whistled. "And you say I'm a crusader. They didn't see it that way?"

Cage cleared his throat and did an imitation of Jake Nelson, a member of the council. "Marshal, we'll take some of these suggestions under advisement, but we are not getting involved in family life. That is not our purview. A husband is the spiritual authority over his own home. We will not interfere with that biblical mandate." Cage's jaw jutted. "He also suggested I'm the one responsible for the crime in this city, and if I can't control it, they may have to make a change."

She gasped. "They wouldn't fire you, would they?"

He chuckled. "No, the mayor backs me, and he's the one who would make that decision. You know what an arrogant twit Mr. Nelson's become since he got on the council. Being the town prosecutor wasn't enough for him. He has his eye on a political career, maybe even running for a state congressman. He was just trying to keep me from causing too much of a ruckus."

"Did it work?"

Cage raised an eyebrow, and she realized what a silly question that was. Her husband was too honorable to allow these men to threaten him with a job.

"So how did your meeting go? Are you going to change the world by the next election?"

She swiped at the tears threatening to spill from her eyes. "Do you wish I had given you a son?"

He set his hand on hers. "Of course not. Penelope is a joy. When I think I could have lost you both..." His Adam's apple bulged. "What made you bring that up?

"I'm trying to make the world better for her, for all young girls, but no matter how hard I try, I can't make any progress."

He stood and pulled her up into his arms. She allowed the tears to flow this time. She always showed determination with everyone else, but she relied on his strength when they were alone.

When the moment was over, she regained her composure. "I can't be a part of their organization."

Cage's mouth fell open. "You've been looking forward to the meeting for a month. Why would you say that?"

"It wasn't all bad. Mrs. Livermore was inspiring. I was able to talk to her afterwards. She's a knowledgeable and enlightened woman. The title of her speech was *What Shall We Do with Our Daughters*. She not only talked about the right to vote but how, if we want the next generation of women to succeed, we must end the consumption of alcohol. So many women are living in poverty and suffering abuse because their husbands drink. Betsy would have loved it."

The muscle in Cage's jaw twitched, and she placed her hand over her mouth. Betsy had asked her not to say anything.

"Why would Betsy have loved it? I didn't know she was that interested in the right to vote."

"She is. She's going to march with me in Elyria next week if her husband gives his permission."

Cage placed her hands in his and gazed into her eyes. "After what happened when we first met, I thought we promised to not keep secrets from each other."

When Lavena had been a journalist assigned to the Ohio Seventh Regiment, she was supposed to do a story on the mysterious Captain Cage Jones, a man she idolized. They had soon fallen in love, but he had a shameful secret that almost ruined their relationship. Things worked out when Cage not only told her the truth but confessed it to his colonel and to his company of soldiers. That was when they promised not to keep secrets from each other.

"Betsy told me Nate isn't the same man he used to be. He pretends to be a good Christian husband and father, but it's an act."

Cage held onto his ear, the one with the scar, a gesture he did when he was troubled.

She let out a sigh. "He has horrible nightmares and wakes up screaming."

"I remember a time when I used to have nightmares like that. Lots of veterans do."

"Cage, he's been drinking... a lot. Betsy says he comes home from the saloon three or four nights a week staggering drunk. She asked me not to tell you."

He slowly shook his head. "I knew something was wrong. He used to stop by the office and have a cup of coffee before heading home, at least two or three times a week. Lately, I only see him at church." He covered his mouth with his hand. "Betsy must be heartbroken."

"She is."

"When I have an opportunity, I'll talk some sense into him. He's always listened to me."

"He listened because you were his captain during the war. You're civilians now."

His posture slumped. "Since he saved my life, we're closer than brothers. That hasn't changed."

"Betsy says most of the problem is he feels useless since he lost his leg. He got his law license, but Mr. Hayes won't hire him because he's a cripple, and he refuses to start his own practice."

Cage rubbed his hand across the scars on his face. "Sounds like he's lost his purpose in life. Maybe I can find a few projects where I can turn to him for help."

Lavena lifted an eyebrow. "Nate is a smart man. He'll figure you out."

He chuckled. "Perhaps, but not right away. I'm pretty smart too, you know." He gave her a kiss on the cheek. "Now, what went wrong at the meeting?"

"After Mrs. Liverpool left, the women discussed what they wanted to accomplish. Cage, they voted to not include Negro women in their organization."

"That's unfortunate."

"Unfortunate? It's sinful. Why did we fight a war to free the slaves if we were only going to allow black men to have rights and not black women?"

"Did they have a reason?"

She couldn't keep in her seat. She stood and started pacing. "They said we need to get more people to see the sense in giving the vote to woman. There's no need to muddy the waters now by including black women. They said they'd take care of that later. Later. Huh." She stopped pacing and sat back down.

"I love you." He set his hand on hers. "Your zeal to make things right is your best quality, but sometimes you're too impatient. You can't force everyone to see the light all at once."

"I can try." A tear fell down her cheek, and she swiped at it.

"I know of nobody who puts more effort into it, but we also have to trust God to change things in His timing."

They'd had this conversation before. "He's not moving fast enough."

He chuckled. "We can't decide His timing. Have you prayed about the Oberlin Suffrage Society and if you should be a part of it or not?"

She let out a sigh loud enough for him to hear. "No."

He squeezed her hand. "What is your favorite scripture passage?"

She glared at him, stuck out her tongue, then quoted it. "Proverbs three, five through six. '*Trust in the Lord with all thine heart; and lean not unto thine own understanding. In all thy ways acknowledge him, and he shall direct thy paths.*'"

"Before you march into the next meeting telling those ladies how sinful they are, don't you think we should pray for them and for guidance on what you should do next?"

She let out a gusty sigh and nodded. She could always count on her husband to remind her where she should put her trust even when she didn't want to listen. "Let's pray for Nate and Betsy too."

He nodded and led her in prayer.

~~~~~

Nate walked along the railroad tracks. It was a beautiful day, one of the few sunny ones they'd had. Yellow and purple wildflowers in a field beside the tracks scented the air. Now that it was May, it looked like spring was here to stay this time after an unusually long winter. It made walking home on crutches easier when he didn't have to worry about slipping on ice and snow or mud caused by the rain they'd had recently.

He stopped at Baldwin's General Store to buy the package of toy soldiers he'd promised Betsy he would get. When he came out of the store, he gazed down the street at the mill, the bakery, and the alley where he'd go if he were headed to the saloon. Even though he didn't head that way as often as he used to, he couldn't help stopping every day on the way home from work and gazing down the street with longing. The only reason that kept him from going more often was the image of what Hanson did to his son.

And the way Nate had treated Betsy after Mr. Hayes decided not to hire him.

He loved his wife and children too much to become that man, so he'd decided to limit himself to a couple of times a week. This week, he'd already been there twice, so even though he wanted nothing more than a stiff drink, he would resist the temptation. Besides, Malachi's fifth birthday was today, and he'd promised Betsy he'd come right home.

Even though he'd stop drinking as much, when he did come home from the saloon, Betsy still waited up for him with his dinner on the stove and tears in her eyes. She'd urged him to stop drinking altogether, but he couldn't do that. She didn't understand what it was like. She should be grateful it wasn't as often. Instead, she now attended temperance meetings once a week instead of once a month, and she was convincing business owners to pay those who signed the temperance pledge more money. Many of them were agreeing. At least she hadn't gone to his boss, Mr. Wilson. Not yet, but it was only a matter of time.

Even though he grumbled about it, he was secretly proud of what she was doing. He might not be able to change the injustices of the world, but at least she was doing her part. He just wished she'd choose another project to get involved with. This one felt like a personal attack on him. He headed home.

As soon as he walked through the door, the aroma of beef stew cooking filled the air. A freshly baked cake sat on the counter ready to be iced, and she was stirring the frosting. A little icing had gotten on her nose. She looked adorable.

He kissed her on the cheek and wiped the icing off with his finger. "I expected the cake for Malachi's birthday, but what are you about? We usually only have beef stew on Sundays."

"What?" She blushed. "Can't a wife fix her husband's favorite meal?"

Something was obviously on her mind. He was glad he hadn't decided to stop for a drink this time. He took her hand, set it on his shoulder, and used his crutches to lead her to the table where he sat across from her. "You have something to ask me or maybe tell me? What is it?"

She sat sheepishly. "It's Malachi's birthday. I didn't want to have this conversation until later, when the children are in bed. Did you stop and get the present?"

He held up the sack of toy soldiers he'd bought. "Where are they?"

She tilted her head toward the stairs. "Upstairs playing with the wooden blocks you made them."

"Then we shouldn't be interrupted." He placed his hand on hers and squeezed to reassure her. "You don't have to cook beef stew to butter me up. Just tell me straight out."

"I want to take the children and go to Elyria on Saturday with Lavena."

"Are you taking the wagon?" Nate asked.

"I would like to."

He gazed into her blue-green eyes, so intense they looked almost gray. Why was she being so evasive? "Are you planning to go shopping? I could get some money from the bank."

"We aren't going shopping."

He stroked his beard. "I see." He didn't see or understand what she was getting at. "Are you planning an outing at Black River with the children?"

"No," she squeaked out.

He let out a gusty sigh. "Betsy, just tell me. Stop making me ask all these questions."

She fiddled with her hands. "There's going to be a suffrage march through Elyria on Saturday. Lavena invited me to march with her."

He furrowed his brow trying to understand why she was so apprehensive. She knew how much he supported the right to vote for everyone. Had he been so irritable that she was afraid to ask even this? "Who's going to watch the children?"

"Nobody." She tapped her fingers on the table then held them together in her lap. "This concerns their future too. We'll take them with us and let them march and hold signs. We'll keep an eye out for them."

Warmth spread throughout his chest. How often had he encouraged her to get involved in something important, something that would take her mind off the temperance society? He grinned so big he was sure his dimples showed. "Betsy, I'm proud of you."

She let out a sigh of relief. "I thought you'd be angry."

"Why would I be? I know this isn't something you'd normally do, marching in the streets, but it's for the betterment of society. That's what I encouraged you to do before…" He glanced at his leg. If only he could be the one out there making the world a better place.

Tears filled her eyes. "Thank you. This is important to me."

He clasped her hands. "Until everyone has equal rights, nobody does. This is for the future of our nation." A thought troubled him. He'd read in *The Wellington Enterprise* that some of these marches had turned ugly. Men who didn't want their women to vote would block their way. Sometimes violence erupted, and police would arrest the protesters instead of the agitators. His jaw set. "If the police or a group of agitators come out against the march, you need to get those children out of there right away."

"Of course. Lavena and I already talked about that. She'll stay in the march, and I'll usher all the children to a safe place. I have no intention of putting them in danger."

"Then you have my blessing."

She would get home late Saturday night which would give him the opportunity to spend the evening in the saloon without seeing her tears.

"One more thing," she said. "Now that the weather is getting warmer, when were you going to build that picket fence to block the children from getting near the train tracks?"

He groaned. Last summer, she wouldn't leave him alone about that fence. "We don't need a fence. You can keep an eye out for them."

"Nate, it's dangerous. I can't watch them every minute."

"And I can't build that fence when I'm on crutches." He hadn't meant to say that, but he wasn't sure he'd be able to dig the holes needed when he was crippled.

"We could hire someone to do it," Betsy said.

"No!" Nate took a breath and let it out slowly to calm his tone. "I'm the man of this home. If a fence needs building, I'll figure out a way to build it."

She pressed her lips together and nodded.

Chapter Six

That Saturday, Betsy and Lavena joined over a hundred women from all over Lorain County for the march in Elyria. Only a few white fluffy clouds dotted the sky. Betsy couldn't help the giddiness mixed with apprehension churning inside of her. The day before, they'd made signs for themselves and smaller signs for the children to carry out of sticks of wood and butcher paper Lavena had procured from the butcher in town.

"Remember," Betsy said to the children as she passed out the signs, "stay with us at all times, and if we tell you to follow me, you hold onto my dress and stay with me no matter what."

"We will, Mama," Malachi said.

Lavena took Penelope's hand. "You, too. If we say it's time, hold onto Aunt Betsy's skirt even though I won't be with you."

"Yes, Mama."

"Perhaps we should move to the center of the protesters," Betsy said. "That way, the children will be protected if anything happens."

"A wise idea." Lavena started making her way toward the center of the crowd with Penelope in tow.

Betsy grabbed hold of Malachi and Naomi's hands and followed her. They passed out the signs to the children and began marching up Middle Avenue through the center of the city. Eventually they would reach Public Square and eat lunches prepared for them by the Oberlin Women's Suffrage Association.

The association invited well-known women speakers, including Antoinette Blackwell, the first ordained woman minister, to talk while they were eating. Betsy couldn't even imagine a woman preacher. She'd never heard of such a thing.

They'd also invited the governor and the mayor of Elyria to attend, although the governor had turned them down. He said he had pressing matters to attend. Of course, he would consider anything more pressing since he was against women's suffrage. At least the mayor would be there.

The main reason the march was held in Elyria, the county seat of Lorain, was because many in Oberlin, including the mayor, had turned against women's suffrage after President Fairchild's speech. The mayor of Elyria was in favor of the cause and offered his city to the association.

Betsy had worried the children would be fussy and lose interest after a while, but they enjoyed the march as much as she did. It warmed her heart to watch them holding their signs and chanting, "Women are citizens too." They weren't the only children in the crowd, and that eased her fears a bit. Ever since Nate had mentioned agitators, she'd fretted about it. She'd considered finding someone to watch them, but Lavena encouraged her to stay with the plan.

She realized now she had nothing to fear. The children loved marching and chanting, and no agitators or police had challenged them. Besides, it was a beautiful, sunny day. Doing something near the beginning of May was always worrisome, but the weather couldn't have been nicer. It was warm, but a breeze kept it from being too hot, and there were the white fluffy clouds expected on a day like this, but none of them turned dark or threatened rain.

Turning the corner, a group of around twenty men dressed in work clothes, jaws set, and brows furrowed, started toward them at a quickened pace. Betsy's stomach churned. The way they approached was purposeful and aggressive. When they reached the women protestors, they halted. Nobody said anything for a few moments. The two groups just stared at each other.

"Should I move the children to a safe distance?" Betsy whispered to Lavena.

"Maybe." Lavena crossed her arms and glared at the men. "Let's see what they want first."

The silence went on too long, and Betsy wondering how her friend could stay so calm. Betsy's whole body was quivering.

One of the men in front, a brute at least six feet tall, finally spoke in a smooth singsong voice his stance didn't match. "Now, ladies. There's no need for you to be out here. You need to be tending to your homes and children instead of..." his voice turned harsh, "...trying to be men."

Lavena pushed Penelope toward Betsy. "They mean no good. Get the children out of here."

"What are you going to do?"

She pursed her lips together. "As soon as the children are safe, I'm going to the front of the crowd to stand with the rest of the association members."

Betsy's stomach now felt as if circus clowns were doing somersaults inside as she moved to the back of the crowd, all three children holding her skirt tightly. When she came across other mothers with children, she urged them to follow her to safety. She heard raised voices behind her.

"If my wife ever dared to do this, I'd show her a thing or two."

"You women are going against who God created you to be."

"Maybe you need a man to teach you how to behave."

She glanced back, but violence hadn't erupted yet. Only ugly words. When they reached the back of the crowd, three other mothers and seven other children had joined them, but she wasn't sure what to do next. She perused the area. Where would they be safe?

A thin elderly woman with her gray hair in a bun called out from her front porch in front of a modest white house. "Over here."

Betsy and her followers moved to the porch.

"You bring them young'uns right up here," the woman said.

Betsy nodded to the others, and they climbed the stairs.

"My name is Mrs. Adams. They're welcome to come inside. I've fixed some cookies I know they'd enjoy."

"That's very kind, Mrs. Adams." Betsy said, unsure of handing the children over to a woman she didn't know. "I'm Mrs. Teagan."

"Call me Grandma, please. Everyone else does. You can come inside too if you have a mind to or watch the goings on from the porch."

"Why are you doing this, Grandma Adams?" one of the other women asked.

"I'll be ninety years old next month. Can you imagine? My pa fought under General George Washington for independence, and my husband lost his leg in the War of 1812."

Excitement stirred in Betsy. Of course, she'd heard stories from the elderly about how their grandparents fought in the War for Independence, but to meet a woman whose pa fought under General Washington was amazing. Lavena had to hear about this. She would want to do a story on Mrs. Adams, but Betsy also wanted to hear how the woman helped her husband get over losing a leg in the war.

She and the other women took their children's hands and followed the elderly lady into the house. The home was much nicer than she expected from the outside. There was a parlor with a fireplace in the front room on the far wall. A divan and decorative Queen Anne chairs lined the wall on the right. A couple more chairs, a harpsichord, and a bookshelf lined the wall on the left. An open rolltop desk in the corner had papers spread out, and an ink bottle and quill set ready to scribble letters. What surprised Betsy the most were the books on the bookshelf. She had to have at least fifty, some of them very old.

As she followed Mrs. Adams into the kitchen through a small door on the left side, she nearly gasped. The kitchen had all the modern conveniences, a stove, an indoor pump, and plenty of shelf space, but it also had a beautiful walnut leaf table with decorative legs and a number of fancy spindle chairs along with a walnut Federal style sideboard and cabinet. Most people probably wouldn't recognize these antiques, but her father was a wealthy cabinet maker and had taught her how to recognize different woods, styles, and types of furniture.

Mrs. Adams began pouring the milk. "Children, sit at the table if you want milk and cookies." A rustling noise filled the room as the children sat. "Growing up, I heard all them high ideas about freedom and equality for all, but that's not true. It took another war to win freedom for the slaves, and even now, only men can vote, don't matter the color of their skin. Only their gender. Us women have always been told to know our place. I can't march. I'm too old, but I can help you ladies with your children. I only wish I could vote just once before I die, but I doubt that will happen. You need to keep on and vote in my place."

Tears welled up in Betsy's eyes, and she was about to say something when shouting started outside. She told the children to mind Grandma Adams and hurried back to the porch to find out if Lavena was okay.

~~~~~

Lavena made her way to the front of the line and locked arms with the other ladies of the society. A few of the men stepped close enough that she could smell the eggs they had for breakfast.

One man over six feet tall and built like a horse said, "My wife wouldn't be out here doing this foolishness. I wouldn't let her. Least we can do is stop you." The men lurched toward them and grabbed and twisted their arms to try to get them to let go of each other.

She tried to keep her arms locked with the women beside her as long as she could, but the tall man managed to break her arm free. He threw her to the ground as if she were a rag doll and attacked her with a knife. Her heart raced faster than a speeding train.

The rest of the men headed into the crowd, and all she could see was limbs and bodies falling around her. *Lord, help us.*

Whistles blew from somewhere, and the men stopped attacking and gradually moved back.

Her chin quivered as she tried to get a clear view of what was happening. Police moved into the crowd of bullies, but would they arrest the protesters or the agitators? The other women who'd fallen stood to their feet, but Lavena couldn't manage it yet. Every muscle inside of her felt like jelly, and her arm hurt. She wanted to let out a cry, but her pride wouldn't let her. She wouldn't show weakness to these ruffians.

Officers of the law grabbed some of the men by the arms and pulled them away.

One officer came toward her. "Are you all right?"

"I'll be fine." She hated how her voice quivered.

He held out his hand to assist her to her feet. "You're bleeding. Are you sure you're okay?"

Lavena looked at the blood dripping down her arm, surprised she hadn't noticed. As bad a wound as it was, she was surprised it didn't hurt. "I'll be fine." She glanced at Betsy watching from the porch of the nearest house. "My friend will help me."

A blur of words came from the crowd of men being forcibly led away.

"They have no right being out here," one man shouted.

A town marshal stepped in front over to them. "You men best mind your business. You keep it up, and we'll throw you in jail."

"What about the women?" the brute who stabbed her asked. "Are you going to let them get away with this?"

"Mayor's orders," the marshal said. "Move on."

The men gradually moved away, some of them checking over their should, obviously realizing they were the ones in trouble. Soon, none of them were left.

When the chaos ended, Mayor Livingstone, the mayor of Elyria, stepped to the front of the protestors. "Forgive me, ladies, for not providing protection earlier. I assumed since I announced how much I support your cause, there would be no trouble."

Lavena held her hand over the gash on her arm to try to stop the bleeding. It was starting to throb, and she felt a little lightheaded. She cleared her throat to make sure the terror she felt didn't reflect in her voice. "Thank you, Mayor. We appreciate your kindness."

"You're hurt," the mayor said. "Do you need assistance?"

"No need." Lavena glanced toward the porch and found Betsy standing there. "My friend will treat my wound."

Mayor Livingstone nodded. "I do hope you'll be my personal guest at the picnic."

"I should warn you, I'm a reporter."

The mayor smiled. "Even better. This story must be written." He turned to the others. "Ladies, I vow you won't be accosted again. My officers will accompany you to the picnic."

As she made her way to the porch, the mayor and protesters continued to the park. When she reached Betsy, a handful of women hurried out of the house with their children and joined the march.

When Lavena saw the horror in her friend's face, she held up her palms. "I'm not hurt badly. Let's gather the children and head to the square."

"Come in the house and let me see."

Lavena delivered a glare, even though she knew she needed treatment. The truth was she was trying to show bravado on the outside to mask the fear threatening to paralyze her.

Betsy nudged her toward the door. "Trust me. While I treat your arm, you'll want to hear the story of the woman who lives here. We'll have time to get to Public Square before the speeches begin."

Lavena followed her into the house and into the kitchen where she was relieved to be able to sit. She was feeling dizzy and a little sick to her stomach.

The only children left at the table were Penelope and Betsy's children.

They were eating gingersnap and molasses cookies and drinking milk.

Penelope ran to her with an entire gingersnap in her mouth and hugged her. "Grandma gave us cookies and milk."

"Don't talk with your mouth full," Lavena reminded her.

"Yes, Mama," Penelope said with her mouth still full of cookie.

Betsy introduced Lavena to Mrs. Adams.

"Oh my," Mrs. Adams said. "You're bleeding."

"Grandma, I'll need some warm water and clean rags." Betsy tore off the sleeve of Lavena's dress so she had access to the wound. "It's not bad, but you're going to need a couple of stitches to stop the bleeding."

Mrs. Adams ran to the sink to fill a pan with water then placed it on the stove. She gathered some rags from a rag basket in the corner.

By now the children were done with their cookies and stared at Lavena's arm with wide eyes. Penelope's lip trembled.

"Children, would you like to see the toys I played with when I was little?" Mrs. Adams said.

"Can we, please?" Malachi asked.

"Pweese," Naomi said.

"I have a whole basket of toys in the parlor. You can play with them in there." She turned to Betsy. "Do you need anything else?"

Betsy started washing Lavena's arms. "Could I also trouble you for some clean thread, a sharp needle, and some honey and vinegar?"

"I'm not sure I have vinegar," Mrs. Adams said.

"Do you have whiskey?"

Lavena gasped. She wasn't about to drink alcohol no matter how bad it hurt.

"I'll get it."

"Bring the honey too."

Mrs. Adams left the room with the children.

"I have never let whiskey touch my lips, and I'm not about to start now."

"No, silly," Betsy said. "You're not going to drink it. I'll pour the whiskey over your cut to prevent infection, but it's going to hurt like the dickens."

Mrs. Adams returned with the needle and thread and went to the cupboard to grab a jar of honey and a bottle of whiskey. "I don't drink, mind you, but I have this on hand for medical reasons. In my day, whiskey was used to treat pneumonia, cholera, and typhoid fever, along with other ailments."

Betsy took the bottle. "It's still used to prevent infection and is used in cough syrup and other medicines."

Lavena nodded. She was relieved to hear the children playing and having fun in the next room where they wouldn't see what was going on.

Betsy poured the whiskey into the wound. Lavena gritted her teeth. It took everything within her not to scream. It hurt so bad.

Betsy threaded the needle and poured whiskey over the needle and thread. "Grandma, why don't you tell Lavena your story while I sew up her arm? She's going to need a distraction."

Lavena could feel the needle moving in and out of her flesh pinching her skin, but she tried to ignore it and listen to Mrs. Adams. It did help to be distracted.

Betsy finished the stitching, rubbed honey over the wound, and bandaged it.

Lavena had to admit that the honey took away some of the sting. "Mrs. Adams—"

"Grandma."

"Grandma. I'm doing a story on this march, or I would stay here all day to hear your accounts. Would it be all right if I came back next week to interview you?"

"I'd love to have you," Mrs. Adams said. "I have stories young people today need to hear."

"Thank you." Lavena turned to Betsy. "Would you watch Penelope Tuesday?"

"No, I won't. I'm coming with you, and so are the children."

"Oh, good," Mrs. Adams said. "I miss having children around. Are you sure you feel all right to walk to Public Square?"

Betsy washed her hands in the sink and pulled down her sleeves. "I'll get the wagon. I don't want you walking that far just yet."

Lavena sighed. As much as she wanted to appear strong, she did still feel a little queasy, and her arm ached. "I'd appreciate it. Thank you."

Betsy went to get the wagon.

"Before you go, dear, let me get you a shawl to cover that torn sleeve." Mrs. Adams hurried toward another room before Lavena could refuse. She returned with a beautiful, knitted shawl.

I couldn't," Lavena said. "This shawl is too nice."

"Nonsense. I have at least twenty of them. Knitting is a passion of mine." She placed the shawl over Lavena's shoulders. "I don't want it returned. I insist you keep this as my gift."

"Thank-you. I'll treasure it."

Lavena and the children said their good-byes. Each of the children thanked Mrs. Adams for the milk and cookies and for letting them play with her toys.

Lavena would not soon forget this day. It was a blessing to talk to Mrs. Adams, and she was proud of the way she stood up to those bullies during the march, but she couldn't shake the sensation of her insides twisting in the same way she would twist laundry to get out the excess water. Everything in her wanted to go home and hide under her bedcovers.

Chapter Seven

With Betsy gone for the whole day, Nate planned to head to the saloon as soon as he got out of work. He licked his upper lip, anticipating the taste of the whiskey going down his throat. Johnnie had already gone to deliver telegrams, so he'd leave as soon as James arrived.

The familiar tapping alerted him a telegram was being received. He quickly dipped his pen in ink and transcribed the message. When he finished, he stroked his beard. The whiskey would have to wait. Cage needed to see this message.

James walked in, and Nate headed to the marshal's office. As soon as he delivered the message, he would head to the saloon. This afternoon, he would buy a bottle and take it home. He'd be asleep before Betsy and the children got home, and if he gargled with some peppermint tea, she might not even know.

When he entered the office, Cage looked up from the desk. "Just the man I wanted to see."

Nate handed him the telegram, and he read it.

To Marshal Macajah Jones, Wellington, Ohio.
Billy Horton robbed store in Black River.
Stop.
Seen riding your way.
Marshall Eli Pritchard, Black River, Ohio.

Cage whistled. "They're getting close. As if I don't have enough to do with all of the petty larcenies, house burglaries, and bar fights in town."

"I didn't know things were that bad."

"Since the cheese factories opened and men here moved here to work, the village has been riddled with crime. Wellington is growing too fast for us to keep up on things. It's not just the law. We need more doctors, more lawyers, even more stores and houses. The only thing we have too many of is saloons."

"It has become more crowded." Nate stroked his beard. "Even the telegraph office is busier than we've ever been."

"I'll have my deputies check out the bank more often." Cage let out a gusty sigh. "We don't have enough officers to patrol. Just between us, I'm praying he stays clear of here."

"Glad I could help." Nate headed to the door and placed his hand on the knob.

"Wait a sec. Something I want to talk to you about."

He let out a heavy sigh and turned back. "What?"

Cage motioned to the chair in front of the desk. "Have a seat."

He sat, even though all he wanted was that bottle of whiskey.

"I arrested a woman this afternoon for petty theft at Baldwin's General Store. She's locked in a cell in the back, and she says she did it."

"And..." He tapped his fingers on the side of his chair.

"She has two young children, and all she stole was some flour and beans."

Nate hated this. Why couldn't his friend come out and say what he wanted? "If she stole from the store, and she admits it, there's nothing anyone can do. Maybe she'll get a light sentence since she only stole food."

"She did it because her husband's a drunkard and gambled away their grocery money. She needs a lawyer."

Nate pulled on his shirt collar. He now knew where this was going. "I can recommend a few good lawyers in town."

"Nate, you beat all, you know that? Quit acting like a dolt. You know as well as I do, if she had to steal food to feed her children, she can't afford a lawyer. She needs your help."

He grimaced. "I'm not a lawyer."

"You have a law license."

He glared at Cage. His friend grinned as if he had already agreed.

He let out a heavy sigh. "Let me meet her."

Cage led him to the back door where the jail was. The cells were separated by mud walls, and the windows and doors had iron bars. Each had a small window that let in the only light. The cells were small, only four feet by six feet. Each cell had a wooden bed with a tick mattress and a blanket. The only other thing in the room was a chamber pot on the dirt floor under the bed. That explained the stench. Most of the cells were filled with men of various ages, all dressed shabbily. Only a few were empty. They walked to the last couple of cells, the only ones with curtains, presumedly for privacy in case any women were jailed.

The curtain to one of the cells was open. A young woman, no older than twenty, sat on the bed staring at the wall as if she were in a daze. Her clothes were faded and looked like she might have received them from a church charity box. Her thin face, stringy brown hair tucked in a dingy bonnet, and dark, lifeless eyes broke Nate's heart. Even though he resented Cage pushing him into this, he would do anything to help her.

"What's her name?" he whispered.

"Gertrude Weber."

"Mrs. Weber, I need to talk to you. Come here to the door."

The woman stood and shuffled over to them, but she studied her feet instead of looking at them.

"I'm your lawyer."

"Can't afford one." She spoke in a heavy German accent.

"I'm doing it pro bono." Confusion covered her features. "I'm doing it for free."

"*Nein*, I don't take charity."

Nate shrugged. "Better than stealing. Has your husband visited you since you've been here?"

She shook her head. "I'm worried about my, how you say, my children. My husband don't look after them. He likes his *schnaps*. Brunhilde's three years old, and Agatha can't take care of her. She's only five. Too young to be by themselves." She grabbed hold of the bars. "If you want to help, *bringen* them to me. "

"If I don't get you out of here tonight, and Mr. Weber isn't caring for them, I'll bring them here until we work this out."

Her eyes started to water, and her voice cracked. "*Danke*. Could you make sure they get fed? They're *hungrig*."

"I'll make sure." Nate followed Cage back to the office. "I'll stop by Baldwin's General Store and see if I can get him to drop the charges. When he hears the circumstances, I'm sure he will." The store was just down the street from the saloon. He could still make it there in time.

"Great idea." Cage grinned. "See, I knew you weren't a dolt."

"Uh huh" Nate crossed his arms. "You could have talked to Mr. Baldwin."

"I could have, but I'm a town marshal. How would it look if I tried to let every criminal I arrest go free?"

Nate knew his friend was deceiving him, but he didn't care. It did feel good to help that woman, almost like when he rescued slaves before the war. Before he lost his leg. "I'll get going. The store closes at five, and it's already quarter past three."

"We'll go together. I have a buggy hitched outside."

Nate narrowed his eyes. "I thought you couldn't get involved, being a marshal and all."

Cage's palms went up. "I'm not. I'm just giving you a ride."

He didn't bother arguing. After they talked to Mr. Baldwin, they'd be close to his house. He could let Cage get back to the office and say he was heading home, then go to the saloon instead and get that bottle.

They rode to the general store in silence. When they arrived, Mr. Baldwin was waiting on a customer buying some seed. As soon as the farmer left, Nate got his attention. "I'm here about Gertrude Weber, the woman who stole food to feed her children."

Mr. Baldwin was a large man with a gravelly voice. He glanced at Cage standing by the door. "As I told the marshal, I'll drop the charges if she pays for the things she took. If I let everyone who comes in here to steal food, I wouldn't make any money."

Nate glowered back at Cage. "So, Marshal, you couldn't talk to him on her behalf."

Cage just shrugged.

Nate let out a heavy sigh. "How much does she owe?"

"Fifty-nine cents."

He reached into his pocket and pulled out some change. After counting out fifty-nine cents, he set it on the counter.

Mr. Baldwin counted the money and dropped the coins into his money bag he kept under the counter. "Marshal Jones, I'll drop the charges."

"You'll do more than that," Nate said. "The next time Mrs. Weber comes in here, I want you to allow her to buy as many groceries as she needs, deliver it to her house, and charge the food and delivery to my account, and I want you to load the food I just paid for in the back of the marshal's buggy."

Mr. Baldwin grinned. "You sure you want to do that? There's a lot of charity cases in town. I'm always getting a hard-luck story from some rascal trying to get something for free."

"I'm sure." Nate hobbled out onto the front porch of the store and sat on the bench next to a barrel of apples.

Cage sat beside him. "Doesn't it feel good to practice law again?"

Nate crossed his arms. "I wasn't practicing law. I just paid that poor girl's debt."

"You helped her when she needed it. Isn't that why you wanted to become a lawyer, to help people when they need it the most?"

Nate wanted to be angry, but he couldn't. It did feel good to help. "I'm close to home now. Head back to your office to let her go, and I'll make my way from here."

"Not a chance." Cage stood. "I'm off work for the rest of the evening. My deputy will handle anything that comes up. We'll stop by the jail to release Mrs. Weber, then I'm buying you dinner at the American House to show my appreciation."

"No need."

"Yes, there is. With Lavena and Penelope still in Elyria until late, I would like some company."

Nate inwardly groaned, but he didn't let his friend see how disappointed he was that he had to spend the evening with Cage instead of with a bottle of whiskey.

~~~~~

When Betsy parked the wagon in front of the marshal's house, it was already dark. Lavena got down and carefully slid sleeping Penelope into her arms.

"You really shouldn't be carrying her." Betsy got out of the wagon and took Penelope from her. "You don't want to tear open those stitches."

She didn't argue. They headed toward the door. When she reached it, Cage had already opened it and stepped out onto the porch. He took the sleeping child from Betsy's arms.

"I'll talk to you at church tomorrow," Betsy said. "Take care of that arm." She headed to the buggy and rode off into the night.

As Lavena removed her shawl, Cage gazed at her torn sleeve and wrapped arm and raised his eyebrow, but he didn't say anything. Instead, he took Penelope to her room to put her to bed. Lavena removed her bonnet and sank into a kitchen chair.

He returned and sat next to her. "What happened?"

"It's late," Lavena said. "You didn't need to wait up for me."

He sat beside her and kissed her on the cheek. "I wouldn't be able to sleep until you were safely home anyway. You didn't answer my question."

"Some ruffians tried to stop the march. One of them pushed me down and stabbed my arm in the ruckus. He had a knife. The police stopped them, and the mayor promised his protection. He even allowed me to interview him after the picnic."

"But your arm…"

"Betsy treated me. She says I'll be all right."

"*Are* you all right?" He gazed into her eyes until it became uncomfortable.

Her eyes burned with unshed tears. "I will be. The incident shook me, but I'll get through it."

"Maybe I should go with you the next time you join one of these marches."

She touched his cheek. She wanted nothing more than having her strong husband there to protect her. "Thank you, but I can handle anything that comes my way."

He chuckled. "Of that, I have no doubt. During the war, you showed more courage than some of my men, but everyone has times when they need help."

One tear fell onto Lavena's cheek, and she swiped at it. She was able to act strong and fearless when it came to everyone else, but Cage knew her so well. He knew how fretful she became in tense situations over the last couple of years.

He ignored the tear. "So other than that, how did it go?"

She was so grateful to him for changing the subject. Telling him how scared she was only made her feel worse. Besides, he knew without her saying a word. She told him about the rally and about Mrs. Adams. "Betsy and I are going to see her again on Tuesday. She insisted we bring the children with us. I can't wait to interview her and to write this story about the march."

He raised an eyebrow. "So, have you decided to stick with the Oberlin Women's Suffrage Association?"

"Yes." She shrugged. "After I prayed about it, I believe the Lord is directing me this way. But I'm still going to bring up allowing all women into the membership from time to time."

He set his hand on hers. "I wouldn't have expected any different from you. I'm glad you're taking Betsy with you, but I want you to keep a revolver in your purse for protection."

"There's no need."

"Yes, there is. I don't want you out that late alone, especially with Billy Horton and his gang around."

Lavena's heart skipped a beat. "He's in the area?"

"I got a telegram today. He robbed the bank in Black River."

"Promise me…" Her voice thickened. "Promise me you'll be careful."

"Only if you promise me the same."

She nodded, but the dread she felt earlier that day returned. She didn't like the idea that her husband might have to face a killer. She cleared her throat. "We won't be gone as long as today. We'll leave early in the morning, and I'll be home in time to fix your supper."

"That eases my mind." Cage filled up the tea kettle and placed it on the stove.

Leave it to her husband to know how much she needed a cup of tea right now. "So, how did it go with Nate? Did you keep him from drinking?"

Cage laughed. "He was on to me the whole time, but he still went along with it. I arrested a woman for stealing a few groceries. Normally I would have talked Mr. Baldwin into releasing her, but this provided a good excuse. I told Nate I needed his help to represent the girl."

"What did he say?"

"He grumbled about it, but he not only got Mr. Baldwin to drop the charges, he paid for a cart full of groceries to be delivered to her family. Afterwards, I invited him to supper at the American House as a thank-you. What could he say? I dropped him off safe and sound at his home after we ate then insisted on coming in for a visit. I only left him an hour ago."

"I can't imagine. Next time, you'll have to be cleverer."

Cage pulled her to her feet and kissed her. "I'll think of something, but even if he sees through me, he can't resist helping those less fortunate than himself."

Chapter Eight

On Tuesday morning, Betsy sat in the parlor listening while Lavena interviewed Mrs. Adams. The children had finished their lunches and cookies and were playing with the toys in the wooden box in the corner. There were spinning tops, toy soldiers, dolls, a rocking horse, and a doll house. More toys than she could imagine one family owning.

Mrs. Adams told them about all the changes she'd seen over the years, not just new inventions like a pump inside the house, telegraphs, sewing machines, and trains, but other changes like speech and fashion, not to mention wars, the expansion of the United States, and the abolition of slavery. As she told her story, Lavena sat at the desk and scratched it onto her paper with her fountain pen.

"My husband, Benjamin Adams was a second cousin of John and Samuel Adams."

Lavena gasped. "You mean the founding fathers, John and Samuel Adams?"

"Sure were. Both my father and his fought in the Revolutionary War under General Washington. I was only a baby when the war started, but I'd became a young woman before it ended. When the last battle was fought in Yorktown, my pa was there, and I remember being so scared he wouldn't come home. But a month later, he did. The war was over, and he had done his part to win our freedom."

"Did you know Abigail Adams?"

"Oh, dear me, I did. My mother was a friend and neighbor of hers. She was a spirited woman, a lot like you, Lavena."

Lavena stopped writing for a moment and blushed.

Betsy suppressed a smile. Mrs. Adams described her friend well.

Mrs. Adams continued. "She was always pestering her husband about the vote for women and ending slavery. I remember being at their house one afternoon visiting her with my mother. Mrs. Adams told her husband that this country's freedoms would never survive if all men and women weren't free. Mr. Adams turned red in the face and said, 'Woman, what would you have me do? I've tried, but nobody listens to me.'" She chuckled at the memory. "In six years, we'll be celebrating this nation being one hundred years old, and we're still fighting the same battles. Nobody will listen."

"That's why I became a journalist." Lavena set her pen down and stretched the fingers on her hand. "I'm trying to get people to listen and to change."

"That's what I want too," Mrs. Adams said. "And I'm glad you're doing your part, but only the Lord can change people's hearts. We can be His servants and do His will, but we can't change people. That's the Holy Spirit's role. Took me a lot of years to learn that. We have to trust the Lord's timing. He's working even if we can't see it."

Betsy took in a deep breath and let it out slowly. *Lord, are You working in Nate? I want to trust You.*

"Now, you sound like my husband," Lavena said.

Mrs. Adams patted her hand. "He must be a wise man."

She let out a snort. "He is, but don't tell him I said so. Tell me about how you met your husband."

"We knew each other all of our lives, but it didn't become a romance until he graduated and came home from Yale. He asked me to take a buggy ride with him, and we were married a few months later. The year was 1795. It was a spring wedding, and we moved to Boston where he opened a law practice. A few years later, the British attacked our ships and seized our cargo. That started the War of 1812. I never prayed as hard as I did when he enlisted to fight in that war."

Lavena pushed the lever on her pen to fill the ink reservoir. "Then, after the war, you moved to the Western Reserve in Ohio."

"Yes. In the Panic of 1819, we lost everything. We both prayed and believed we needed a new start somewhere else, so we packed up the children and moved here."

"How many children?"

"Sixteen." Mrs. Adams pulled her handkerchief out and dabbed her eyes. "Only four made it to adulthood."

"I'm so sorry," Betsy said.

"Those four have grown into fine citizens and have made me proud, but the medicines we have today weren't around back then, and nobody knew about things like germs and what caused infection. Lots of families suffered loss."

They were all silent for a moment, and Betsy glanced toward her healthy children and let up a silent prayer of thanks. Families still suffered loss today, but hopefully, with the advancement of medicine, at some point in the future, most children would live to adulthood and beyond.

"Anything you care to add on the record?" Lavena said.

Mrs. Adams looked puzzled. "On the record?"

"It's a newspaper phrase that means, you don't mind if we report it."

Mrs. Adams chuckled. "You young'uns are always coming up with new words. I suppose that's all I have to say on the record."

Betsy bit her lip. "May I ask you a question? It wouldn't be in the article Lavena's writing."

"Yes, of course, my dear."

"You said before that your husband lost a leg in the war. My husband is a lawyer also, and he lost a leg during the war between the states."

Mrs. Adams walked over to her, sat beside her, and took hold of her hands. "I'm sorry, child. I know how difficult that can be for a wife. Does he have nightmares?"

"Not only that. He started going to the saloon and drinking, and he won't practice law. He says nobody wants a cripple representing him." Betsy started pouring out the entire story of what she and Nate had gone through. She couldn't believe she was telling all of this to a woman she'd only met a couple of days ago, but she couldn't keep silent another moment. Even Lavena looked surprised by things she hadn't told her.

"Your story sounds very much like mine. My husband started drinking and feeling sorry for himself as well. What have you done to help him?"

"I comfort him when he has nightmares, and I've asked him not to drink. I also joined the Wellington Temperance Society. We're trying to convince businesses to pay men more if they sign the pledge not to drink. And I pray."

Mrs. Adams patted her hand. "Prayer is vital. However much time you've been praying, pray more, and trust God to show you what to do to make your husband's life more difficult while he drinks."

Betsy furrowed her brow. "More difficult? But I want to be a good wife."

Mrs. Adams gazed at her for a moment. "Do you wait up for him and keep his supper warm on the stove?"

Betsy nodded.

"Do you get up and make breakfast for him when he's been drinking all night?"

She nodded again.

"When he yells at you or says harsh words to you, do you keep silent? Do you lie to his boss about his drinking or hide it from his friends to protect his reputation?"

She remembered lying to his boss a couple of times when he was too sick from the drink to go to work. She dabbed the perspiration off her forehead with her yellow embroidered handkerchief. The temperature seemed to rise at least ten degrees. "Yes, to all of those, but how can I stop doing things for him and still be a loving wife?"

Mrs. Adams smiled. "I did the same things at first, but God showed me I was making it easier for my husband to drink. I sat him down and had a serious talk. I told him I would not keep his meals warm or make his breakfast on the nights he decided to keep company with a rum bottle instead of with me. I would not lie or hide his depravity. He never raised a hand to me although he did pound on the table or throw things, but I told him that if he threw things or said horrible insults, the children and I would stay with my parents for a couple of days until he apologized. I told him I loved him and would remain his loving wife, but I wouldn't put up with his shenanigans anymore."

Betsy could scarcely believe what she was hearing. Was it really that simple? "So, he stopped drinking after you told him that?"

Mrs. Adams snorted. "Oh, my, no. Things got worse. He drank more than ever, and said really mean things, but I did everything I said I would do, and I trusted God to direct my paths. It took a couple of years of me on my knees and doing what the Lord led me to do before my husband finally repented."

"That's not encouraging." Betsy dabbed her tears with her handkerchief.

Mrs. Adams put an arm around her. "I can't say if your husband will repent or not. All I know is he'll be lost if you don't partner with God and fight for your marriage. And the Lord will give you the peace and grace to get through it. Are you ready to do that?"

Betsy realized she hadn't been really praying for Nate. She'd been praying for him to be a good husband and stop drinking to make her life easier. If she did what Mrs. Adams said, her life would get harder. She squared her shoulders. She would pray fervently for her husband and marriage and trust the Lord to answer, come what may. Whatever He directed her to do, she would obey. She was ready to fight even if things got worse.

~~~~~

That afternoon, the sun bore down brightly on Nate when he left the office. Cage stood outside the door, apparently waiting for him.

"I need your help," Cage said.

Nate groaned, knowing whatever his friend was up to would keep him from going to the saloon. "What is it this time?"

"Come with me?"

He propped himself onto his crutches and followed Cage to the marshal's office. When they got inside, Cage motioned for him to sit.

"Doug Hanson beat his wife again."

Nate's jaw tightened. "How badly is she hurt?"

"A black eye, a bruised lip, and a broken arm. Dr. Clark treated her. He says she'll be all right in a few weeks."

Nate slammed his fist on the desk and glared at Cage. "I know. You can't arrest him because there's no law against beating up your wife. The law needs changed."

"I did arrest him."

Nate's mouth fell open. "I can't believe you did that. What are the charges?"

"Assault. If he'd beat up someone other than his wife, I'd charge him, so I decided to do something."

"Is the prosecutor going to bring this to trial?"

"No. I talked to Mr. Nelson, but he won't budge." Cage stood and paced a few steps. "If I want to keep him in jail, I need some other lawyer to prosecute this case. Do you know of anyone?"

Nate sputtered as he realized what Cage wanted him to do. "It will be thrown out. You know as well as I do, there's no law against beating your wife. If there was, Betsy's sister might have survived her abusive marriage."

Cage's brow furrowed. "I know, but he could get a year in the penitentiary for assault. It shouldn't matter that the victim is a family member."

"It won't work."

Cage pulled on his ear. "Probably not, but if we keep bringing these cases before the judge, sooner or later, someone will do something about it."

"You're loony, You know that."

A smile crossed his friend's mouth.

"I know. I'm just as crazy as you are."

"Come on." Cage headed for the door. "I got the buggy hitched. I'll drive you home, and we can talk more about how to make this case."

Nate almost said no. He really wanted to get drunk, especially if he was going to try this impossible task. Instead, he followed Cage to the buggy.

~~~~~

Betsy didn't say anything most of the way home, and it irritated Lavena. She loved what Mrs. Adams had said, and she wanted to know what her friend was thinking. Betsy was demure and sweet most of the time. People could and did take advantage of that, including her husband. What most people didn't know was she also had a determination and stubbornness that could not be defeated. This was the women she knew in Oberlin and during the war. Lavena prayed that was coming to the surface, but she couldn't keep silent any longer.

"So, what are you going to do?"

Betsy shrugged. "I was quiet because I believe God gave me direction while we were praying. I was trying to work it all out in my mind."

"Well?"

"First I'm going to pray for my husband's salvation like never before."

She knew that glint in Betsy's eyes. She wasn't only going to pray.

"Are you going to write articles like you said you would do about the evils of drink?" Betsy continued.

Lavena smoothed her skirt. When she'd brought it up before, Betsy acted like she wasn't sure about it. "If you want me to."

"Oh, I do. The march for suffrage inspired me. I plan to organize protests in front of the saloon on Friday and Saturday nights. We'll carry signs and sing hymns. Maybe you can write about that too."

"Of course," Lavena said.

"I'm sure the temperance society members will agree to it. We have a meeting tomorrow night. Reverend Fowler is a member. I'm going to talk to him about preaching in front of the saloon while we're protesting." She shrugged. "But first, I'm going to have a conversation with my wayward husband."

A smile spread across Lavena's face. Her friend's fire was back.

~~~~~

When Betsy got home, she expected Nate to be out drinking, but he wasn't. Instead, he was sitting at the table discussing some court case with Cage. After greeting her husband and Cage, she settled the children and started supper. "Are you staying?" she asked the marshal.

"No, I have to get home."

After Cage said his good-byes and left, Betsy turned to her husband. "After the children are in bed, I want to talk with you about something."

He nodded. "I have something to discuss with you as well."

That was all that was said for the rest of the evening. After supper, the children went right to sleep, obviously worn out from their journey to Elyria.

She came back into the kitchen and sat at the table where Nate still was brooding. "Did you want to go first or shall I?"

He wiped his hand across his lips. "Did you tell Lavena about our... my difficulties?"

A lump formed in her throat. "Yes, I did. She's my best friend, and I needed to talk with someone."

"I assumed so. She must have told Cage. He keeps coming up with projects for me to do."

"Projects?"

"Lawyer projects." Nate lowered his eyes. "I've put you through a lot, haven't I? I mean it's bad enough the nightmares and..." he pointed to his missing leg, "this. But I haven't been the husband you need." The muscle in his cheek twitched. "Not just the drinking. I'm treating you like you're responsible for my misery." His voice hitched. "I'm so sorry."

She reached out to take his hands in hers. "That must have been some talk you had with Cage while I was gone."

"We didn't talk about that, but it was obvious he knew."

"Does this mean you won't go drinking again?"

His lips pressed together in a slight grimace. "I'm not going to lie to you. I don't want to stop. I've tried to slow down, but it's hard. I feel so hopeless about my situation, and when I get that way, well... Whiskey helps."

It wasn't what she wanted to hear, but at least he was being honest for a change. "If you turn to God, I know He can help you get through this."

His jaw twitched. "Where was God when I lost my leg?"

She wanted to say He was right there keeping Nate alive, but she didn't. "I have something to tell you that might upset you."

He stroked his beard. "What is it?"

Betsy's mouth grew dry, and she swallowed before answering. "When we were first married, and you told me when you left to rescue slaves for a whole year, it was something you had to do. I understand that a little better now because there's something I have to do."

His brow furrowed. "Are you leaving me?"

She gave his hand a squeeze. "No, I'm not leaving you. I promised you that during the war."

"Then what?"

"I feel as strongly about the dangers of drink and how it's ruining families as you did about freeing slaves. Helen was married to a drunk, and he ended up killing her."

Hurt flashed in Nate's eyes. "Have I ever laid a hand on you even when I was drunk?"

"No, you haven't. If you did, then I would leave you. But you have banged the table with your fist and thrown things, and you have said really hurtful things."

The muscle in Nate's cheek twitched. "I'll try to do better."

"I hope so, but either way, I'm going to meet with the Wellington Temperance Society tomorrow evening after supper and make plans. I hope you'll stay sober and watch the children, but if you don't, Lavena will take care of them."

"Of course, I'll watch them." His voice had an edge to it, and he pulled his hands away. "What plans?"

"I'm going to ask Mr. Hayes and other businessmen to talk to the mayor and the city council about prohibiting alcohol in this village just as it is in Oberlin. If they agree, Wellington will become a dry town. If not, the men will continue their efforts to convince the businesses in the town to get their employees to sign a pledge not to drink. At some point, this will include the telegraph office."

Nate's eyes widened. "You're going to talk to my boss."

Betsy swallowed the lump in her throat. "Not yet, but at some point, one of the men will."

"I never thought you would turn against me like that. That money supports you and the children."

"And it pays for your whiskey."

He wiped his hand across the back of his neck.

She didn't expect him to take this well, but she needed to tell him the rest. "I'm going to talk to Reverend Fowler about…" Maybe she was telling too much. She didn't want him to stop going to church.

"So, what are you planning to do? You mentioned what you've asked the others to do, but you must be planning some little scheme of your own since you feel so strongly about this." A hint of sarcasm emphasized his words.

"I hope you don't go to the saloon again, but if you do, you'll find a group of women near the entrance carrying signs and singing hymns. I'll be the one leading them."

The muscle in his jaw twitched. "Betsy, no. This is different than the suffrage march. You don't know what kind of men go there. I can't let you do it."

"Horsefeathers. There will be a large group of us. They aren't going to attack us with so many carrying signs." She gave him a faint smile. "You could order me not to do this, but I'm asking you not to. You didn't take me along on your slave rescues before the war or give me a say in your leaving me alone for an entire year, then again for months at a time. I'm your wife, so I don't have that luxury. I have to obey you, but this is important to me. I'm asking you not to forbid it."

"What about the children while you're singing your hymns? Surely, you're not going to take them along this time."

"I wouldn't do that. We'll only be out on Friday and Saturday nights when the saloon is its busiest. I'm going to ask Mrs. Hayes and Mrs. Fowler to care for the children at the church unless you're willing to take care of them. If they can't and you won't, I'll drop them off at Lavena's."

He gazed at her with a blank expression. Finally, he spoke. "It seems you've thought of everything."

She shrugged. "So, are you going to forbid it?"

"No. If I decide to go drinking, I'll plan it during the week when I won't run into your do-gooders."

Betsy's eyes burned with unshed tears. She wouldn't let him see her cry. "Good, but there's more."

Nate glowered at her. "Go ahead."

"I can't stop you from drinking, and I'm not going to try anymore. No more nagging or cajoling, but I would like you to talk to Cage or Reverend Fowler about it. They might be able to help you."

"That's not going to happen."

"That's up to you. I don't have any control over what you do, but I'm going to tell you what I've decided. I won't go out of my way to tell people you're a drunk, but I'm not going to lie for you anymore or hide what you're doing. If Mr. Wilson or even the whole town finds out, so be it."

"I never asked you to lie."

"No, but I did it anyway to hide the shame of what you've done."

Nate nodded as if he couldn't deny the truth anymore.

"There's more. If you come home drunk, I won't wait up for you or keep your supper warm, and I won't get up early to make your breakfast the next morning. I'll only serve meals to a sober husband."

He let out a gusty sigh. "Anything else."

"If you ever berate me or the children or scare me again by pounding your fist on the table or worse, I'm moving in with Cage and Lavena and taking the children with me."

"I thought you weren't leaving me." His voice had a pleading tone.

"I'll move back after you sober up and apologize."

Nate tried to take Betsy's hand, but she pulled it away. She knew he would try to charm her like he always did, and she needed to stay strong.

"Have I ever berated you except that one time when I didn't get the job with Mr. Hayes?"

"Yes, often. You don't even realize how often. Then there's the throwing things and sometimes even getting in my face and yelling at me. How do you think that makes me feel after finding out that my sister was being abused by her drunken husband for years before he finally killed her?"

Then something happened she didn't expect. Nate started sobbing.

Chapter Nine

The next day, when Nate left work, he headed to the town hall where Judge Murphy would have a hearing about Doug Hanson's assault charge. Cage would meet him there with Hanson in tow. The town hall was a two-story brick building on Main Street only a block from the telegraph office. Two courtrooms and a meeting room were on the first floor, and offices were on the second. There was some talk about building a new town hall since the village was growing so fast, and they might need additional courtrooms, but so far, it was only talk.

Nate walked into the courtroom and found Cage already there sitting beside handcuffed Hanson. Doug's hair and beard were straggly, and his clothes were dingy and dirty. From the look on his face, he was in the midst of a huge hangover.

The courtroom was small with three benches on each side that seated maybe twenty people at the most, a desk and wooden chair where the judge sat, and a chair beside the judge for witnesses to sit when they testified. Two large twelve-pane windows allowed plenty of light inside, and there were chairs under one of the windows where the jury sat. The jury chairs and benches were empty since this was only a hearing.

Nate tried to stay focused on what they were about to do, but his mind kept wandering back to the things Betsy said. Everything she said about him was true, and he couldn't shake the tightness that gripped his chest. The irony wasn't lost. He was about to prosecute a drunk for the way he'd treated his wife, when he had become a drunk who had often berated his own wife.

Judge Murphy walked in, and everyone stood. He pounded his gavel, and they sat back down. "Court is now in session. Is everyone here?"

"Yes, your honor," Cage answered.

"Where's Mr. Nelson?"

Nate stood. "Your honor, I will serve as the prosecutor in this case."

"Name?"

"Nathaniel Teagan."

Judge Murphy read his notes. "It looks here like Mr. Douglas Hanson is accused of assaulting a woman. Is that right?"

"Yes, sir," Nate said.

"What is the name of the woman he's accused of assaulting? And why isn't she in the courtroom today?"

He groaned inside. He was hoping the judge wouldn't ask that so soon in the case. "Her name is Mrs. Nancy Hanson. She's Doug Hanson's wife."

The judge's eyes widened.

"He beat her so badly, she has a black eye, a tooth missing, and a broken arm."

The judge glared at him. "Mr. Teagan, do you have a law degree?"

"Yes, Your Honor."

"Then you know there's no law against a man beating his wife. I wish I could throw him in jail and lose the key, but I must follow the law. As distasteful and reprehensible as his actions are, there's nothing I can do about it."

"Your honor, she should have the same protection under the law that you would give any other woman?"

"I see what you're trying to do, Mr. Teagan, and I am sympathetic." He rubbed his jaw. "All right. I'll allow it for now, but I need to hear from Mrs. Hanson."

At this point, Cage stood. "Your honor, I saw her injuries myself, and Dr. Clark can verify them, but she's afraid to come to court to accuse her husband."

Judge Murphy leaned back in his chair. "Did she tell you her husband caused these injuries?"

Cage looked down. "She said she fell down the stairs."

Nate let out a groan. Cage didn't tell him Mrs. Hanson lied about the incident. He made him look like a fool in front of the judge.

"Do you know how many cases I hear every day? I don't appreciate my time being wasted like this." The judge beat his gavel. "Mr. Hanson, there may not be a law against it, but if it were up to me, you would rot in jail. Case dismissed." The judge walked out of the courtroom.

Hanson chuckled, stood, and held out his hands for Cage to unlock the shackles. Cage unlocked them, and Hanson turned to Nate. "You have no call to judge me. You ain't no different. You just don't have the backbonel to get your own wife in control. Leave my family alone." He walked out of the courtroom.

Heat rushed to Nate's face. "Cage, why did you have to make me look like a fool? Isn't it bad enough having strangers on the street pity me for being a cripple?"

Cage set his hand on Nate's shoulder. "We both knew this case would probably be dismissed."

He stepped away. "But you never told me Mrs. Hanson lied about what happened. Even if I could have convinced the judge to have a trial, that little detail would have been good to know. We never had a chance, and you didn't even bother to tell me."

Cage held his palms up. "I'm sorry. I was afraid you wouldn't take the case."

Heat rushed up Nate's back. "How many impossible battles did I follow you into during the war? Do you really think so little of me that you couldn't trust me with the truth? If I'd known, I would have warned you, but I still would have brought this to court."

Cage sank onto the bench. "You're right. I should have trusted you."

Nate sat beside him. "Why didn't you?"

He grabbed hold of his ear. "You've changed. You're not the same man who saved me from that fire. You drink too much, and you feel sorry for yourself. You're making your family's life miserable, and we're not close like we used to be. It's like you've given up on God and yourself."

He couldn't have said anything that hurt Nate more.

~~~~~

Betsy had contacted all the members of the Temperance Society. They all agreed more had to be done. Mr. Guthrie, the publisher of *The Wellington Enterprise*, was pleased Lavena wanted to write a series of articles on the evils of drink and about how women's suffrage would benefit the temperance movement.

Rev. Fowler, the young fiery preacher with dark curly hair, was most helpful. He promised to attend the protests in front of the saloon at least once a week to call out for those poor souls to repent and to preach a sermon on the evils of drink, and he would preach about strong drink at church for the next few Sundays. Mr. and Mrs. Hayes agreed to contact local businesses who had not yet agreed to pay more to men who signed the pledge and convince them of the merits of such a policy. It was a boon to the employers not to have workers who were drunks.

Betsy's part in all of this was to contact wives all over the village to attend the next temperance meeting and to organize them to protest. Men might reconsider if they had to make their way through a gaggle of women carrying signs to get to the saloon. Mrs. Hayes and Mrs. Fowler agreed to watch the children during the protests.

The first woman she planned to contact was Mrs. Hanson. Afterall, that poor woman knew better than most the danger of having a drunk for a husband.

She rode the wagon down Liberty Street to where the woman lived. She had never been on this side of town before. The houses were small, usually only two rooms. Some of the bigger houses housed as many as five families in them, and they shared a kitchen. Most of the men who worked at the cheese factories lived in this area of town. She knocked on Mrs. Hanson's door.

A thin woman in her thirties with reddish-brown hair answered.

"May I help you?" Her voice was weak. She had sad brown eyes and wore a simple brown dress with a dingy, stained, dark green apron. Her right eye was bruised, and she wore a sling on her left arm. Betsy wondered if Mr. Hanson had inflicted those wounds.

"Hello, Mrs. Hanson. I'm Mrs. Teagan. Your son Johnnie works with my husband."

The woman didn't answer or offer to let her in. She just stood there, hand on the door, as if ready to close it at a moment's notice.

"I'm the one who treated your son's wounds."

Mrs. Hanson bit her lower lip. "Thank you for that. Everything's fine now. If you could just leave us be—"

Betsy interrupted her. "We have something in common. My husband drinks as well, and…" She hated admitting Nate's faults to a complete stranger. "I thought if we wives bind together, we might be able to do something about it."

Mrs. Hanson's forehead furrowed. "Don't I have enough trouble without you do-gooders making it worse?" A baby cried from inside the house, and she closed the door without another word.

A do-gooder? Betsy was only trying to help. She knocked on the next door and received the same cold response. By the time she got to the fifth house, she was about to give up.

A young woman carrying an infant answered. She couldn't have been more than eighteen and was dressed simply like the others. "May I help you?"

Betsy introduced herself and said why she was there.

"I'm Mrs. Green," the woman said. "Won't you come in?"

Betsy entered the small home. A table, a couple of benches, and a cradle were the only furniture surrounding the tiny hearth. Mrs. Green placed the baby in the cradle, and they sat at the table. Betsy told her why she was there.

"My husband has worked at the cheese factory for a year now. He's always fussing about the men drinking away their hard-earned money instead of supporting their families. He's a God-fearing man. I know he'd like me to do what I can, but I have a baby to care for. How could I go off carrying signs in front of a saloon?"

"Mrs. Hayes of the Temperance Society has a solution for that. She and Mrs. Fowler, the pastor's wife of the First Church, will care for the children while we're protesting."

"Then count me in," Mrs. Green said. "I know I can get some of the other ladies in this neighborhood to join. When shall we do it?"

"We're going to meet at First Church on Wednesday morning around the tenth hour to make our plans."

"Wednesday it is. I'll be there, and I know I can bring at least five other ladies."

Betsy left a bit more encouraged. She might not know the women of this area of town, but Mrs. Green obviously did.

She knocked on the next door down. A young woman with blond hair, in her early twenties, answered the door. "Hello, I'm Mrs. Teagan."

"Mr. Nathaniel Teagan's wife?" the woman asked with a strong German accent.

Betsy paused for a moment. How did she know Nate? "Yes, he's my husband."

"Come. Come. I'm Mrs. Weber, but call me Greta." The woman ushered her into the small kitchen. Two young children played in the corner.

Betsy sat at the table. "Greta, you speak English very well."

"*Ja*, I try. I moved here from Germany a few years ago with my husband."

"How do you know my husband?"

"It's a little *peinlich*, how you say, embarrassing."

"You don't have to tell me, but if you do, I'll keep your confidence."

A blush spread over Greta's face. "I was arrested for stealing food from Baldwin General Store."

Betsy patted her hand, hoping this girl would not feel judged by her.

"My husband, he likes his *schnaps*, um, beer. He drinks a lot. Sometimes when he does, he plays cards with the men at the saloon. A couple of weeks ago, he lost everything he earned from the cheese factory. We didn't have any food in the house, and the children were *hungrig*. They cried at night. One day, I couldn't stand it, and I stole some flour and beans from the store. Mr. Baldwin caught me and took me to the marshal. Marshal Jones put me in a jail cell. I was never so scared and humiliated, but mostly, I was worried about my *kinder*… um… children."

"I can't imagine," Betsy said. "What happened?"

"I only was there for little time when Mr. Teagan came to the jail and asked me what happened. About an hour later, Marshal Jones let me out and told me I could go home." Greta wiped the tears off her face with her apron. "Mr. Teagan had paid off my debt and told Mr. Baldwin to deliver a wagon full of groceries to me. Mr. Teagan told him to charge them to his account. I've never been so happy. I told my husband I wanted to start going to church to thank God for this miracle. He told me to do as I please, but he still drinks, and I worry he will do something like this again."

Betsy blinked away the tears forming in her eyes. Nate hadn't told her what he'd done. It reminded her of the man he used to be, always wanting to help those in trouble. "Would you like to join us and do something about our men who spend too much time in the saloon?"

"How?"

Betsy told her about their plans to protest.
"I will do it."

Chapter Ten

A couple of weeks later, Nate stepped out from the telegram office into a dreary day. As he pulled on his overcoat, the heavens opened, and a deluge of rain dumped onto his head. His coat didn't shield him from the downpour, and drops of water rolled down his neck into his shirt. He wished he'd brought his oilcloth. he would wear as a cloak on days like this. He would be drenched before he was able to make it home.

Each step became more cumbersome. He almost fell when his crutch sank into the mud. He had to yank at it to pull it out while trying to keep his balance with one leg and the other crutch. He walked along the track, avoiding any other mud puddles forming in the dirt and trying not to think about how cold, wet, and miserable he was. He stopped for a moment and glanced at the next road sign, Dewolf Street. If he were going to the saloon, that was where he would turn. Clay Street where his house stood was only a block further.

His mouth watered. He hadn't had a drink since Betsy chided him for what he had become, a horrible husband and father who had mistreated his family. Then what Cage said about him changing… He'd decided right then to give up drinking.

Since then, he'd had frequent headaches and a hard time sleeping. He realized it was stopping altogether that caused these symptoms and made him irritable, but he tried not to show it to Betsy or the children. All of it was harder than he thought it would be.

He glanced down the street, longing for a glass of whiskey. It would help him sleep. What would be the harm in one glass to warm him up? Afterall, he was drenched, and the wet clothes were making him shiver. While he was in there, the storm might slow down. It might even stop raining. Then he could make his way home.

He leaned on his crutches. Had he so soon forgotten how drink had caused Hanson to beat his boy to a pulp and give his wife a black eye and broken arm or that Betsy's sister was beaten to death by a man who wouldn't stop drinking? He let out a sigh and started to walk on, then stopped again. He had promised himself he'd stop, but even as he scolded himself for it, he turned and headed down Dewolf. Each step grew heavier. Why couldn't he resist the temptation? It would be all right. This time, he'd only have one drink. Nobody could fault him for one drink in this weather.

He thought about his children, Malachi with his blond curls and Naomi who always greeted him with open arms calling for Papa to pick her up. He almost turned back, but he kept walking. He passed Baldwin's General Store, then the boxing mill, only half a block from the saloon.

Steam rose from the brick plant and joined the rain clouds above that were still emptying their water on his head. A loud clank and hum sounded from the factory and joined with the rain beating on the rooftops. The only thing louder was when thunder crashed mirroring his crashing mood.

He wanted that drink so bad. He reached the alley where the saloon sat and looked up at the roughhewn logs and wooden porch. He shouldn't be there. Deep inside, he heard a voice warning him this was dangerous. If he had one drink, he might have another… and another. He made his way up the steps and through the swinging door.

Cigar smoke whirled about, and a couple of men were drinking themselves into oblivion even though it was still early. The men at the mills and the cheese factory didn't leave work until at least six o'clock. He might have to rise before dawn, but at least he was able to be home from work in the middle of the afternoon. So why was he here instead?

He glanced around at the men's faces, hard chins, glazed over eyes, and slumped shoulders. They had nothing to live for but the next drink. A tightness covered his chest. Even with the loss of his leg, and his law career gone, he still had Betsy and the children.

He didn't belong here. Only one drink, and then he'd go.

~~~~~

Betsy looked out the window, and bit her bottom lip. The storm was still going strong, and even though dark clouds blocked the sun, sheets of lightning lit the sky. A moment later, thunder as loud as her heartbeat rumbled.

The children played in the corner of the kitchen with the spinning tops Mrs. Adams had given them. They wanted to stay close to her during this tempest. If things got any worse, they would take refuge in the fruit cellar under the house. She would have ushered everyone there already if she hadn't worried about Nate. It had been over an hour since he was due to arrive home.

She tried to convince herself that the storm delayed him. Either he'd taken shelter near the telegraph office, or maybe he'd sheltered somewhere else on the way home. It didn't help. In her heart, she knew he'd stopped at the saloon for a drink.

He had stopped drinking altogether since they'd had their conversation two weeks ago, but he still had bouts of feeling sorry for himself. The nightmares hadn't stopped, and he'd tossed and turned at night, but at least he had stopped drinking. That was improvement, wasn't it? Eventually he'd go back to being the man he once was. Unless he stopped at the saloon tonight instead of coming straight home and reassuring her that he wasn't caught in this storm.

Pounding on the roof caused Betsy to glance out the window again. The sky looked grayish, almost green. She couldn't wait any longer. She needed to get the children out of danger.

She blew out the oil lamp, placed a candle and flint in her pocket, and got oilcloths to cover their heads. She kept old blankets and pillows in the cellar for emergencies. They'd sleep there for tonight.

"Children, I need you to listen to me. We're going outside, and I want you to keep these cloths over your heads. The fruit cellar doors are right beside the porch. That's where we're headed. We'll be safe there."

"Ma, I'm scared," Malachi said.

Naomi started crying.

"It will be all right. Malachi, hold on to my dress." She picked up Naomi, covered her with the oilcloth, and headed outside.

It was dark, but the frequent lighting strikes lit the way. Hail began to pound on the ground, and one of them hit her forehead as she and the children hurried down the stairs and toward the door to the cellar. She had to set Naomi down to open the door, and the child clutched her legs and screamed. She got the door open and ushered Malachi inside. She had to sweep Naomi into her arms to get the child to move into the shelter. Even then, the girl's thrashing and screams make it difficult. A loud roar thundered in her ears, and she glanced at the sky. A twister was headed toward them. She rushed inside, set Naomi on the top step, and closed and latched the door.

In the darkness of the cellar, Naomi's screams turned into sobs, and Malachi was now crying also.

"Sit on the steps until I get the candle lit." Betsy's hands shook, and it took three tries to strike the flint and light the candle. She carried Naomi down the stairs with Malachi holding onto her dress. When she finally reached the landing at the bottom, she had them sit against the far wall. She retrieved the oil lamp she kept on a shelf and lit it with the candle, then blew the candle out. Then she grabbed the blankets, sat in between the children, and covered them up.

The roaring grew louder, and her insides quivered.

"Please, Lord, don't allow the tornado to touch down. Keep us safe."

"What about Pa?" Malachi asked. "Is he okay?"

"Of course he is." Betsy placed an arm around each of them. "Wherever your Pa is, I know he's all right." She prayed that was true.

The roaring that sounded like a train grew louder, and the thunder still crashed as loud as it did before.

Nate had stopped drinking. He had sheltered in town. She tried to convince herself, but what scared her the most was what Mrs. Adams had said when they visited her in Elyria. Things would get worse before they got better. Nate giving up whiskey so easily after their talk told her this wasn't over.

While they sat against the wall and listened to the fierce wind blowing and the rain hitting the door to the cellar, she prayed for Nate. When she heard what he had done for Greta Weber, something in her had changed. She saw a glimpse of the way Nate used to be, and her love for him grew. She imagined this was only a small amount of the love God felt for him.

She no longer prayed he would stop drinking to make life easier for her and the children, or that he would become the man he used to be so she could have a happy home. She placed her husband in the Lord's hands and asked Him to do whatever it took to bring Nate to his knees, and she pledged to do the same, no matter how difficult.

The roar of the wind grew louder until it was deafening and rattled the cellar door. Naomi screamed. The door blew off.

~~~~~

It was long after dark before the storm died down. Nate left where he had taken shelter for the past six hours and headed for home. Very few of the streetlamps were still lit. Most of them had blown out with the glass broken around them. A couple of the poles had toppled along with a few trees. One tree had fallen onto a house. Nate rushed over to see if they needed help, but the family was in their cellar when the tree hit, and they assured him they had things under control. Tree limbs had blown around, and debris littered the yard. One tree was pulled out by its roots and had landed in a field. It could have been much worse, but the strong winds had done their damage. Only the aftermath of the storm needed cleared away.

Unless the twister had hit elsewhere, maybe his house. He walked as fast as his crutches allowed. He needed to make sure his family was safe.

He took another couple of steps when his crutch sank into a puddle, this time causing him to fall headfirst into the mud. He barely placed his arms out in time to break the fall. He sat there for a moment, shaken. His arms bore scratches, and his clothes were drenched and muddy, but he believed nothing was hurt badly. The problem was how to get to his feet, foot, when the ground was so soft and there was nothing around to hold on to. He tried to raise onto his foot with only his arms against the ground to support him, but it was too slippery, and he couldn't get the leverage he needed.

Glancing around, he found a small tree that hadn't blown over around ten feet away. He placed his crutches across his lap and scooted, using his hands and leg, through the mud and puddles. By the time he got to the tree, he was thoroughly wet and miserable. It still took at least a half hour to stand upright, partly because of the mud and partly because he was still shaky from the fall. He started for home again.

When he finally approached his house, small hail stones and tree branches littered the yard, but nothing major seemed amiss. The house looked unharmed.

He climbed the porch steps and entered the kitchen. No lanterns were lit. They had probably already gone to bed. He lit a candle and made his way into their bedroom as quietly as he could considering the thumping noise his crutch made.

Betsy's form was not under the covers. He pulled them back. She wasn't there. Where could she be? Panic gripped his stomach. Surely, she wouldn't go out in this storm. Perhaps, the children were afraid of the thunder, and she'd gone upstairs to comfort them and had fallen asleep.

Nate made his way to the staircase, blew out his candle, and placed it in his pocket. He couldn't carry the lit candle and hold onto the rail and his crutches. He hated climbing the stairs, but he did, one stair at a time. When he reached the top of the staircase, he steadied himself, lit the candle, and headed to Naomi's room. She wasn't there. He hobbled down the hallway to Malachi's room. No sign of them. The back of his throat ached. Where could they be?

After traveling to the staircase, he sat on the top step. He tried to calm his breathing as he struggled to reason where they might be.

The fruit cellar. Of course. When the weather got bad, Betsy would have ushered the children into the cellar to protect them in case a tornado touched down. Normally, they would have been back by now, but the children had probably fallen asleep.

As much sense as that made, Nate couldn't calm his pounding heartbeat until he made sure they were safe. He placed the crutches on his lap and bumped down the stairs on his bottom then headed outside. When he reached the storm shelter, the door to it was gone. It felt like an anvil rested on his chest.

He tried to reassure himself, to stop panic from overtaking them. Even if they had been down there when the door blew off, the cellar was dug deep. He wanted to call to them, to see if they'd survived the storm, but he paused for a moment. He wouldn't want to wake his sleeping children. He sat at the top of the stairs. He wasn't sure he could make it down to find out they weren't there and try to climb back up. His arms and leg ached from the strain, and he was shivering because of his wet clothes. Exhaustion overtook him, but he had to know if they were all right.

He whispered loudly, "Betsy, are you down there?"

"I'm here," came her soft voice.

The relief nearly did him in. Tears welled up inside of him. He had never considered himself an emotional man, but this was the second time he'd wept in two weeks.

"I'll be right down." He didn't have the strength left in his body to make it down on crutches, so he placed them on his lap and bumped down the stairs on his bottom as he'd done inside. The soft glow of the lantern on the shelf near his wife lit his way. When he finally reached the ground, he used the railing to pull himself up then hobbled to where she sat with his sleeping children on either side of her under a blanket. "Thank God you're all right." He reached to kiss his wife, but she pulled away.

"Where were you?" she whispered. "From your appearance, I suspect the saloon. I was worried sick."

Nate held his hands out to calm her. "I wasn't at the saloon. I mean, well I did go there."

She pressed her lips together.

"But I didn't have anything to drink. I thought about it and decided not to."

"Then why are you home so late, and why are you soaking wet?"

He wiped his face with his hand. "Betsy, please listen."

She didn't say anything, but it was obvious from her raised eyebrow, she didn't believe him.

"I was headed home, but the storm grew so fierce. I took shelter at the mill. When the storm finally ended, it was late, but I still headed straight home. I was worried about you."

Her shoulders relaxed a little, she leaned back against the wall. At least, she didn't say anything more.

"My crutch got stuck in a puddle, and I fell." He pulled up the torn sleeves on his arms and showed her the scratches. "That's why I'm so wet and muddy."

Her face softened, and she touched his arm gently. "Those need treated so infection doesn't set in."

"It'll wait until morning." Nate touched her face and kissed her. This time she didn't pull back.

When the kiss ended, she stood. "I'll be back. That wound needs treating, and we need to get you into some dry clothes. Tomorrow, we'll talk some more about this, and if you did have that drink, I want to know the truth." She headed up the stairs.

Nate sat against the wall, relief sweeping over him. His family was okay, and he'd resisted the temptation to drink. *Thank You, Lord.*

It surprised him that the prayer came so easily. He hadn't prayed since he lost his leg in the war over six years ago.

Then he realized what Betsy said. They needed to talk. She didn't believe him. Had she finally decided to leave him and take the children to live in Philadelphia with her parents? He wouldn't blame her if she did.

He shook his head. God allowed him to become a cripple, and now he was about to lose his wife and family. He had devoted his life to the Lord, and this was what he got for it. He was a worthless human being.

I have so much more for you. Just trust Me.

There was no doubt where the voice was coming from. God spoke to his spirit, but he couldn't listen. He couldn't get his hopes up. He wouldn't.

Chapter Eleven

Nate had left early the next morning for work, but Betsy was worried about him. She had treated the scratches on his arms with garlic and honey-soaked bandages to prevent infection, but he had been in those wet clothes for a long time. He was so exhausted after she'd treated him and got him into dry clothes that he decided to spend the rest of the night in the cellar. He just didn't have the energy to climb those stairs. She wasn't keen on waking the children either, so she went back to her bedroom, wound up the clock, and brought it to the cellar where they all slept that night.

When the alarm bell rang, she was the only one who woke. She had to wake him out of a sound sleep to get him to make it to work on time. At least she convinced him to let her harness the horse to the wagon so he could ride to work. He was too tired to make that trip with his crutches no matter what he said. The conversation they needed to have about where he was the night before would have to wait.

After he left, Betsy woke the children so they could come into the dry house. She got them cleaned up and changed their clothes. An hour later, when she and the children were eating breakfast, Nate came back through the door coughing violently. When the coughing subsided, his voice sounded weak.

"The telegraph lines are down from the storm. It will be a week before they get them all repaired."

"Papa," Naomi ran to him wanting to be picked up.

"Not now." Betsy took her hand and led her back to the table. "Eat your breakfast."

When Naomi obeyed, she walked over to him and kissed him on the cheek. Her brow furrowed. He was hot, too hot. "You're burning with fever. Get in bed, and I'll get you some medicine."

"I haven't unhitched the wagon yet."

"I'll do it. Go."

He didn't waste any time making it to the bedroom and collapsing on the bed without even taking his shoe off. That worried her even more, considering he would normally not rest during the day no matter how bad he felt. He started coughing again.

She didn't like the sound of that cough. She pulled his shoe and sock off, propped his crutches by the bed, and covered him with the blanket.

"Thank you." He sounded weak, too weak.

She went to the kitchen and heated a kettle of water on the stove. By now, the children had finished eating and had gotten down from the table.

"Is Papa all right?" Malachi asked.

"He's sick, but I'll do my best to make him feel better."

"Papa." Naomi started to whine.

"None of that," Betsy said. "If you want to help your Pa, go upstairs and play."

The children ran up the stairs. Since they'd received all of their new toys from Mrs. Adams, it didn't take much to get them to play in their rooms when it was too wet to go outside.

She ground some mustard for a mustard plaster then poured some tea leaves and honey in a teacup. The honey would help the cough. Next, she poured a little water in a tin cup, mixed in some ground salicylic acid, a medicine made out of willow bark, and stirred it vigorously. She carried it into the room and handed it to him.

"What is it?"

"Some salicylic acid mixed with a little water."

"That stuff tastes terrible." Another coughing attack.

"Drink," she said. "It will help with the fever."

He held his nose and drank the awful concoction.

She hurried back to the kitchen. The kettle wasn't boiling yet, so she went outside, led the horse into the barn, and unhitched the wagon. Then she took the pitchfork and pitched some hay into the horse's stall. She rested on the pitchfork for a moment longer. As much as she wanted her husband to be the man she'd fallen in love with, she still loved him for better or for worse. She decided she would believe his story that he went into the saloon last night but decided not to drink although it still sounded implausible to her. She hoped she wasn't making a fool of herself.

~~~~~

After four days, the cough and congestion hadn't improved, and Nate was still warm with fever. Betsy knew she needed to have Dr. Clark stop by.

Someone knocked on the door, and when she answered, Lavena was there with Penelope.

She invited them in. "I forgot I was keeping Penelope today."

"Is Nate still under the weather?" Lavena asked.

"Yes, and I'm concerned about him. This seems more than just the common ague."

"Cage is too busy with the storm damage to worry about a child in tow," Lavena said. "I'll take Penelope to the suffrage meeting. No need to take on an additional child when you're caring for Nate."

"I'll keep her. When she's around, she occupies my children and keeps them from being underfoot."

"If you're sure," Lavena said.

Betsy nodded.

"Penelope, kiss your ma good-bye, and go upstairs to play."

The child did as she was told.

"I do have one favor to ask," Betsy said.

"Anything."

"Could you stop by Dr. Clark's office before leaving town and ask him to stop by?"

"Of course," Lavena said.

They said their good-byes, and she left.

Betsy spent the next four hours trying not to fret. She gave Nate another mustard plaster and some tea with honey, fed the children lunch, read them a story, and put them all down for a nap, but the doctor wasn't there yet. Meanwhile, every few minutes, she would hear her husband in the other room having a coughing fit.

There were only a few doctors, too few for a village this size, and ague would not be considered urgent, especially since Dr. Clark knew she would give the standard treatments. The young doctor had served in the war in the Ohio Seventh Regiment, the same unit as Nate. He'd known her then as a nurse and knew she was capable in treating most illnesses, but she still wanted her husband checked out, and she hoped the doctor would bring some cough syrup that was a little stronger than the tea and honey she'd been making.

She finished kneading some bread, when a knock sounded on the door. She opened it and stood with her hand on the door frame. "Thank you, Doctor, for coming. I've been treating him with mustard plasters, salicylic acid, and tea with honey, but that cough worries me."

Dr. Clark curled the edge of his handlebar mustaches and grinned a little. "May I come in?"

Heat flushed her face, and she moved away from the door. "I'm sorry. Of course."

He entered the room. "Has his fever come down at all?"

"He feels cooler than he did, but I still think he's running a fever. The congestion is a little better since I had him lean over a bowl of boiling water with a towel over his head, but I've been giving him a treatment every few hours, and it always comes back."

"Has the mustard plaster given him any blisters?"

"No, I take it off after twenty minutes, and I've only given him one a day."

"You've done everything right." Dr. Clark touched her hand. "Where is he?"

She led the doctor into the room where Nate lay on the bed having another coughing spell. He stopped coughing and tried to sit up.

"You stay where you are." The doctor opened his medical bag and pulled out a thermometer, a stethoscope, and wooden tongue depressor. First, he took his temperature with one of those new six-inch thermometers that only took twenty minutes to get an accurate reading. Betsy was a little surprised he'd purchased one. Most doctors didn't bother with the newer gadgets, but then, Dr. Clark was a younger doctor who always wanted to keep up with the latest techniques. Then, he listened to his heart and lungs using his stethoscope.

He turned to Betsy. "Could you hold the lamp up so I can see easier?"

She took hold of the oil lamp and held it up as he took the tongue depressor, stuck it in Nate's mouth, and looked down his throat.

He set the depressor, the stethoscope, and the thermometer back in his bag and pulled out a bottle of medicine. "He's still running a fever, but it's not a dangerous one. His ague is running its course and should be better in a couple of days. I would discontinue the mustard plasters and steam treatments, but I'm concerned about his throat. His tonsils are red and inflamed. They'll eventually heal, but I want him to use this cough syrup three times a day. This bottle should last a couple of weeks, but I don't believe he'll need it more than three or four days."

"What's in it?" she asked.

"Honey, herbs, a little opium, and some alcohol."

"Alcohol?" She gasped. "I don't want him to take alcohol."

"I don't mind," Nate said then started coughing again.

Betsy turned to her husband and glared at him. "Hush." She sat in the chair next to the bed. "Does he really need to take this? I mean, is it really that bad? I could continue to give him tea with honey."

Dr. Clark stroked his mustache. "With a throat that red, there could be complications. Of course, it's up to you, but I strongly urge it."

Betsy nodded and took the bottle. He was doing so well resisting the temptation to drink. At least she hoped he was. He'd admitted going to the saloon the evening of the storm, but he said he resisted the temptation. She wasn't sure since he was so eager to take the medicine. She only hoped this didn't make things worse.

~~~~

Lavena was enjoying the meeting. Since she was a member of the Oberlin Suffrage Association, she could participate and report on it at the same time. The other members were thrilled that she kept the public informed.

Mrs. Allison stood to speak and was recognized. "Ladies, I have secured a permit to march right here in Oberlin in two weeks. Even though the mayor is against the right to vote for women, he's agreed that we have a right to protest and will guarantee our safety."

The other women exclaimed.

"Isn't that wonderful?"

"Maybe President Fairchild will listen."

"Let's do this."

A knot formed in Lavena's stomach. If they were accosted in a town where the mayor supported them, would they be safe protesting here where the mayor was not sympathetic to their cause?

Mrs. Allison waited for the noise to die down then continued. "We'll end the march in front of First Church on the Oberlin College campus by the historic elm tree. I'm hoping we can convince Father Charles Finney to address us, but since he travels so much for his meetings, that may not be possible."

Lavena touched her arm, the one that was stabbed. She had to figure a way out of this. She couldn't march. Not again, and not in Oberlin. Here, everyone would be against them. The law might not step in and protect them from the agitators this time."

"We have yet to secure a speaker," Mrs. Allison said. "But I have been in correspondence with Lucy Stone. She can't come to the march, but she said if our society journalist would write an article about the march and what has been going on in Oberlin, she would feature it in her new periodical, *Women's Journal*. Mrs. Jones, could you write such an article?"

All eyes turned to Lavena. How could she possibly say no when she was the one who originally suggested they contact Lucy Stone. "Of course," she squeaked out. She cleared her throat. "It would be an honor."

"Wonderful," Mrs. Allison said. "We'll meet in front of the church on June eleventh. Pray for decent weather. Meeting adjourned."

On the way home, Lavena couldn't help but think about the day she was attacked. By the time she picked up Penelope and arrived home, she thought she might be sick.

Cage kissed her on the cheek. "How did the meeting go?"

"Great," she said trying to keep the dread out of her voice. She hurried to dish out the soup she'd had simmering on the stove all day.

As they sat at the table to eat, Cage prayed then gazed at her like he could look right through her. "Could you give a few more details?"

Lavena took a bite of soup. "They're having another march, this time in Oberlin."

"Can I go, please?" Penelope said. "I can hold my sign."

"Not this time."

"Why not?" Cage wiped his mouth with his napkin. "You took her last time."

"Because... because it's not safe. I was attacked last time. Don't you remember?"

"When is the march?" Cage asked.

"June eleventh."

"I believe I can arrange to be off work that day."

"Why?" Lavena asked. "Why would you take off work?"

"To go with you. That way Penelope can go too. Between the two of us, we can keep her safe."

Lavena swallowed. The dread in the pit of her stomach wouldn't go away. If she did go to the march, she didn't want her child anywhere near there. "I don't want Penelope there."

"Please, Mama." Penelope put her hands together as she pleaded with her eyes.

Maybe it would be all right if Cage were there with them. She would feel a lot safer. "All right. We'll all go."

Chapter Twelve

It had been almost a week since Nate came down sick, but now that he'd finished the cough syrup, he was now feeling well enough to get back to work. He just wished he'd had more to take with him. Betsy had warned him about using so much of it, but it made his throat feel so much better.

Since the telegraph lines had to be repaired, he hadn't missed any work due to sickness. He was glad about that, but now that he finished his first full day of work after recovering, he felt flushed and tired.

As he walked out the door of the office, he started coughing. He needed more cough syrup, so he headed to Dr. Clark's home and office. Dr. Clark was across the street from the telegraph office on Kelley Street, so he didn't have to go out of his way.

He walked over there and knocked on the door. Mrs. Clark answered the door. She was a pleasant woman with kind eyes and a crooked smile.

"I need to see Dr. Clark," Nate said.

"Come in." She ushered him into a small waiting room with three wooden chairs. "My husband is seeing a patient right now, but if you wait here, he'll be out in a moment."

Nate nodded as she walked out of the room then went to the first of the three chairs and sat. He glanced up at the grandfather clock in the corner. Five minutes past two. He leaned his head back, but that made him want to cough, so he sat up straight. As the clock ticked on, his lower back started hurting. Even the chairs at the telegraph office were more comfortable than this.

He glanced at the clock again. He'd been waiting a full thirty minutes. He thought about leaving. It really wasn't that important, but he wanted that cough medicine. It made him feel better. He stood and paced for a while then sat back down. What was the doctor doing, performing surgery? He let out a gusty sigh.

Finally, as the clock chimed three, the doctor came into the room with a boy who had his arm in a cast and a woman Nate assumed was his mother.

"You be more careful, Tommy," Dr. Clark said. "And no climbing trees until that cast comes off."

"Thank you, Dr. Clark." The woman left with her son.

The doctor looked at Nate. "I'm glad to see you up and around.

How's your cough?"

"Better," Nate said. "But it's still bothersome, and I ran out of cough syrup. I wondered if I might get some more."

Dr. Clark raised his eyebrow. "You're out already?"

"Yes, I am." Nate stood. "So, if you could just give me another bottle, I'll be on my way." He coughed a little to make his point.

"I'd like to look at that throat first." Dr. Clark opened the exam room door. "Right in here."

Nate huffed out a breath. "I don't need an examination. I just need some more cough syrup."

The doctor crossed his arms and said nothing. Finally, Nate went into the examining room and sat on the bed.

Dr. Clark took a stethoscope and listened to his heart. Then he spent twenty minutes taking his temperature. Finally, he looked down Nate's throat while holding a tongue depressor in his mouth.

"You look fine. " Dr. Clark said. "You don't need any more cough syrup."

"But I told you, my throat hurts."

Dr. Clark gazed at him a little too long. "I'm not giving you any more. If your throat still hurts, I'm sure your wife will fix you some tea with honey. You should be fine in a couple of days."

Nate climbed off the bed. "But I need that cough syrup."

"You took two weeks of cough syrup in three days. You're not getting any more from me."

"What kind of a doctor are you, not giving me the medicine I need?"

Dr. Clark crossed his arms but didn't say another word.

Nate stormed out of the room and slammed the door. He headed to the saloon. The medicine had alcohol in it, so a stiff drink would work just as well.

~~~~~

It was long past time for Nate to be home. Betsy walked into the bedroom, grabbed the bottle of cough syrup off the table, and looked inside. It was empty. Empty. The doctor gave it to him three days ago and said there was enough for two weeks. When Betsy tried to give him the doses of medicine, he growled that he would take care of it himself. Now she knew why. As she feared, the cough syrup gave him a taste for alcohol again which explained his absence. He'd gone to the saloon after work.

After tucking the children into bed and changing into her night clothes, she bowed on her knees by the bed and prayed. *Lord, what should I do now?*

She already knew. She needed to turn out the oil lamp and go to sleep. In the morning, she wouldn't rise early to make his breakfast.

Lying in the bed, she tried to sleep, but she couldn't. The rope bed wasn't tight enough for only one person, and she wouldn't use the wedge to tighten it when her husband would be home soon. At least she hoped he would. After a while, she gave up trying, but she didn't bother getting out of bed. It wasn't the bed keeping her awake. She couldn't stop fretting about her husband. Since she wasn't going to sleep anyway, she spent the time praying for Nate.

Maybe this was a one-time thing. He'd just gotten over a cold. He'd stopped drinking before that cough medicine. He might realize what he'd done and get back on the wagon. At least he didn't mind her prohibition activities. He even encouraged it before he started drinking again.

Of course, he didn't know he might very well run into the ladies if he picked the wrong day to go to the saloon. At the last meeting, they'd decided to stagger the days to make sure the men didn't plan their visits to avoid them.

Lord, make him realize the errors of his ways. Convince him to stop drinking again.

Soon, she heard the door to the kitchen open and footsteps coming into the room. She could smell the alcohol on him even before he came near. Everything in her wanted to let him know she was awake. She wanted to tell him how disappointed she was in him, but she didn't. The Lord gave her the strength to keep her eyes closed and her breathing steady.

"Are you awake?" His voice slurred.

She kept silent. She heard him winding the clock then felt the bed move when he sat on it. His shoe thumped against the floor, and she heard the crutches prop against the wall.

"I wish you were awake. I'd tell you how sorry I am."

She felt a tear slide down her cheek, but she didn't respond. Was God working on his heart?

He lay down, and soon she heard his soft snoring.

After a while, she fell asleep as well.

He screamed out, "No! Don't shoot."

She woke with a start. She rubbed her eyes and took his trembling body in her arms.

"I'm sorry." His breath was ragged. "I didn't... I'm sorry I woke you."

"It's all right." She massaged his back soothing him. "It was only a dream." She held him like that until the trembling stopped and his breathing became normal. "Go back to sleep."

She settled into the covers when she heard Naomi crying. Nate's screams had awakened the girl. She let out a sigh and headed up the stairs to comfort her daughter.

At least, she'd decided not to get up early and make Nate's breakfast.

She would need the sleep.

~~~~~

Nate sat at the telegraph desk and wiped his hand over his face. It had been a slow day, and he needed a drink. Betsy had been asleep when he returned home the other night. He'd expected her to wait up even though she said she wouldn't. She didn't even fix his breakfast the next morning. When he came home yesterday, she greeted him with a kiss as if nothing had happened. He expected her to say something about what he'd done, but she didn't say a word. That was worse than her nagging him.

He should go home after work. She didn't deserve a drunk for a husband, and he should do his best not to be that man. He let out a sigh. No matter how much he wanted to resist, he would be at that saloon tonight. When James entered, he nodded, made his way out the door, and headed to the railroad tracks.

"Nate." Cage's voice. "I'm glad I caught up with you."

Nate groaned and turned toward the voice.

Cage shook Nate's hand. "I need your help."

"Another woman who needs her grocery bill paid?"

Cage pulled his ear. "Not this time."

Nate wanted to ignore him and head toward the saloon, but Cage was too good of a friend. He'd find out what the problem was even if his friend was using it as an excuse to get to him.

"There's a young woman who needs a lawyer."

"Have her hire Mr. Hayes. He'll do a good job."

Cage wiped his hand across the scar on his cheek. "Nate, this is important."

A knot formed in Nate's gut. "Why? What's wrong?"

"Come to my office, and I'll tell you the whole story."

Nate followed Cage to the jail. Cage offered him a cup of coffee, and they both sat.

"The woman's name is Eliza Johnson. She's a spinster who takes in laundry to make a living."

"Okay." Nate wasn't sure what this had to do with him.

"Miss Johnson was attacked last night and forced to…" Cage starred at his coffee cup. "She did his laundry, and when he came to pick it up, he forced himself into the house and had his way with her. I have the man in a jail cell back there." He motioned to the door that led to the cells. "A man witnessed the attack, but he was too late to stop it. He made sure the girl got the medical help she needed. Miss Johnson tried to fight and was hurt pretty badly. Then he came to get me."

"Wellington has a town prosecutor. I'm sure Mr. Nelson can handle it."

"He won't bring it to trial. You know he refuses to prosecute any case if there's a chance he'll lose."

Heat flushed through Nate. "Did he say why he thinks he'll lose? Is she known for cavorting with men?" Even if she did have a reputation, that didn't excuse what the man did, but it would explain why Jake Nelson wouldn't bring it to trial.

Cage brow furrowed. "She was a good Christian girl. She's never been with a man before. She lives with her parents, although they weren't there when the attack happened. They'll attest to her virtue. And there are bruises showing he acted without regard to her feelings."

Nate cracked his knuckles. "If she has a good reputation, there are witnesses, and she has bruises from the attack, what's his problem? It sounds like the kind of case he likes, one that will get him lots of publicity."

A vein pulsed in Cage's neck. "He doesn't think he can get a conviction because the man is white, and the girl is a Negress."

Nate stood and pounded his fist down on Cage's desk. "I can't believe someone in his position would be so yellow-bellied. He's an affront to the legal profession."

Cage nodded. "We both already knew that. He's only concerned about his political ambitions. So, you'll prosecute the case?"

Nate sat back down thinking of a number of reasons he couldn't and shouldn't do it. "I can't ask my employer to give me time off for a whole week. That's how long the trial might last. And I need time to prepare. I don't know how I could possibly manage it."

Cage grinned. "If that's all that's stopping you, I talked to Judge Murphy. He'll agree to you prosecuting the case, and he'll wait a week for you to prepare. He said he'd open the courtroom at 2:30 every day during the trial. Since you get off at two, it shouldn't be a problem. So, you'll do it?"

What if he failed to convict the man? The girl would be worse off than she was now. What if the jury couldn't look past the fact that he was a cripple and she was black? He wiped his hand over his mouth. He was more yellow-bellied than the prosecutor. "It looks like I don't have a choice."

His friend slapped him on the back. "I knew I could count on you. I've written down her address, the name and address of the witness, and all the information you'll need." He handed him a folded sheet of paper.

Nate nodded and tucked the paper in the pocket of his trousers. "I'll get started on this right away." He shook hands with Cage and left the office. If he were going to do this, he needed that drink more than ever. It didn't take him long to get to Dewolf Street where the saloon could serve him up some liquid courage. He turned and headed down the street past the boxing mill. Singing filled the sky. A group of ladies from the sound of it, singing, *Oh, Why Not Tonight*. As he drew closer to the alley where the saloon was located, the words sounded louder.

> *Oh, do not let the Word depart,*
> *And close thine eyes against the light;*
> *Poor sinner, harden not your heart,*
> *Be saved, oh, tonight.*

The song used to be one of his favorites, but now the words pricked his heart. He wanted nothing more than to close his eyes to the light and harden his heart in a bottle of whiskey. When he turned down the alley, he knew why the music came from there. The ladies were carrying signs and singing hymns in front of the saloon, and his wife was leading the choir. Before he could turn away, her eyes locked onto his making his cheeks burn with shame. He turned and hurried away as fast as his leg and crutches could carry him.

What were they doing there? It was Wednesday, not Friday. Didn't Betsy say they'd protest on Fridays and Saturdays? Not today. Not Wednesday.

A lump formed in his throat and threatened to choke him. He glanced toward the sky with the bright sun shining light on the darkest of places and shielded his eyes. "Why not today, huh? Lord, I don't want Your bright light shining on me. Let me stay in the shadows."

He let out a gusty sigh and pulled out the paper Cage had given him. Since he couldn't get a drink, he might as well work on the case.

~~~~~

When Betsy and the children arrived home, Nate was sitting at the table writing notes on a piece of paper. He folded the paper and set it aside. She didn't say anything, just hurried to dish out the vegetable soup she had simmering all day on the stove. He didn't say a word while she sliced and buttered bread, poured milk, and set the children at the table.

After saying the prayer, they ate, and all she could hear was the clattering of silverware in the bowls. Finally, she could have no more of the silence between them.

"I saw you today."

"I know." His voice was soft. "I didn't expect you there on Wednesday."

"We decided to change the days we went. That way, the men trying to avoid us wouldn't know we were there."

"Like me."

"Yes." She took a sip of milk. "I suppose now you're going to forbid me from protesting and having anything to do with the temperance society." Even though she tried to stay calm, she had already determined in her heart that if he came against what she was doing, she wouldn't stop. This was more important than her husband's objections.

Nate kneaded the back of his neck, and she braced for his answer. "No, I don't want you to stop. What you're doing is important." He lowered his gaze. "You even stopped me from drinking."

She covered her mouth with her hand. She was almost afraid to believe what she was hearing. Was God beginning to do a work in her husband?

"I'm sorry." Nate's voice thickened. "I won't be going there again."

"How can I believe you? You've stopped drinking before, but you always go back."

"True enough. This time, I mean it."

She swallowed back the lump in her throat. "Why the sudden change?"

"We can talk about that later." He pointed to the children.

She glanced over. They'd finished their soup. It was obvious the only reason they were sitting there so content was because she'd promised them some cookies she'd baked earlier that day. She'd taught them they wouldn't get the treat unless they stayed at the table and didn't cause a fuss. She stood and grabbed a couple of cookies then turned to the children.

"You can each have a cookie, but I want you to play quietly upstairs. If you do that until bedtime, I'll give you another cookie then."

Malachi and Naomi grabbed the cookies and headed upstairs so quickly she didn't even have a chance to tell them to not get crumbs all over. No matter. She'd sweep up the crumbs later. She sat by Nate.

"Now, why have you decided to quit drinking this time? Surely it's not because you were embarrassed to see me out in front of the saloon. You never considered my feelings before." Her voice had an edge to it, but she couldn't manage an even tone.

His Adam's apple bulged. "I talked to Cage today."

She narrowed her eyes wondering what his friend could possibly say to change his ways.

"He told me about a woman who was raped."

Heat flushed her face.

"He caught the man, and there's plenty of proof he did it, but the prosecutor won't bring it to trial because the woman is black, and the man is white."

She pulled on the collar of her dress. "Oh, my."

"He asked me to prosecute the man, and I agreed." He placed his hands on hers. "So, you see, I won't drink because it might hurt this case. This might be my chance to become the lawyer I wanted to be and help those who need it."

She pulled her hands away. "If all of this is true, why did you go to the saloon tonight?"

He looked down. "I was afraid I'd fail. I thought one drink would give me the courage I need. When I saw you there, I knew I was wrong. I need to stay sober if I want to help this girl."

Betsy pulled close to him and kissed him. "I'm glad." She hoped he meant it this time, but what would happen if he didn't win the case?

Chapter Thirteen

Lavena visited *The Wellington Enterprise* with Penelope in tow to drop off some stories. The first was about the suffrage march in Oberlin. She saw now how foolish she was for worrying. The march went well, and there was no trouble. No mobs of men confronted them, and the police department in Oberlin was on hand to make sure they didn't. She was glad Cage had come along. That kept her from feeling as anxious, but it scared her that she needed him there so badly.

The second story was a harder to write. *The Wellington Enterprise* was doing stories on crime in the area. At least the articles didn't blame her husband. According to the newspaper, the fault was with the city council for not providing more money for law enforcement. The editor also wrote an opinion editorial about how most of the problem was that the council wouldn't ban alcohol in the village. Each reporter covered a different crime.

Her assignment had been a colored woman who was raped by a white man. She felt heartsick for the woman who had been assaulted. Her stomach tightened as she remembered a soldier during the war who tried to assault her. If Cage hadn't stopped him, she didn't know what would have happened.

She'd already interviewed everyone in the case and reported that the trial would start tomorrow. When Betsy had told her Nate was representing the woman and had stopped drinking so he could remain sober while the case was open, she was thrilled for her friend. She only hoped he would stick with it after the man was convicted.

After dropping off the stories, fixing Penelope supper, and delivering her to Mrs. Fowler at the church, she headed to the saloon to report on tonight's protest. She wanted to be there to support Betsy, but she also planned to do a story about the protests in front of the Bonnie and Sons Saloon. There had been several protests so far led by Betsy. Now the number of women coming out had doubled in size.

This event tonight would be spectacular. Rev. Fowler had planned to bring a wagon to the saloon and preach to the men going inside. He would urge them to give up their sinful drink and climb aboard the wagon to give their lives to their Savior. He was a fiery preacher who was sure to cause the men to pause. He even preached once a week in a field near Liberty Street where the cheese factory workers lived. From the reports she'd heard, every week, men gave their lives to Jesus and were baptized in a horse trough they'd brought to the field.

As she arrived at the saloon, Rev. Fowler was already preaching on top of his wagon to some men headed to the door. Betsy, and around ten other women, stood near the door with signs. Whenever Rev. Fowler paused, they would sing hymns. The men ignored them and entered the saloon.

Lavena strode to Betsy. "Last week, you had fifteen women. How come there are only ten tonight?"

"Over twenty women arrived at the church. We formed into two groups and one group is in front of the Mudoch Saloon on Liberty Street."

Lavena placed her hand on her chest. "Do you think that's wise? That's not a very safe area of town."

"Horsefeathers," Betsy said. "Half the women protesting live on Liberty Street. They're twelve women strong. They should be able to handle any problems. Besides, your husband assigned two deputies to make rounds nearby. We sent one of them with the other women."

That sounded like Cage. He always encouraged Lavena to ruffle feathers, but often, he made sure she was protected when she did. That was why she had the courage to attend the march in Oberlin. "Sounds like you have it all figured out."

The whistle blew to signal the end of the working day for the factories, and a few minutes later, a group of men sauntered to the saloon. Betsy and the other women started singing *Amazing Grace* at the top of their lungs. Lavena couldn't help joining in.

When the song was finished, Rev. Fowler started preaching. "While your wives and children are at home waiting for you, will you squander your time here on whiskey? Repent and return to your families."

A few of the men stopped and listened for a moment, then headed another direction. Some of the men ignored the preaching and hymns and marched inside the saloon. What caused a knot in Lavena's stomach was the four men who, instead of going inside, stood glaring at the women in a way obviously meant to scare them.

Betsy sang louder as if she wanted to show they couldn't intimidate her, but Lavena swallowed back the lump in her throat. These men had the same look in their eyes as the ruffians who'd confronted them in Elyria and who had pushed her to the ground and stabbed her arm.

Doug Hanson stepped in front of the men as if he were the biggest toad in the puddle and faced Betsy. A sneer covered his features. "You women better skedaddle if you know what's good for you. Get on back to your children and your cooking."

The men behind him started cackling. The women stopped singing their hymns, and Rev. Fowler stopped preaching and headed to stand with the women.

Cage had told Lavena how Hanson had beaten his wife and son, and there wasn't a thing he could do about it. Her heart raced so fast she was sure it would beat right out of her chest. Surely the man knew if he did anything to a woman who wasn't his wife, he could be arrested.

Betsy set her jaw and gazed at him as if he were only a minor annoyance, like a mosquito buzzing around her head, but she didn't say a word. How did she remain so composed?

Mr. Hanson wet his lips. "This is a place for men." He raised a fist to her face but didn't swing it. "If you don't leave, we might have to fix your flint."

Betsy showed an intense calmness that surprised Lavena. "You forget, sir, I'm not your wife. If you lay a hand on me, you'll end up in jail for a lot longer than one night."

Lavena gasped. *Please, Lord. Protect my friend.*

Mr. Hanson chuckled, and the men behind him followed his lead, but Lavena noticed he didn't lower his fist. "You don't belong here. Leave now, or I'll teach you a thing or two."

Rev. Fowler stepped in front of the women. "The Lord is on our side, and I won't have you accosting these ladies."

"Careful, preacher." Mr. Hanson shook his fist in Rev. Fowler's face. "Your collar won't protect you here."

Deputy Caleb Brown, one of Cage's strongest and best men, came running up to the crowd. "What's going on here?"

Mr. Hanson lowered his fist, stepped back, and gave a slight smile that didn't reach his eyes. "These women and this," he snurled up his nose, "preacher are blocking the door. We just asked them to kindly move."

The deputy raised an eyebrow. "Hard to believe. I've passed this area ten times in the last hour, and they never once block the door. Doesn't look like they're blocking it now either."

Betsy shrugged. "Men have been pouring into that saloon since we got here. We haven't blocked their way once."

"That's true." Lavena's voice cracked. "They've been staying on the porch away from the door."

Deputy Brown set his jaw and stared down at Mr. Hanson. "If you want to go into the saloon, I suggest you do it now and stop causing trouble."

Mr. Hanson looked like he might protest, but he didn't. He and the men wandered into the establishment.

Deputy Caleb turned to the women. "I'll keep patrolling, but some men who come in here are dangerous. I'd feel better if you'd all go home."

Betsy placed her hands on her hips. "We're not going anywhere."

The deputy nodded. "Suit yourself, but I can only do so much. I can't be here to protect you all the time."

"No need. The Lord is our rear guard." Betsy turned to the other women and led them in a hymn.

> O why not tonight?
> O why not tonight?
> Wilt thou be saved?
> Then why not tonight?

Lavena's legs felt like they might give way, and she sat on the edge of the wagon. Her heart raced faster than a horse galloping at full speed, and she struggled to catch her breath. How could Betsy be so fearless in the face of danger when she, the champion of women's rights who had challenged the norms of society and had reported on more than one battle during the war, couldn't stop trembling.

~~~~

The trial of Ralph Peterson went faster than Nate had expected. The only defense Mr. Peterson's lawyer put up was that Eliza Johnson was a former slave in Kentucky, and slave women were often used for breeding. Therefore, she must have had sexual experience. Mr. Peterson stated that Miss Johnson propositioned him for money, then she changed her mind.

It was a preposterous defense considering how many character witnesses Nate had called. That and the testimony of the witness who saw Miss Johnson struggling against Mr. Peterson and the doctor who documented the bruises and the rough way Miss Johnson had been treated was sure to convict Mr. Peterson.

As the jury was dismissed to deliberate, Nate let out a sigh. He felt pleased with himself for the job he had done. Even more, he'd made sure justice was served.

A hand on his arm made him look up.

Miss Johnson stood there with tears in her eyes. "No matter what happens, thank you."

He set his hand on hers and nodded. When he left the courtroom, he left word for the bailiff where he'd be, and headed to Cage's office. He felt sure the jury wouldn't take long and wanted to be close by when the verdict came in. Cage sat at his desk and glanced up when Nate opened the door.

"Come in." Cage pulled out a chair and headed to the stove in the corner to get Nate a cup of coffee. "How did it go?"

Nate took the cup and sat. "Better than expected. I don't believe there's any way the jury will find Mr. Peterson not guilty."

Cage poured himself a cup. "I don't know. Juries are tricky, and the accuser is colored."

Nate raised an eyebrow. "In this day and age? We fought a war to free the slaves, and some colored men are even running for Congress. I could understand them not believing her if we were in the deep south, but this is Ohio, the state that had an underground railroad stop in every county, not to mention the place where the Oberlin/Wellington Slave Rescue happened before the war. They'll convict him."

"I hope so," Cage said.

A warmth travelled through Nate. "I want to thank you."

"For what?"

"For not giving up on me. I know I've been a fool, drinking too much, insisting I can't do anything because of this leg, and well…" He swallowed back the lump in his throat. "All of it. You didn't give up on me. That's the only reason I had the courage to try this case."

"You're welcome. I knew you had it in you. You just needed a shove."

Nate gulped his coffee. "I've made a decision, and I want you to be the first to know. I'm going to rent some office space and hang out my shingle. And the drinking is over with."

"That is good news." Cage placed his hands around his cup. "I hope you mean it no matter what the verdict."

"You don't need to worry about that. I told you the evidence was clear. Ralph Peterson will be found guilty."

The bailiff opened the door. "The jury is in. The verdict will be read in ten minutes."

Nate stood. "See, I told you. The evidence was so great, they didn't even need time to convict. Probably unanimous on the first vote." He started toward the door.

"Wait." Cage stood. "I'm going with you."

They headed up the stairs to the courtroom. When they got there, everyone already was in place. He walked over to Miss Johnson and squeezed her hand then took his place in front. Cage sat next to his wife two rows behind them.

"Stand for the honorable Judge Murphy," the bailiff said. The judge came into the room and pounded the gavel. "Court is in session. Be seated. Bring in the jury."

The bailiff had the jury file in and take their seats. From their faces, Nate didn't what they were going to say. He couldn't understand why his heart was beating as loudly as the judge's gavel. He knew it would be a guilty verdict. Under the circumstances, what else could it be?

Finally, the judge read the charges. One count rape, one count assault on a woman. "Do you have a verdict."

The foreman of the jury stood. He was a scrawny man with thick glasses and a squeaky voice. Sweat beaded his forehead even though the windows were open and nice breeze came through. "Yes, Your Honor."

"Read the verdict."

"We find the defendant..." He cleared his throat. "Not guilty on both counts."

Nate gasped. Surely, he heard wrong. A lump formed in his gut.

Mr. Peterson let out a loud whoop as the soft crying of Miss Johnson told Nate it was no mistake."

"You're free to go, Mr. Peterson," the judge said.

Peterson headed toward the girl. "I'll come by again soon." He touched her cheek.

Heat shot up Nate's back.

The girl winced, and Nate's hands turned into fists. He raised his fist to hit the man.

Cage grabbed his right arm in full swing and pulled it back then stepped in front of him. "Mr. Peterson, you're free to go, so I suggest you go, now!"

The man held his palms up and left. Miss Johnson ran into the arms of her parents and sobbed.

Nate brushed through the crowd toward the door. Cage grabbed him by the arm, but he pulled away.

"Wait," Cage said.

He didn't wait. He hobbled down the courtroom stairs and burst outside. Cage's voice sounded behind him, but it sounded more like an annoying buzz, one he didn't care to hear. He hobbled toward the saloon. It was his fault. If the girl had had a competent lawyer, this wouldn't have happened. The evidence was overwhelming. All the jury could see was a cripple. He was foolish to think he could make a difference.

~~~~~

Lavena sat stunned. They actually let the rapist go with all the evidence against him. How could anyone feel safe with men threatening women in the street, and men assaulting women and not paying for it? A shiver went through her.

The bailiff motioned toward her. She looked around. Everyone had left the courtroom while she was in this fog, and she hadn't even noticed. She picked up her lap desk and left the courtroom so the bailiff could lock up. Then she sat on the bench in the hallway and wrote her story about Ralph Peterson being freed by the jury. She didn't bother to hide her disdain for the verdict in her writing. If Mr. Guthrie wanted to edit it, he could, but she'd write the truth.

When she'd finished, she headed to the newspaper office with this story and the account of the protest at the saloon. She'd walked this path many times, and it was still daylight, but she felt unsafe, as if someone were following her. Her heart beat faster.

She looked back. Nobody was there.

When she got to the Reninger Building and dashed inside, she climbed the stairs to the second-floor newspaper office. Men were working at various desks, but they seem ominous. How many of them accosted women in their lifetimes and got away with it? She tried to catch her breath and headed to Mr. Guthrie's office. Only when she walked inside and closed the door did she feel safe. She trusted her publisher.

"So," Mr. Guthrie said. "What happened?"

She had to force herself to speak. "They let him go."

"I was afraid of that. Hard to get a conviction on rape anyway, but with the victim being black..."

She handed him both stories. He nodded, and she rushed out of the office and ran down the stairs and outside without even saying good-bye.

Once outside, she closed her eyes and leaned against the brick wall. She tried to calm her racing heart, tried but failed. She opened her eyes and looked around. A couple of men walked past her on their way somewhere. Or maybe they planned to double back.

She ran along Mechanics Street then Cortland as fast as she could trying to get home. As soon as she reached the house, she ran up the steps and inside, then closed the door and tried to calm her heavy breathing.

Mrs. Farmer, an elderly lady who lived next door, stared at her with concern. She'd agreed to watch Penelope since Betsy was protesting at the saloon. "Are you all right? You look like you've been chased by a ghost."

"I'm fine," Lavena panted out. "I was hurrying too much. That's all."

"You need to be careful. A lady should never rush anywhere. She should always walk slowly with grace."

"Thank you, Mrs. Farmer." Lavena tried not to be annoyed with the woman's antiquated ideas of womanhood, especially since most of the population agreed with her. "I appreciate you watching Penelope."

"No problem at all dear, although I don't believe a mother should work. It's not seemly."

"Yes, ma'am. I'll consider what you're saying." She'd say anything to get the lady to leave."

"Miss Penelope is in her room playing. I'll be on my way." Mrs. Farmer left and closed the door behind her.

Lavena sank to the floor, wrapped her arms around her legs, and sank her face into her arms and sobbed.

~~~~~

Nate turned into the alley. Great. The women, including his wife, were there in full force, singing their hymns and carrying their signs. Betsy stood in front leading them.

Pausing, he stared at them. There were other saloons in town, but he didn't want to walk that far. He wanted a drink now. He strode toward the door, his gaze focused straight ahead so he wouldn't see the hurt in his wife's eyes. Still, out of the corner of his eye, he noticed her drop the sign and scurry toward him.

She grabbed his arm. "Please, Nate, why are you doing this?"

He stopped for a moment and swallowed back the lump in his throat. "I lost, Betsy." His voice was thick. "That poor women didn't get justice because I was her lawyer."

Her eyes grew wide. "I'm sure you did everything you could. It's not your fault."

He placed his hand on hers. "I'm a cripple. That's all the jury could see." He pulled away and walked into the saloon.

Chapter Fourteen

Betsy hitched the wagon, bundled the children into the back, and headed toward the telegraph office. The summer sun shone brightly, not matching her mood. She'd awakened every night with Nate screaming from another nightmare. Sometimes, he woke the children.

Since the trial, he was back to getting drunk at least three times a week, sometimes more. She'd kept her promise to not wait up for him and not get up the next morning to make him breakfast. And she continued protesting in front of the saloon twice a week. He never stopped on those days. If he did go toward the saloon, he'd stop, let out a heavy sigh, and continue home. At least he had enough shame not to pass by her and the protestors on his way to get drunk.

Even though he'd started drinking again, he still encouraged her to attend the temperance meetings and protests. The meetings were going well. The owners of most of the mills and the cheese factories and many businesses in town had agreed to pay a bonus to the men who signed the temperance pledge to not drink. They saw the sense in it. Men who didn't drink were better workers and took less time off.

This afternoon, when Nate got off work, they were going to ride to the fairgrounds and have a picnic together. She had some news for her husband that she hoped would cause him to consider giving up the whiskey. She was expecting another child in around six months. She hadn't wanted to tell him before because she wanted to be sure she didn't lose the baby. She'd had a couple of miscarriages early in the pregnancy before and one last year. The last thing he needed was to be disappointed again. She knew he would be pleased. He loved being a father, and he'd always wanted a house full of children.

When he heard the news, she was sure he would stop drinking. Afterall, he had stopped before. Once that dreaded cough syrup had tempted him, and another time when he blamed himself for the not guilty verdict against the rapist. He'd stop again. She was sure of it. Didn't him agreeing to this picnic prove he cared about her and the children?

She pulled up to the telegraph office. Nate was waiting outside. He climbed into the wagon and flicked the reins.

As they turned onto Main Street, shots fired. Cage and his deputy, George, rode past them in the direction of the gunfire.

Nate pulled the reins back and shouted to his wife. "He might need help. Get the children and go to Lavena's. I'll meet up with you later."

Betsy didn't waste any time. Nate had told her dangerous outlaws were in the area, and he would want to help his friend. She got the children down, and Nate turned the wagon and headed in the direction Cage rode.

She took the children by the hands and started walking toward Lavena's house near the jail. Her friend would be worried.

~~~~~

Lavena heard shots, and her stomach hardened. "Stay here," she said to Penelope then ran to the door and opened it. Betsy and her children stood there, her hand raised to knock. Lavena pushed past her, but Cage was no longer in view. "What happened?"

"I'll tell you in a minute." Betsy entered the house and told the children to go to Penelope's room to play.

Lavena placed her arm over her stomach. The way it was churning, she thought she might lose what she'd eaten for the noon meal. "Now." She tried to keep her voice calm, tried but failed. "What happened?"

Her friend filled a kettle with water and placed it on the stove. "I'll make us some tea."

"Please." She hated the desperate tone in her voice. "Tell me. Is Cage all right?"

Betsy placed Lavena's hands in hers. "Shots came from the direction of the bank, but the grocery store, the bakery, and the saloon are in that direction too. Cage and Nate both took off to find out what's happening. I really don't know anything yet."

A million thoughts raced through her mind. "Billy Horton and his gang. It had to be him." Her eyes burned with unshed tears. "They're robbing the bank." She paced as she tried to remember to breathe.

"We don't know that," Betsy said. "It could be some rowdy men shooting off guns. Come sit down."

Lavena's heart pounded fiercely, and she couldn't catch her breath. She felt light-headed and dizzy. Her vision blurred, then everything went black.

~~~~~

Nate turned the wagon and followed Cage. He wasn't sure where the shots were coming from, but the saloon was in that direction. So was the bank. He lost sight of the marshal and his deputy and urged his horse to go faster. They might need his help.

As he neared the bank, he spotted Cage's gray horse and Deputy George's brown mare tied to the railing in front of the bank along with a couple of horses he didn't recognize. He pulled up to the bank and grabbed his crutches before climbing down. He looked around. The street was empty which he expected. People would take cover as soon as they heard the gunshots. Where was Cage?

Dread went through him. Cage was in the bank with whoever was robbing it, probably Billy Horton and his partner.

Shots boomed through the air.

~~~~~

Lavena woke to a foul odor and coughed. She was on the floor, and Betsy held smelling salts to her nose.

"Get that away from me." She pushed the bottle away. "What happened?"

"You swooned." Betsy offered her a hand, and she got to her feet.

"I don't swoon."

"You need to sit until you're feeling better."

As much as she didn't want to admit how weak she felt, Lavena sat in her rocking chair by the stove.

Betsy handed her a cup of water. "Drink this. You were breathing too heavily. That can sometimes bring on light-headedness and fainting."

Lavena closed her eyes and shook her head slowly.

Betsy placed a cool, wet cloth on her neck. "Just rest a few minutes. You'll be all right."

"Are they back? Are they all right?"

"Not yet." Betsy sat and leaned toward her. "I heard more shots, so I don't know."

Lavena tried to hold back the tears, but a sob escaped her. "What if..."

Betsy held her hands. "This isn't the time for fear. We need to pray for them. We can trust in the Lord to bring them back safely."

Lavena fell to her knees and cradled herself with her arms.

Chapter Fifteen

Nate grabbed his rifle out of the back of the wagon and hobbled to the bank as quickly as he could. He might not be able to stand on one leg without crutches, but he could shoot straight. He wouldn't let Cage face Horton alone.

He struggled with the steps, and before he could get to the entrance, Cage came out holding the outlaw by the scruff of his collar and pointing a gun at him. "I'm glad you're here. Can I use your wagon?"

Nate nodded. "Were there any more of them?"

"Yeah, the other two are dead. Horton, here, surrendered." Cage pushed the outlaw toward the wagon. "We need to hurry. They shot the bank teller."

"Tyler?"

Cage nodded. "He's still alive, but he needs a doctor. George will stay with him and do what he can. When we get to my office, fetch Dr. Clark. It might be too late, but…"

"Say no more. Betsy's at your house. I told her to take cover there. I'll send her to help too."

"Good idea."

Nate climbed into the wagon as Cage handcuffed Horton, pushed him into the wagon, and climbed up himself, keeping his eyes and handgun always pointed toward the outlaw.

As soon as they climbed off the wagon with the prisoner, Lavena and Betsy came running out of the house. They must have told the children to stay inside, because only the women came out.

Lavena ran to Cage. Her face was pale, and her eyes were red and swollen. "Are you all right? Where's George? Is this Horton? What happened?"

"Bank robbery." Cage turned his body to shield the women from his prisoner even though he no longer could do anything to hurt them. "Lavena, I'll tell you all about it later, but for now, Tyler's been shot. George is with him, but he needs help."

Lavena closed her eyes and nodded. Nate could have sworn she'd been crying, but that didn't make any sense. She wasn't the type of woman to weep.

"Nate, get the doctor." Cage pulled Horton into the jail.

Nate headed toward the wagon, but Betsy passed him.

"Stay here with Cage." She climbed in the wagon. "He might need you. I'll get the doctor and head to the bank. Lavena, stay with the children."

Before he could say a word, she took the reins and rode as fast as the horse would go.

Lavena wiped her hands on her apron and sauntered into her house.

A lump formed in Nate's throat as he headed to the jail. He knew why Betsy wanted to handle getting the doctor on her own. He looked down at his missing leg. She could manage faster than her crippled husband ever could.

By the time he hobbled into the marshal's office, Cage had already locked Horton in a cell in the back.

Horton yelled obscenities. "You're a dead man. Just wait 'til I break free." Then he used some words even Nate wouldn't say.

Cage walked in from the back where the cells were and slammed the door shut. They could still hear the obscenities, but at least they were muffled.

"Betsy went for the doctor." Nate stroked his beard. "I guess she figured she'd be more help than I could." He swiped his hand against the leg of his trousers, the leg with the stump. "Do you need my help?"

"I'm fine," Cage said. "Maybe you'd better get back to the telegraph office."

Nate couldn't help clenching his jaw. "I was about to leave for the day anyway." Now Cage wanted to get rid of him. He stood and made his way to the door. "I can meet Betsy out front."

"Before you go, there is something I'd like to talk to you about." Cage sounded serious, maybe too serious.

He turned back toward his friend. "What's on your mind?"

Cage sat on the edge of his desk and crossed his arms. "You're my closest friend."

Nate's chest tightened. It was obvious he planned to talk to him about his drinking again. This wasn't the time.

"Why don't you sit down?" Cage said.

He sat because he couldn't think of how to leave without his friend chasing after him.

"I remember you getting drunk a couple of times during the war. From what you said, you'd never touched the stuff before then."

Heat flushed up Nate's back, but he kept his tone steady. "I stopped drinking over a month ago."

"I heard, but you started up again after the verdict at the trial."

"Mind your own business."

Cage delivered a glower that almost made him take a step back. "This is my business. You saved my life more than once during the war. I owe you."

He blew out a gusty sigh. "Fine. Say your piece."

"It wasn't your fault the trial went the way it did. We took a big risk trying a white man for raping a black girl. Hatred runs deep even in Ohio."

"And…"

"You're not the same man since you lost your leg. During the war, you became my brother. You were there when I needed you the most. Now that you're in trouble, I want to be there for you."

Nate clenched his jaw, unwilling to give in to the emotion rising inside of him. He didn't want to show how weak and worthless he had become, not even to his friend. "I don't need any blasted help." He didn't mean to use that kind of language, but he didn't appreciate his friend interfering, and he wasn't about to say what he really was thinking. "I might be a cripple, but I get along pretty good most of the time."

Cage stared at him, a sad expression crossing his face. "I know you can get around fine. I probably know it better than you do, but that's not what I'm talking about. You're feeling sorry for yourself, and you're blaming God for your troubles."

A gasp came out before Nate could hold it back. How did his friend know? He hadn't even told Betsy. "What makes you think that?"

"It's not just the drinking. You got your law license, but you're not doing anything with it. You resent every time I ask you to help someone who needs it like it's a bother. You've given up."

"I tried to be a lawyer. I tried to get a job with Mr. Hayes. He wouldn't hire me." Nate couldn't help his tone getting louder. "Do you know why he wouldn't hire me? Because of this." He pointed to his missing leg. "But you convinced me to put away my misgivings and try the case against Ralph Peterson, and we know how that turned out. It wasn't because Miss Johnson was black that Peterson got away with it. It was because she had a blasted cripple for a lawyer. Besides, I know what you're doing."

Cage grabbed his earlobe. "I don't know what you mean."

"You've been giving me these jobs to do because you pity me. Can't you see it only makes things worse?" He rubbed the back of his neck. "Just leave it be."

"I've been trying to show you have what it takes to be a lawyer. You lost one case. That doesn't mean you give up."

"Watch me."

"So what if Mr. Hayes won't hire you? Why haven't you set up your own office? I know you have money saved. You could quit the telegraph office tomorrow."

The curses from the other room had stopped, and all Nate could hear was his pounding heart. "Who…" He cleared his throat. "Who's going to hire a man with one leg for a lawyer?"

Cage sat on the edge of his heavy oak desk. "If you wore your artificial leg in court, nobody would notice, but your wife says you won't even bother to put it on."

"It rubs me raw." It didn't really since Betsy knitted him that sock, but he wouldn't admit it. He didn't want to wear it.

"So, be a man and get used to it. You need to stop drinking for your family's sake."

"I've tried to stop. I can't." The raw honesty of the statement formed a lump in Nate's throat.

"You won't be able to until you turn your life over to God and ask Him to help you. He wants you back."

Heaviness swept over Nate. His shoulders slumped, and he leaned on his crutches. He wouldn't have taken this rebuke from any other man, but he and Cage had gone through a lot together during the war. "I don't know how to fix this." He hated the crack in his voice. "I always wanted to help people, to do something for the betterment of society. Now I can't even help you when you're facing down a bank robber or go for help in time to save Tyler. That's why my wife sent me in here. She knew she could get to the doctor faster."

The ache in his throat threatened to choke him. "I'm in constant pain, and what's worse, the pain is coming from the leg that's no longer there. I can't even get on the floor and play with my children."

Cage swept toward him, put his hand on Nate's shoulder, and squeezed. "Lord, my brother is hurting. He feels useless even though You have a plan for him. Help him come back to You. Let him see You haven't deserted him. In Jesus' name, Amen."

A sob escaped Nate, and he worked to contain himself. "Thank you. I'll try. That's all I can promise."

"Trying isn't enough. Unless you surrender this to God, you'll fail. He's the only one who can help you through it."

Nate wiped his face. "I thought you decided not to be a preacher. You said you weren't good at it."

He chuckled. "I'm not, but I want to be a good friend."

"You are, Cage. You are."

~~~~~

Dr. Clark asked Betsy to stay and help while he removed the bullet. He was the only doctor in Wellington who appreciated her training as a nurse.

After removing the bullet out of Mr. Tyler's thigh, the doctor asked Betsy if she wanted to stitch up the bank teller.

"I do." She put on one of his surgical aprons, took the needle and thread out of the pan of alcohol, and made the stitches. "How is he doing?"

"He lost a lot of blood." Dr. Clark washed his hands. "But the bullet lodged in some fatty tissue in his thigh. It didn't do any serious damage."

She was grateful that the patient wasn't awake while she stitched him up. She knew Dr. Clark didn't like to use more chloroform than necessary. She missed being a nurse, and she appreciated the doctor giving her opportunities like this. Who knew? If she hadn't been a wife and a mother, she might have made a fine nurse, or even a doctor.

She chuckled to herself. The only woman doctor she'd ever heard of was Elizabeth Blackwell, and she was only able to treat former slaves and Native American women and children. No white families would allow her to doctor them. She had heard there were women doctors out West where doctors were scarce, but she didn't know of any.

She finished the last stitch, removed her bloody apron, and washed up in a basin of clean water. "Thank you for letting me help."

He nodded. "You were of great assistance. He should be all right in a few days as long as infection doesn't set in."

Betsy bit her lower lip. Infection had killed more soldiers on the battlefield than bullets. If they hadn't removed Nate's leg when they did, infection would have most likely killed him. She was glad medical knowledge about infection and germs had grown. Alcohol to wash surgical supplies and doctors washing their hands before and after treatments had greatly reduced infections. Even the honey and vinegar ointment she used prevented it.

"I must get back to my husband and children now." She waved goodbye, climbed aboard the wagon, and headed to Lavena's home next to the marshal's office. She would talk to Lavena and gather up the children first. It would be easier on Nate if he could rest a little longer. As late as it was, they'd have to have their picnic another day. She'd save the news about another child on the way until then.

When she got to the house, the children were still playing in the other room, so she sat across from her friend. "When you were worried about Cage, you became agitated and fainted. I assume this wasn't the first time. When did it start?"

Lavena let out a sigh. "I should have known I couldn't keep it from you. After the war, I started fretting about little things. I tried to give them to the Lord, but to no avail. I told Cage about it, and he suggested I memorize Proverbs three, verses five and six."

"*Trust in the Lord with all thine heart; and lean not unto thine own understanding. In all thy ways acknowledge him, and he shall direct thy paths.*"

Lavena nodded. "I want to trust in the Lord, but I've always been confident about doing things on my own. It's difficult."

Betsy let out a sigh. "I do understand that. It's so hard to trust God when my husband won't stop drinking. I've often quoted the same verse."

"It got worse after I almost died delivering Penelope and was told

I..."

"I know." Betsy patted her hand.

"I talked to Dr. Clark about it. He said my hysteria is caused by what happened to me during childbirth. He said I have a wandering womb. He treated me for it, but it did no good."

"I'm so sorry."

"When the treatments didn't work, he gave me some laudanum and told me to take a little every time I'm troubled, but I've done enough articles about that stuff to know how addictive it is. I was managing to handle my fears, then at the suffrage march when that man stabbed me..." Lavena took a sip of tea. "I was so frightened. Since then, it's gotten worse. I used to be the one who ran into the fray. Now, I'm not sure I can even go to another march, let alone the protests in front of the saloon. And it makes it worse that Cage has such a dangerous job. Every day when he leaves here, I fret he might not come home. How do I regain my courage?"

"I don't know." Betsy wrapped her hands around her cup. "Quoting that scripture and prayer are good ways to start, but that doesn't mean everything will work out the way we hope. All we can do is trust the God who gives hope to fill us with His peace. Can I pray for you?"

"Yes, please." Lavena's voice was timid like a small child.

Betsy laid a hand on her shoulder and prayed she would learn to trust in God to give her the peace she needed. Then, she realized she need to trust in the God who gave hope and peace for her situation. She prayed the same thing for herself. She hugged her friend. "I must go. Nate will wonder what's taking so long."

After saying their good-byes and getting the children settled in the wagon, Betsy entered the office next door. Cage and her husband sat across from each other. When they saw her, they both stopped talking abruptly.

"How's Tyler doing?" Cage asked with an impassive expression as if she hadn't interrupted them in a serious conversation.

"The bullet didn't hit anything vital. It will take a couple of weeks of bedrest. Unless infection sets in, he should recover without any problems."

"Good news." Cage turned to Nate. "Before you go, I have a favor to ask."

"Another mission to help those in need?" Nate's tone had a sarcastic edge. What was that about?

"No," Cage said. "This time, I really do need your help."

"Anything," Nate said. "What do you need?"

"I have to take Horton to Columbus by train to stand trial. We'll leave in two days, but I'll have to sign a statement about what happened in Wellington before I go, so we won't make it back until late Friday night."

The Aftermath

Betsy wasn't sure, but based on Cage's concerned look, he really needed Nate to come along. She knew Lavena would appreciate it.

Nate stroked his beard. "Why don't you have the trial here?"

"He committed crimes all over the state. They want him in Columbus, and it's not wise to go alone with a killer."

"I don't know, Cage. I have work. Why don't you take one of your deputies?"

"I could, but we're already shorthanded. We need extra men as it is with the rise in crime. I sure don't want to leave and take another deputy with me. It will leave the village unprotected."

"I'd need to talk to my boss first," Nate said. "If it's all right with him for me to take a couple of days off, I'll do it."

Betsy let out a sigh of relief. She was worried her husband would say no.

"One thing." Cage placed his hand on Nate's shoulder. "If you go along, you to stay sober."

The muscle in Nate's jaw twitched, and Betsy worried he might change his mind.

"If I go…" Nate jabbed his finger into Cage's chest. "…you don't have to fret about me staying sober." He swiped his hand across the back of his neck. "Do you really think so little of me?"

Cage shook his head. "If I did, I wouldn't have asked you along."

Her husband stood there a couple more moments staring at his friend. "I'll let you know what my boss says. Let's go, Betsy." He grabbed her hand and escorted her out the door.

Chapter Sixteen

On the train ride to Columbus, Nate didn't say anything. Even if he had wanted to talk to Cage, he wouldn't have said anything in front of Horton. As the train chugged along, he let his thoughts drift. Since there were only two seats on each side with an aisle in between, Cage sat beside the outlaw, and he sat behind them.

He was still angry at his friend, but they'd always been straight with each other, and he had no right to bellyache about Cage telling him the truth now. Maybe it wasn't Cage he was angry with. He resented God allowing him to lose his leg, but he had to admit that was getting old. God was sovereign and allowed things like this to happen during war. Nate was the one who volunteered for the dangerous assignment. God didn't force him to become a spy. As much as he hated what had happened, he realized that sometimes he stirred up the rage at God to give him an excuse to drink. He wasn't ready to repent yet, but he didn't really blame the Lord for what he had become, at least not anymore.

His real ire was toward himself. He had nobody to blame but himself. He wanted to be a good husband, a loving father, and a good man, but he wasn't. He was a drunk. Cage had every right to remind him to stay sober on this trip.

Would he have committed to doing that if Cage hadn't mentioned it? He didn't know.

One thing that kept going through his mind was the suggestion he open his own law practice. Even though he accused his friend of giving him opportunities to use his knowledge of the law out of pity, he enjoyed helping people and practicing law. So why didn't he go ahead and do it? He knew he'd done the best he could for Miss Johnson. Although he used it as an excuse to go back to drinking, he had to be honest with himself. It wasn't his missing leg that made the jurors vote the way they did. It was their own prejudices.

He had enough money to start a practice. That wasn't the problem. They had plenty saved at the bank. When his father died during the final days of the war, and his mother died soon after, he sold their plantation in Tennessee for pennies on the dollar to carpet baggers in the area, but he still made a tidy sum from it. The money both he and Betsy made during the war, him as a soldier and her as a nurse, wasn't much, but since they'd spent very little of it, it added up to a nice nest egg by the time the war ended. They'd spent some on their house and saved the rest. There was plenty left.

If Horton had gotten away with robbing the bank, he would have stolen their money as well. Was God keeping it safe so he could use it for this very reason?

Dare he risk their savings on this foolish venture?

When he thought about it before, he'd always concluded that he couldn't practice law with only one leg, but he knew the truth. It wasn't his missing leg that stopped him from practicing law now. It was the demon drink that had hold of him. He couldn't consider it until he was able to leave the whiskey behind for good.

The train chugged into the Columbus station. Horton leaned over to Cage to say something, and Nate leaned forward in his seat to hear.

"You can let me go," Horton whispered. "I have lots of money hidden away. I could pay you a thousand dollars. More than you'd make in years as a lawman." He tilted his head back. "You could share it with your friend. He wouldn't say anything."

"Shut up," Cage said.

"This is your only chance. You could say I got away." Horton chuckled. "If you turn me over, I'll escape. I'll make a deal with someone else. I can promise you that, and when I do, you're a dead man."

Cage ignored the threat, pulled Horton to his feet, and escorted him to the exit. Nate followed close behind.

When they left the station, two men with badges were waiting for them. As the men escorted Horton away, the outlaw turned his head back and shouted. "You're a dead man, Marshal. You hear me? Dead."

Cage turned to Nate. "Let's get something to eat."

"Aren't you worried?"

He grinned. "No, I'm hungry."

Nate nodded and headed to the restaurant with his friend. If Horton ever did escape, he would have to go through him before he ever got to Cage.

~~~~~

A few days later, Betsy met Nate at the telegraph office as he came out the door. He had agreed to take her on the picnic they'd missed when Billy Horton robbed the bank.

"Time to go." She fanned herself. "The children are in the wagon, and I've packed a picnic basket and blanket." She looked at the white fluffy clouds in the sky. Not one of them looked like rain. "It might be a little hot, but it looks like we're going to have a beautiful day."

Nate nodded and followed her to the wagon. He took the reins and drove them to the fairgrounds just outside of town. They rode in silence. She wanted to ask him about the trip to Columbus, but something was on his mind, so she waited.

When they had arrived, the children took their new ball and ran off to play.

"Not too far," Betsy said. "Make sure I can see you and listen for when I call."

"Yes, Mama," Malachi said.

She spread out the blanket while Nate brought the picnic basket over.

"Shall we eat now?" he asked.

"Let's give the children a little more time. It's still early."

He nodded and sat down beside her on the blanket.

"How was the trip?" Betsy asked.

"I did a lot of thinking."

She swallowed, not sure where this was going. "About what?"

He took her hand in his. "I haven't been a good husband or father, but I'm going to do my best to stop drinking and be a better man."

A smile spread across her face, but a nudging inside warned her she should guard her heart against him breaking it again. She so wanted to believe him. "That's good news. So, you'll sign the pledge not to drink."

"I'm not sure I can do that yet." He shrugged. "I don't want to sign until I'm sure I can stop drinking. If I can make it a month without a drink, I'll sign it."

She blinked to keep tears from forming in her eyes. Until he signed the pledge, how could she believe he would stay sober?

"I have more news."

She swiped a residual tear off her face. "What?"

"If I can stay sober, I'll put on that artificial leg and open a law office."

"Really." The tears started again, but this time, they escaped her eyes and rolled down her cheeks. "I know you can do it with the Lord's help."

He pulled his hand away and spoke in a faraway voice. "Yes, with God's help."

She didn't understand the change in his demeaner, but she decided it was time to change the subject. "Now that you've agreed not to drink, could you build that fence in the back?"

"Oh, Betsy." He let out a sigh. "I'll try."

"The reason I asked is because I also have some news."

Nate perked up a little. "What is it?"

"I'm with child."

His eyes widened, then he kissed her. "I love you. I'm going to try my best to be the husband you deserve."

She wanted to believe him, but she couldn't help seeing the doubt in his eyes. If he wasn't even sure he could do it, how could she trust him?

~~~~~

On Sunday, Nate hitched the wagon and took his family to church.

He'd been angry with the Lord for so long. Maybe it was time to surrender. He felt the Holy Spirit wooing him back, and it was only a matter of time. Going to church reminded him the Lord hadn't given up on him. In Jesus' eyes, he wasn't worthless. Cage's prayer made that reminder more real than ever. Then the news of another child on the way... He needed to repent and ask God to help him, so why didn't he?

They sang three hymns. The first two were some of Nate's favorites, hymns he'd often sung at First Church in Oberlin where the fiery evangelist and president of the college. Rev. Charles Finney, preached often during his years there. Rev. Fowler was very much like Rev. Finney, only younger.

When the third hymn played, the only reason Nate stayed in the building and pretended to sing was so people wouldn't know the song was about him. The name of the hymn was *Behold the Dying Dunkard Man*. Each verse got progressively worse, but the chorus made him want to crawl under the pew.

> *Help us to feel for drunken man,*
> *In all his sin and wo;*
> *And let our bright example teach*
> *The way he ought to go.*

Betsy's voice sang loud and clear throughout the song, but she never looked over to him. Thank God for that. It finally mercifully ended, and Rev. Fowler came to the pulpit.

"Today's sermon is about the sin of drunkenness. Some of you here today might be imbibing in that sin, but Christ wants to set you free."

Nate groaned inside. Rev. Fowler had been preaching this too often lately.

"Some may say the Bible doesn't say drinking is a sin, that Jesus turned water into wine, but the Bible doesn't encourage you to leave your family behind and visit saloons for the sole purpose of filling your belly with whiskey. The sin of drunkenness has enslaved you until you no longer realize what you've done to your family.

"Others say, 'I drink in moderation.' Do you? If it has no hold on you, why not give it up?

"Let's start with Isaiah 5:11. 'Woe to those who rise early in the morning to run after their drinks, who stay up late at night till they are inflamed with wine.' I challenge you to say that stopping at the saloon to have a drink pleases the Lord when First Thessalonians five, verse 6 admonishes us to be sober."

On and on Rev. Fowler went quoting every verse about the sin of drunkenness and the admonishment to be sober. He quoted Proverbs,

The Aftermath

Luke, Ephesians, and more verses from Isaiah. He talked about how wives and children were affected by their husbands being enslaved to strong drink, and how drink caused more than one husband to berate or even beat his wife and children, but even those who didn't abuse their families broke their hearts and spirits by not being godly examples and spiritual leaders of their homes.

With each passing moment, Nate felt more hopeless and worthless than he did before. He knew he had sinned grievously. There was no way around it. The preacher was right. Strong drink had enslaved him. He'd promised Betsy he'd try to stop drinking, but he hadn't signed the pledge because he wasn't sure he could stay away from it.

He didn't know if he was ready to give it up or go to the altar and repent, especially when the sermon was about drunkenness. Only a few people knew he drank. How would it affect his reputation if he admitted it in front of the entire congregation?

No, today wasn't the day. He needed to stay sober for a little while longer for Betsy's sake and to prove he could do it. Then he could come to God and repent in private. He didn't need to do it at a church service with everybody knowing.

While the resolve to do better set his jaw, he listened more intently.

Rev. Fowler continued his sermon. When Nate was sure he was finished, he ended with this. "I am calling on every member of The First Church of Wellington to sign the temperance pledge to never drink alcohol again."

A flash of anger heated his face. This had to be Betsy's doing.

"I have met with the board, and we unanimously agree. Anyone who doesn't sign is no longer a member of this church."

Nate's heart pounded in his chest, but he took steady, slow breaths to keep an even temper while in the midst of the congregation.

"Anyone who does not sign this pledge may attend, but until he repents publicly, he will not be allowed to become a member, take communion, or receive any other sacraments of the church."

They might as well hang a sign around his neck that said, "drunkard." This was reprehensible. He glanced at Betsy who didn't avert her eyes from the preacher. She must have told them what he'd been up to at the meetings. Didn't she realize how this would affect his reputation, the reputation of their family? He couldn't start a law office if everyone thought he was a drunk. How could she do this to him?

With each word the preacher said, Nate grew angrier. As soon as the altar call was given, he stood, grabbed his crutches, and walked out of the church.

Once he got out on the street, he didn't trust himself to go straight home. If he didn't calm down before his wife arrived, he wasn't sure he would be able to remain civil. Instead, he headed to the saloon.

~~~~~

After the service ended, Betsy grabbed hold of the children's hands and rushed past the parishioners out onto the front lawn to escape the pity-filled looks she received. She wiped her cheeks and told the children to stay put.

Cage and Lavena hurried over to her with Penelope in tow.

"Children, you can play together on the church lawn but stay close," Cage said.

The children ran off together. Giggles showed they didn't know the disaster that had befallen their family.

Lavena gave her a hug. "I'm so sorry."

She appreciated their support. She had been so flustered when the preacher announced the new church policy. She honestly didn't know he'd planned to do that. Then when Nate walked out, she'd never been so humiliated. Pain gripped her chest and throat. He would blame her.

Cage pulled on his ear. "I'm not sorry."

Heat flushed her cheeks. "But he'd stopped drinking. He just wanted to wait to sign the pledge to make sure he could manage it. This drove him right back to the saloon."

"Now hear me out." His brow furrowed. "We're all worried about Nate, but not just his drinking. I'm more worried about his relationship with God. Until now, he was able to pretend everything was fine. Now, the church has called out his sin, and he doesn't like it."

Betsy swiped at a tear running down her cheek. "I didn't mean for it to go like this. I'm the one who encouraged Rev. Fowler to preach a series of sermons about the sin of drunkenness, but I didn't expect him to remove Nate's membership if he didn't sign the pledge. He'll think I planned it. He'll be so angry, and I don't blame him. He's probably at the saloon drowning his troubles in a bottle of whiskey. What do I do?"

"You pray for him." Cage extended his hands so Lavena and Betsy could grab hold of them. "We'll all pray for him."

Betsy grasped her friends' hands tightly, and they prayed like she had never prayed for him before. They not only prayed he would stop drinking and feeling sorry for himself but that God would restore him to the man he was before, that He would do whatever it took to get Nate on the right path.

After the prayer, Betsy took her blue embroidered handkerchief and wiped the tears from her eyes. "Now, I have to go home and face him. If he's there."

"You won't face him alone," Cage said. "We're having Sunday dinner at your house tonight. If Nate doesn't show up until late, we'll put all the children to bed and stay there until he does."

Betsy swallowed hard. "Won't he be angry if we ambush him like that?"

"He might." Cage swiped at the back of his neck. "But he needs to know we who love him most aren't going anywhere, that we care about him, and we'll confront him because we want him to make things right with God."

Lavena patted Betsy's arm. "It will be all right. You'll see."

Betsy hoped so. But it might make things worse than ever.

Chapter Seventeen

Nate headed to the saloon at a swift pace after walking out of the church. He couldn't go home after what happened. He wasn't sure he could keep a civil tone after what his wife had done. He was almost ready to sign the pledge and turn to God. Then she had to go and convince the pastor to revoke his membership? How could she humiliate him like that?

He brushed through the doors into the dark saloon and stepped to the bar. "Give me a bottle of whiskey."

The bartender didn't waste any time. He was probably happy to have the business. Most men didn't drink on Sundays even if they'd been here all night the evening before. Drunks during the week and churchgoers on Sunday morning. The irony was not lost on him.

He threw a coin on the bar, grabbed the bottle, and sat at a table in the corner. Only one other man was at the table across the room, Doug Hanson, but he'd already drank enough that he slumped over the table with his eyes lowered. He'd probably be passed out soon.

Nate opened the whiskey bottle, poured a drink, and swallowed it down in one gulp. Then another. After that, he sat there for hours, staring at the bottle. When he found out another child was on the way, he'd promised he would try to not drink again, and he had meant it. So why was he here? He drank one more glass and corked the bottle. Then he sat there until well after sundown staring at the almost full bottle he'd paid for.

What's wrong with me?

His stomach grumbled reminding him he hadn't eaten since this morning. He'd missed the noonday meal and supper. He thought about going home so he could at least get something to eat, but he couldn't bring himself to do it. He wanted to wait until Betsy had gone to bed.

Everything he'd gone through over the last few years rolled through his thoughts. He went to Oberlin College on a mission from God. He was going to be a lawyer and champion those who had nobody to speak for them. He'd even planned not to marry so he could devote his life to his mission.

Then he met Betsy, one of the female students at the college. She was so pretty with her blond hair, blue-green eyes, and fair skin. Even though most of the women dressed in an austere style, Betsy wasn't afraid to be herself. She came to classes in satin hoop-skirt dresses wearing elaborate hats and carrying matching embroidered handkerchiefs. She'd mesmerized him.

As the week passed by, he got to know her better and not only was attracted to her looks but to her kindness and warmth. She'd told him that all she'd ever wanted was to marry a godly man who served the Lord and cared for those who needed help. Her mission was to marry such a man and make a home with him, partner with him, encourage him, and raise children who loved God and others.

He fell in love with her and began to realize a woman like Betsy would be an asset to his law career and his mission. He married her the day after graduation.

Two weeks after that, he was arrested along with other Oberlin students for rescuing a slave from slave catchers in the Oberlin-Wellington Slave Rescue. Three months later, he was released and decided to go to Tennessee to rescue slaves. He felt it was his obligation since his father owned men and women who worked his plantation.

Betsy begged him to take her with him, but he refused. She was from a wealthy family and was too delicate for an excursion like that. Besides, it was too dangerous. He didn't want to worry about his wife getting hurt or captured.

When he returned, he promised he wouldn't leave again, but he did three more times. In the first two years of their marriage, they were together only a couple of months. Then the war broke out, and he was one of the first to enlist without even telling her first. He didn't blame her for threatening to leave him. Two years later, she wrote him a letter saying she meant it, that their marriage was over. He was devastated. That was the first time he'd ever touched a drop of liquor.

The hurt he'd nursed was what led him to become a spy who'd eventually been shot by the Union Army while wearing a Confederate uniform. That was when he lost his leg, but Betsy showed up without any pity in her gaze. She poured herself into nursing him back to health even though he was the one who betrayed her love for him. Now, he was betraying that love again.

The only light in the saloon was the lit candles on each table. The sun had gone down a long time ago. He checked the pocket watch she'd given him when they married. After midnight. He hadn't realized he'd been here so long. Betsy would have gone to bed hours ago.

Time to go home. Even though his wife did talk to Rev. Fowler about him, he had no call to be angry. She did it because she loved him. At least, he wouldn't be going home drunk this time. He glanced at the bottle then poured one last drink before pulling his coat around himself. He needed that drink in case she waited up for him. He took a few steps, then walked back to the table, and corked the bottle and tucked it into his coat pocket.

He would hide it under the porch before going inside.

No sense wasting a good bottle of whiskey. Besides, if he decided he needed a drink, he wouldn't have to go to the saloon. Betsy wouldn't know.

He stepped out into the night. The air was brisk and cool for summer, and the dark clouds hovered over the night sky. They matched his mood. He walked along the train tracks toward his home.

When he got to the house, the lantern in the kitchen shone through the window. He was surprised she'd waited up for him. He'd wanted to slip in bed and put off this conversation until tomorrow afternoon after work. He tried to be quiet while he hid the bottle under the porch and covered it with some dirt so it wouldn't be discovered. He rubbed his hands together and blew on them. The nip in the air chilled him. Or maybe it was the chill of hurting the only person who really loved him.

~~~~~

Betsy lifted her head from where it was propped on her arms at the kitchen table. She was sure she heard something. Footsteps and the thumping of crutches sounded on the porch. She, Lavena, and Cage had been waiting all evening for Nate to come home. She'd begun to worry that he'd found somewhere else to sleep it off. Even when he was drunk, he didn't usually come home this late.

She touched her friend's arm to rouse her. "Lavena, Cage, he's here."

Lavena wiped the sleep out of her eyes, and Cage stood at the door, his jaw set.

Betsy smoothed out her church dress. "You don't suppose he's too drunk to listen to us? Maybe you two ought to just go home and get some sleep. Lavena can fetch Penelope in the morning."

"If he is drunk," Cage said, "we'll douse him with cold water until he sobers up. He isn't going to get out of it this time."

Betsy nodded.

Nate walked in the door, and his eyes grew wide. "I'm glad you're still up. Cage, Lavena, I didn't expect you to be here." He kissed Betsy on the cheek and shook Cage's hand.

Betsy's thoughts scrambled as she bit the inside of her cheek. She smelled a hint of whiskey, but he wasn't staggering drunk like she expected. He couldn't have surprised her more if he'd come riding into the house on the back of an elephant.

Cage rubbed the scar running along his face. "Nate, we're here because we need to talk."

"No need." He poured himself a cup of the coffee brewing on the stove. "I apologize for leaving the church like that. I should have stayed, and Betsy, I forgive you."

"Forgive me?" Betsy sputtered. "For what?"

"For having the preacher revoke my membership unless I signed the pledge even though I'd stopped drinking. It was wrong of you, but I love you, and I forgive you."

Betsy glared at him. "I didn't do that."

Nate raised an eyebrow.

"All I asked was that Rev. Fowler do a series of sermons on drinking and encourage members to sign the pledge. I didn't know he was going to revoke membership and deny communion to anyone who didn't sign."

Nate stroked his beard. "I should have known you wouldn't do anything to betray me. I shouldn't have walked out like that, and I'm sorry I went to the saloon. As you can see, I only had a couple of drinks. I didn't get drunk, but it won't happen again."

Cage placed a hand on Nate's shoulder. "Why don't we sit down?"

Nate crossed his arms. For a moment, Betsy was afraid he would refuse. "I've already heard it all in church. Besides, I only had three drinks all night, well, four if you count the one I had before I left. I didn't get drunk, and I'm not going to. I told Betsy I would try not to drink from now on, and I will. I was just upset about what happened at church."

Cage raised an eyebrow. "You went to the saloon tonight, and you did drink. What happens the next time you're upset. Are we supposed to consider it virtuous because you only had four drinks?"

Nate let out a heavy sigh and plopped into the chair then shrugged. "All right. Go ahead and say what you have to say. I'd like to get some sleep."

Cage sat across from him, and Betsy and Lavena sat on each side.

"I'm not here to preach Bible verses at you," Cage said. "You already heard those at church."

Nate's mouth flattened. "Then why are you here?"

"Because we care about you, you big idiot." Cage wiped his hand over his face. "Look at what you're doing to your wife and children. It's not just about the drinking. It's about your relationship with God and about feeling sorry for yourself. So, you lost a leg during the war. Do you know how many men lost more than a leg? I still have scars on my face and in my heart from when I was burned, and Colonel Creighton never did make it home. His wife had to rely on her relatives to support her. Not to mention the other soldiers we lost."

~~~~~

Nate's chest squeezed tight as if someone were lacing a corset around him. "I know."

"Do you?" Cage stood and started pacing. "Because you don't act like it. You were a part of something greater than yourself, a part of God's holy mission to hold this nation together and to free those oppressed by their slave owners. Now you're going to give up everything God has called you to because you can't get over your own pride about losing a leg." He said the last part with a sarcastic tone.

With every word Cage spoke, Nate slumped a little more. Everything his friend said was true. He combed his fingers through his hair. What could he say?

"Then you've made your family suffer the indignity of making everything about mollycoddling yourself over what happened to you. When are you going to start being the husband and father they deserve? Do you know how many times Betsy has shared her sorrows with Lavena? My wife and I have prayed for her and you every day, that you would wake up and come to your senses. The drinking isn't the worst of the way you're acting. It's just the most noticeable."

Nate glanced up and looked into his wife's tear-filled eyes, and his heart broke. She deserved better than him. He should leave her now and spare her any more pain, but he couldn't do that. He loved her too much. All he could do was hang his head in shame for what he'd done.

"I'm so sorry."

"If you mean that, you won't just apologize to her. You have some repenting to do to God."

Nate nodded.

Cage took a piece of paper out of his pocket and slapped it on the table. "And if you really are sorry, you'll sign this pledge."

Betsy quickly placed a pen and a bottle of ink in front of him.

Nate let out a sigh, dipped the pen in ink, and signed the document. He wasn't sure he'd be able to live up to it, but he would do his best.

Then, the three of them stood around him and prayed for him. Tears came to his eyes, and he knew he needed to repent to God, but he couldn't manage it. Not yet. He'd become the man Betsy deserved, then he'd go to God. He would give up drinking and try to be a good husband and father. That was all he could do for now.

A week later, Nate stood in front of the church and presented a signed pledge.

Chapter Eighteen

A couple of weeks later, when Johnnie came to pick up the telegrams to deliver, Nate asked him how things were at home.

"Pa still goes to the saloon every night, but at least he got another job, this time at the boxing mill."

"I'm glad to hear that." He placed a hand on Johnnie's shoulder. "With money coming in again, maybe you won't have to work as hard."

A grimace covered the boy's features for a moment. He shrugged and delivered a half-hearted grin. "I still have to work plenty hard. My ma wouldn't have enough to feed my brothers and sisters if I didn't."

"But now that your father has a job…"

"They don't pay him as much as some of the others 'cause he won't sign the temperance pledge. He's plenty mad about that, but what money he does make, he spends at the saloon anyways, so I ain't gonna be quitting my jobs anytime soon."

Nate wiped his hand across the back of his neck. "I'm sorry to hear that."

"Just the way of things." Johnnie grabbed the telegrams. "No need fussing about it. Instead, I try to remember God is my Heavenly Father, and I can count on Him to help me."

He raised an eyebrow. "I've never heard you talk about God before. I didn't even know you and your family went to church."

"It's been recent. I heard Rev. Fowler preach in the field in my neighborhood."

Nate remembered hearing something from Betsy about Rev. Fowler preaching in the area of town where the migrant cheese factory employees lived. He had no idea anything came of it.

"I prayed and gave my life to God right then. I even got baptized in the horse trough they have there."

Nate lowered his gaze. This impoverished boy with a drunk as a father managed to do something he couldn't bring himself to do, surrender his life to God.

"I stop my deliveries and sneak to the field to listen every time Rev. Fowler comes around to preach. Course I have to work twice as hard to get everything delivered afterwards, but it's worth it. The reverend even started a boy's Bible study, and Mr. Baldwin lets me take a break once a week to go to it."

Nate's brow furrowed. "Why do you have to sneak?"

"I want to go to church, but both Pa and Ma don't like it, so I never managed it. Pa says if he catches me at church, he'll give me a whooping I won't soon forget, and Ma says God don't listen to our prayers."

"Sometimes He doesn't."

"Mr. Teagan, you should know better than that. I hear you go to church every week. Don't the Bible say something about how we all have trials in this world, but we should be happy because Jesus overcame the world?"

Nate couldn't help but remember a time he would have quoted that verse. "Says something like that, but how do you trust God when your father is... well, the way he is?"

"God don't have nothing to do with the way my pa acts. Jesus gave His life for everyone, and if my pa won't accept Him, that's on him. I couldn't go through this hardship if the Lord wasn't with me the whole time." With that, Johnnie headed out to make his deliveries.

Nate couldn't shake the feeling the Lord had used Johnnie and his situation to speak to him. He couldn't remember the last time he spent any time playing with his children, and he never talked with them about God or prayed with them. He left that to Betsy.

He had prided himself in being a better father than Doug Hanson. He'd stopped drinking, hadn't he? But he knew the truth. He wasn't the father he wanted to be, and in a few months, he'd have another child.

James came into the office a few minutes later, and Nate headed for home. Today, he was going to be the father his children deserved. He was going to spend time playing with them and talking with them about their Heavenly Father. Even if he wasn't on speaking terms with God yet, he wanted his children to be Christians.

He hurried home, and when he entered the kitchen, Betsy was kneading bread. He kissed her cheek. "Where are the children?"

"Outside playing."

He nodded. "I'm going out back to play with them."

She raised an eyebrow. "You're going to play with them?"

"Don't look so surprised."

He made his way to the back yard and looked around to see where they were. He couldn't find them anywhere. His gaze moved to the railroad tracks. Adrenaline shot through him. They were sitting on the tracks. He ran toward them as fast as he could on his leg and crutches. "Malachi, Naomi, come here right now!" As much as he tried to keep his voice calm, the panicked tone burst forth, but the children didn't hear him. They didn't even turn to look at him.

A train whistle blew.

"Betsy, help me!" He hurried toward the tracks as fast as he could. A glimpse of the train appeared in the distance. The lump in his throat threatened to choke him. "Malachi, Naomi," he screamed. "Come here now!"

The children looked up and stood, but they didn't move off the tracks. The train was coming closer every second, and the whistle blew a warning that stabbed Nate's heart. He tried to go faster but fell to the ground. Tears welled up in him. "No!" *Lord, please save them.*

A blur moved past him, and just as the train bore down upon his children, Betsy snatched them from the tracks.

He collapsed onto his back and pressed his fists into his burning eyes.

His wife chiding the children and telling them they couldn't play outside alone again until they were older and their tearful apologies barely reached his ears. They were safe, but not because of him. If she hadn't come out when she did, both of his children would be dead, and it would be his fault. What kind of a father couldn't protect his children from danger?

She came toward him and placed her hand on his back. "It's okay. They're fine."

That only made things worse. He should be the strong one, not her.

Reaching her hand out, she said, "Let me help you up."

He brushed her hand away and struggled to get to his feet—foot—even though it took a while. By the time he'd risen, the children were inside, but she waited by the door, apparently worried her cripple husband couldn't make it in on his own.

"Don't wait supper for me." He walked past her toward the tracks that would lead him to the saloon.

Sometime later, when he entered the smoke-filled room, his heartbeats had finally calmed, but the guilt and anger that he almost let his children die because of this blasted leg did not. He ordered a bottle of whiskey and sat at a corner table. Pouring a glass, he downed it in one gulp and waited for the warmth to fill him. It didn't ease the pain, so he drank another glass and another. He wasn't sure how long he had been drinking, but the bottle was empty. Even the numbness the whiskey produced hadn't deadened his anger at God or himself. All he could see was that train barreling toward his children.

~~~~~

Betsy paced the kitchen floor. She hadn't seen or heard from her husband since he took off. She knew he was distraught. Seeing the children on those railroad tracks had upset her too. She had never been so scared, not even during the war when she'd heard Nate had been shot, but she didn't desert her family. She was the one who stayed and disciplined Malachi and Naomi, then calmed their fears. She was the one who fed them and prayed with them when she put them to bed that night.

She was the one who gave them extra cuddles after what had happened and reassured them she still loved them.

He ran off. She hoped he wasn't at the saloon, but she knew deep in her heart, that was exactly where he was. Even so, he should have been home by now.

She placed her hand over her growing stomach. She'd always wanted a large family, but she'd never planned to be both father and mother to them. When she married a godly man who had just graduated from a Christian college, she'd never planned to have a drunk for a husband. It didn't bother her that he'd lost his leg. What troubled her was that he'd lost his relationship with God, and she didn't know how to change him back to the man he had been.

When he stopped drinking and signed the pledge, she'd started to hope that he might be changing. He even acted like he'd gotten things right with God. Today ended all of that. Now, she knew it was a lie. He only signed that pledge to appease them. Was there any hope? Would he ever change back to the man he used to be?

She gathered Malachi and Naomi around her. "Children, we're going to pray for your papa."

"Me too?" Naomi asked.

"Yes, you too. He needs us all to pray. Let's hold hands." They held hands. "Proverbs three, verses five and six says, 'Trust in the Lord with all thine heart; and lean not unto thine own understanding. In all thy ways acknowledge him, and he shall direct thy paths.' Lord, we are trusting in You with all our hearts. We don't know what to do. Direct our paths. Save my husband, not just from the drinking. He needs to repent and turn to You. He needs to acknowledge You as Lord and let You direct his path."

"Lord, help Papa," Malachi said. "Make him a good papa."

"Amen," Naomi said.

"Okay, children, time for bed."

After she'd tucked the children in, and they drifted off to sleep, she went back to the kitchen. She sat at the wooden table with her Bible open in front of her. "Lord, You said You would direct my paths. Show me what to do or how to believe for my husband." She turned to First John and began reading. When she got to First John chapter five, verses fourteen and fifteen leapt off the pages.

She read it out loud. "*And this is the confidence that we have in him, that, if we ask any thing according to his will, he heareth us: And if we know that he hears us, whatsoever we ask, we know that we have the petitions that we desired of him.*"

When she read it, a warmth filled her. She had confidence that God heard her prayers for Nate and would answer them. Nate would repent and come back to God. She spent some time thanking and praising God.

The Aftermath

Lord, is there anything else You would have me do?

She remembered the passage Rev. Fowler preached last week in the book of James. He said that in the early days of Christianity, they would anoint a person's head with oil and pray for him if he were sick, and he would recover. He had even spent money on some olive oil he had shipped to him. He said from now on, they were going to pray for the sick the way the Bible prescribed. The demon whiskey that had hold of Nate was a spiritual sickness. Of that she had no doubt. But how could she anoint her husband's head without him knowing?

She pulled her jar of lard off the shelf and dabbed her finger in it. She didn't have any olive oil, and she'd run out of butter, so it would have to do. Walking into the bedroom, she sat on Nate's side of the bed and wiped the lard on the pillow in the shape of a cross. He'd be too drunk when he got home to notice the slippery substance. If he did notice, she'd have to think of something else, but she would anoint his pillow every night until she saw a change.

That night, she didn't toss and turn until he got home and safely in bed. In fact, she must have been sound asleep when he staggered in because she didn't hear him come home or feel the bed move. When she woke at dawn, without the help of the alarm on the clock, he was still asleep beside her. She glanced over at the clock.

Six o'clock. She shook her husband. He stirred but didn't wake. She shook him again. "Wake up. You're late for work."

He groaned, sat up, and looked at the clock. "I forgot to wind the clock last night. I'm late." He grabbed his crutches and rushed to get his clothes on.

"I'll hitch the wagon," Betsy said. "It'll be quicker than walking." She ran outside and hitched the horse to the wagon then ran back again.

Nate was dressed but looked hungover. His breath still smelled of whiskey.

"Thank you." He hobbled to the door. Before he left, Betsy handed him an apple and a couple of leaves of peppermint from the plant she kept in the window. "Too late for breakfast, but the apple will tide you over."

Nate stared at the peppermint leaves.

"For your breath. Suck on them on your way to work."

He nodded and rushed out the door.

She walked out onto the porch and watched him climb onto the wagon and ride off. When he was gone, she swiped a little lard onto her finger and wiped it on his pillow in the shape of a cross.

"Lord, You said if I ask anything according to Your will, You'll hear me and give me what I desire. I'm asking You to save my husband, no matter what it takes."

She felt the Lord speaking to her spirit, telling her to continue what she was doing. To pray for her husband and anoint his pillow every day and to continue her work with the temperance society no matter what her husband said. That surprised her. He'd been supportive about her being involved even when he was drinking. Was that about to change?

Chapter Nineteen

Nate rushed into the office a full half hour late. He'd sucked on the peppermint leaves the entire trip there, but the apple was still in his hand. His head hurt, and his stomach churned. He wasn't sure he could eat even if he did have time.

Sam Shaffer, a scrawny older man with gray hair and glasses, scowled at him. "You're late. I had to cover for you even though I've been up all night."

"I'm sorry." Nate hurried to the desk. "I overslept."

Sam sniffed the air. "Is that why you're late? You've been drinking?"

Apparently, the peppermint didn't work well enough. "Last night, I had some cough syrup. I think it has alcohol in it."

"Do you think I'm muddle-headed or something? I know a drunk when I see one." Sam slammed the door on the way out.

Nate groaned and sat at the desk. Sam was a member of the church and was there when he presented the signed pledge. What was worse, Sam had a tendency to gossip. By Sunday, everyone would know. His membership would be revoked, and his reputation ruined.

He tried not to dwell on that. There was nothing he could do about it now. Instead, he concentrated on transcribing messages. It was a couple of hours before his stomach calmed down enough for him to eat his apple. He took one bite when Mr. Wilson, his boss, walked in.

He set the apple down and stood, hoping his breath wouldn't give him away.

Mr. Wilson leaned against the wall and crossed his arms. "I ran into Sam at the barbershop."

Nate could feel the heat flushing his face.

"He told me you'd come to work late and that you'd been drinking."

A heavy sigh escaped him. No use in denying it now. "I was drinking last night, and I overslept this morning. I didn't have time to tidy myself up before coming to work. I was a half hour late. I'll make it up to Sam."

"Look, son." Mr. Wilson placed a hand on Nate's shoulder. "I don't have a problem with having a drink once in a while. I even drink a glass of wine at dinner every night. I'm not one of those do-gooders who want you to sign a temperance pledge to work here, but when it affects your work…"

Nate let out the breath he didn't realize he was holding. Mr. Wilson was a drinker. He'd understand. "It won't happen again, sir."

"See that it doesn't." Mr. Wilson wiped his hand over the back of his neck. "You'll make it up to Sam by taking the night shift for two weeks. I told him he could have your shift."

Nate's jaw tightened.

"And if your job is affected by your drinking again, I'll have to find someone else. Is that understood?"

He kept his tone steady. "Yes, sir. I understand."

"Good, then I'll expect you back here at ten o'clock tonight. After a few night shifts, you'll realize why Sam was angry about you coming in late." Mr. Wilson left the office.

Nate sank into his chair. It could have been worse. He could have been fired, so why did he feel as if an anvil were sitting on his shoulders? It wasn't just the night shift or the dressing down at work. By Sunday, everyone would know he was a drunk. They'd realize why Betsy was so involved in the temperance movement.

He spent the rest of the day, when he wasn't transcribing messages, thinking about it. He'd have church membership stripped from him, probably in front of the whole church, but even that wasn't the worst of it. People at church, people he respected, would treat him differently. It was bad enough having their pity about losing his leg. Now, they'd send those pitiful looks toward his family and privately comment about his poor wife and what she had to suffer through. The more he considered it, the angrier he got. If she hadn't joined the Wellington Temperance Society, none of this would have happened.

By the time he rode home from work he'd decided what he needed to do. First, he would not set foot in that church again. Rev. Fowler would have to remove his membership without him there to witness it. He wasn't about to be shamed in front of the entire congregation.

Next, he would let Betsy know that her activities with the temperance society would have to cease. Enough was enough. He was the head of the home, and he would forbid it.

Betsy was a sensible wife. She'd realize she needed to obey him. He'd also let her know he wasn't even going to try to stop drinking anymore. Either she'd accept him for who he was, or she'd leave.

A knot formed in his stomach. Since he lost his leg, he always knew someday she'd leave him. Better to have it happen now than live like this waiting for the heaviness on his shoulders to crush him.

He walked into the house. The children played blocks on the kitchen floor while Betsy kneaded bread.

She wiped her hands on her apron, sauntered up to him, and kissed him on the cheek. "I'm glad you're home."

Nate nodded to their bedroom. "We need to talk."

She followed him to the bed chamber and closed the door. "What's wrong?"

He sat on the wooden chair and motioned for her to sit on the bed. He took a deep breath and let it out slowly. He didn't want to get angry or yell. He just needed to explain the way things were going to be from now on. "Things didn't go well at work today. Mr. Wilson says if I come to work in a drunken condition or am late because I was drinking again, he'd fire me."

Betsy glanced at his pillow. "The peppermint didn't work then?"

"No, it didn't." He scowled at her. "He also said that I have to work the night shift for two weeks as a punishment. I have to be at work at ten o'clock tonight."

"Then I'll let you alone so you can get to sleep. I'll keep your supper warm so you can eat before you leave." She stood and started to leave.

"Stop!" It came out a little harsher than he meant it. "Sit back down. There's more."

She sat on the bed with her brow furrowed. "Go on."

"I've tried to stop drinking. You know I have, but I can't do it. I don't even want to stop anymore. I won't go to the saloon more than three times a week for your sake, but you're going to have to love me as I am if you want to stay married to me like you say you do."

Tears filled her eyes, and one dripped down her cheek making him feel like a louse, but he continued. "By Sunday, the church will know I've become a drunk, so there's no need for me to pretend. I won't be going to church with you and the children anymore, but you still have my permission to attend if you want to."

Her chin trembled.

He tried to ignore the hurt in her gaze. "There is one thing I require of you. As your husband, I forbid you to embarrass me again by protesting in front of the saloon. I'm also ordering you to stop going to those temperance meetings. You will give them your resignation by tomorrow."

She wiped the tears off her face with her hand and stood. "I've listened to you sputter this nonsense. Now, I'm going to tell you what I've decided. I will love you and stay married to you unless you leave me, abuse me or the children, or betray our vows, and there's nothing you can do about it. I can't control what you do, but I will continue to pray for you to repent and give up the drink every day. I won't stop going to church with or without you, and I won't stop protesting or going to temperance meetings. God has directed my path, and I'll obey you only when you don't order me to do something God has instructed me to do."

The heaviness on Nate's shoulders moved to his stomach. "You will obey me, or I'll… I'll… I won't come home in the morning."

The color drained from her face, but her tone stayed calm. "I'll wake you up at eight, and I'll keep your supper warm for you." She started toward the door.

Heat traveled up his back. At that moment, he noticed something staining his pillow. "What is that?"

"Lard," she said. Then she walked out of the room and closed the door.

Lard? Why would there be lard on his pillow? He didn't have time to worry about it now. He had to get some sleep before work tonight.

She'd think about what he said. She wouldn't go against his orders. An unease settled over him. He'd given her an ultimatum, but he wasn't sure he would follow through on it. He would never leave her and the children.

~~~~~

Betsy closed the door of the bedroom and asked the children to go to their rooms to play. Once they were out of sight, she stepped onto the porch. The trees blew, and there was the smell of rain in the air. As soon as she closed the front door, she crumpled to the floor of the porch and sobbed. Rain started pouring, and the wind picked up so that it was blowing in her face, but she didn't move.

"Lord, I don't understand. He's getting worse, not better."

Trust me.

It was the only response she got.

After she was able to get hold of herself, she went inside, finished kneading the bread, and started cooking supper. It was easier to manage her distress when she busied herself with activity. She did trust God, but that didn't make it any easier.

After the children ate, and she got them ready for bed, she woke her husband. She didn't say a word as he rose to dress for work. The rain still pounded against the house. She grabbed an oilskin cloth from the trunk and set it on the bed. Even with the oilskin, he'd still be drenched by the time he walked there if he didn't take the wagon, but she wasn't going to suggest it. Let him decide for himself what he was going to do.

She grabbed the plate she had warming by the stove and set it on the table with a glass of milk. He came in and started eating, but neither of them said a word. She finally sat on the bench at the table next to him.

He finished up his last bite of bread and washed it down with the last of his milk. "I'll take the wagon tonight. I don't want to walk in this rain."

She didn't say anything.

"Thank-you for getting out the oilskin. It will help."

Betsy nodded. She was afraid anything she said would be choked out by the knot in her throat.

"So have you made your decision?" Nate said the words while concentrating on tying his boot. He wouldn't even look at her. "Are you going to obey your husband, or do I have to find somewhere else to live?"

"I won't quit the temperance society. I won't disobey God." She was surprised she was able to say it without showing the storm stirring inside her.

"Then, I won't be here in the morning." Nate wrapped the oilskin around him. "Think about how stubborn you're being. Do you really believe you're honoring God by disobeying your husband?"

She crossed her arms. "I won't quit."

He strode out the door.

Betsy dipped her finger in the lard, went to her bedroom, and wiped it on his pillow. If he didn't come home, he wouldn't be sleeping on this pillow, but she didn't know what else to do. She blew out the lantern and prayed until she fell asleep.

~~~~~

The next morning, she set the alarm early enough to make Nate breakfast. If he came home. If he didn't, she would have to feed his breakfast to the children. She swallowed back the lump in her throat. She wouldn't be able to eat even though her morning sickness had subsided. She placed her hand on her stomach. Her children would either have a drunk for a father or no father in the home at all. She swiped at the tears threatening to spill out of her eyes and placed a cast iron skillet on the stove where she would make the eggs and bacon.

The thump of Nate's crutch sounded on the porch outside, and her heart skipped a beat. She poured the eggs into the skillet.

Nate came inside, walked up to her, and kissed her on the cheek. "You can continue with your temperance activities, but I don't want to hear a word from you about my drinking."

"Breakfast will be ready soon."

He sat at the table. "Good. After I eat, I need some sleep."

He didn't say another word during breakfast, and she couldn't think of anything to say. When he finished eating, he got up, went to their bedroom and closed the door.

Lord, please help me.

~~~~~

Nate tossed and turned but couldn't sleep even though he was exhausted from working all night. When Betsy hadn't reacted as he'd expected, he hadn't known what to do. He dwelled on it all night at work. It was the first time she'd refused to do as he said. Maybe Lavena was rubbing off on her.

He did appreciate that she made his dinner before work and got out the oilcloth for him. She was being so nice despite her determination not to quit the society. He did the only thing he could do. He threatened to leave her. He was shocked when she still refused. Since it was an empty threat, he didn't know what he was going to do. He wasn't going to desert his family.

He'd finally decided the only way to save his pride was to give his permission while ordering her not to say another word about his drinking. She didn't refuse that request, but she didn't agree to it either. He wasn't sure what to make of that. She wasn't acting like herself.

At least she didn't have to worry about him getting drunk over the next couple of weeks. After working all night, and riding home in a constant drizzle, all he wanted to do was sleep.

He finally dozed when he heard a bang coming from the kitchen, followed by loud giggles. He got out of bed, grabbed his crutches, and made his way to the room.

The children were on the floor playing blocks and had apparently knocked down the blocks, spewing them all over the kitchen. Betsy wasn't paying attention to them at all. She was churning butter.

"Can't you keep those children quiet? I'm trying to sleep!"

Betsy looked up from her task. "They can't play outside. It's raining."

Heat flushed through his body. "They can be quiet. Children should be seen, not heard!" He said it harsher than he meant to.

Naomi started whimpering, and both children ran to their mother.

Betsy hugged them and let out a gusty sigh. "I'll try to keep them from making noise."

"Thank you," he said through gritted teeth. "That's all I ask."

He went back into the bedroom and lay down, but now he couldn't go to sleep. His muscles were too tense, and the constant rain beating on the roof kept him awake. Instead, he lay there listening to see if the children made any more noise. It didn't take long before there were more quiet giggles and then quiet tones he couldn't hear clearly.

Grabbing his crutches, he went back into the kitchen. Betsy had the children on her lap and was telling them a story. He delivered a glare and went back to bed.

As he was starting to doze, he heard that bang again. He strode to the kitchen. The blocks were all over the floor again. His heart pounded with anger. "Do you need a spanking, children? Is that what it will take to keep you quiet?"

Now they both sobbed loudly. Betsy moved in front of them and delivered a glower so fierce, he almost took a step back. "Go back to bed. I'll hitch up the wagon and take them to Lavena's."

Just then thunder accompanied the hard rain.

A cold chill from inside Nate's gut dissipated his irritation. "Don't do that. Not in this storm."

She leaned down and hugged the children who were still crying loudly.

He felt like a louse. "I'm sorry." He placed a hand on Naomi, but she flinched. "I didn't mean to yell. I just need some sleep."

"It's all right." Betsy patted the children's backs. "Papa didn't mean it." She glanced back at him, and her tone changed to have an edge in it. "Go back to bed. I'll take them upstairs and find something quiet for them to do."

He nodded. This time, as soon as his head hit the pillow, he fell asleep, but Betsy woke him for supper far too early to suit him. How would he manage two weeks of this without pushing away his children?

Chapter Twenty

The next day, after Nate went to bed, Betsy started a pot of beans and ham on the stove to cook all day and gathered the children into the wagon to take them to Lavena's house. She would have to return home before supper to wake him, but she didn't want another day like yesterday. She understood he needed to get to sleep and tried to keep the children occupied, but she couldn't keep them completely quiet for two weeks. That was impossible. And her husband had been so hateful. Ever since she started anointing his pillow and praying for him every day, things had gotten worse, not better.

Lord, did I really hear Your promise that Nate would repent, or did I just want it to be true so much that I imagined it?

The rain had subsided, and the sun was shining, but the ground was still muddy and wet. By tomorrow, the ground would dry up, and the children could play outside. She remembered what happened the last time they played outside alone. She would have to set a chair out there so she could work on her mending or do some gardening while they were playing. She didn't want to leave them out there alone.

Maybe she could buy some lumber, a hammer, and some nails at the store. If Nate didn't want to build a fence to protect their children, she could build it. How hard could it be? Of course, she would have to wait to build the fence until he worked days again. The pounding of the hammer would probably wake him, but she could stop at Baldwin General Store and order the supplies.

Only three more days until Sunday. Would he really skip church? He'd never missed a church service unless he was sick and couldn't manage it. To think he would stop going altogether was startling.

She drove to the general store and held the children's hands as they entered. "If you behave," she said to them, "I'll let you both have a licorice."

"We'll be good, Mama," Malachi said.

She walked up to the counter where Mr. Baldwin was standing. "I would like to buy supplies to build a picket fence."

Mr. Baldwin raised an eyebrow. "For your husband to build?"

She let out a sigh. "No, I'm building it."

"Do you want the wood pre-cut into pickets? That will cost more."

She couldn't imagine how much time she would spend sawing the wood. "Yes, please."

"How much lumber will you need?"

Heat flushed her face. "Um, enough to build a fence on one side of my property." For a furniture maker's daughter, apparently, she knew nothing about fencing.

"And how big is your property?" At least Mr. Baldwin didn't sound impatient.

"I'm not sure." She hated sounding so ignorant. "How would I measure that?"

Mr. Baldwin gazed at her as if he could see right through her. "Do you have some string?"

"I have some in the barn at home."

He nodded. "Take the string and lay it down where you want to build the fence. Cut or mark the string, then bring it back here, and I'll order the supplies. You'll also need fence posts to nail the pickets into place, plenty of nails, and a shovel."

"A shovel?" she asked.

"You'll have to dig holes in the ground to place the fence posts." Mr. Baldwin's brow furrowed. "Do you know how to build a picket fence?"

"No, I was hoping someone could tell me how."

"It's hard work for a woman," he said. "When you come back with the measurements, I'll give you the name of a handyman who can help you build it."

She remembered how Nate reacted when she suggested they hire someone. "I sort have wanted to build it myself."

He gave her a slight smile. "He's reasonably priced. I'll give you the name anyway, and if you run into trouble, you can call on him."

She nodded then glanced at her children standing on either side of her without making a peep but staring at the candy. She bought each of them a licorice. "I'll be back with the measurements."

He nodded, and they left.

She hoped she didn't sound as dull-witted as she thought she did, but it didn't matter. Since her husband wouldn't build that fence, she needed to. She and the children climbed into the wagon and headed toward Lavena's house.

When they reached her friend's house, Betsy tied up the horse, gathered the children, and knocked on the front door.

When Lavena answered, her face brightened. "What a surprise. I'm so glad to see you." She ushered them in. "So, what's wrong?"

"Naomi, Malachi," Betsy said, "go play with Penelope."

Lavena added, "Why don't you all play in your room? I'll let you know when lunch is ready."

They did what she said with lots of noise and giggles.

The Aftermath

"I didn't know what else to do." Betsy pulled out her handkerchief and blew her nose to keep from crying.

Lavena started a kettle of water boiling on the stove. "I'll fix us some tea, and you can tell me all about it."

Once the tea was poured, Betsy poured out everything that happened that week. "So, I came here this morning because I don't want the children upset. I knew they could play here with Penelope without being yelled at." When she finished, she dabbed her handkerchief across her face to wipe away the tears. She hadn't meant to cry, but she couldn't help herself.

Lavena touched her arm. "I'm so sorry. You're welcome any time."

Betsy sipped some tea. "Mmm. I love Assam tea." She took another sip and wrapped her hands around the cup. "I'm not leaving him unless he breaks our wedding vows with another or abuses the children or me physically. Besides, I was praying for him, and the Lord gave me a verse to hold onto."

"What verse?"

"First John five, fourteen and fifteen."

Lavena reached for her Bible sitting on the shelf, turned to the Scripture, and read it out loud. *"And this is the confidence that we have in him, that, if we ask any thing according to his will, he heareth us: And if we know that he hear us, whatsoever we ask, we know that we have the petitions that we desired of him."* She set her Bible down. "What a wonderful promise."

Betsy looked down. "He also told me to anoint Nate's pillow and pray for him every day and to not give in when Nate ordered me to resign from the Wellington Temperance Society or give up protesting in front of the saloon. I assumed God would move on Nate, but he got worse instead of better."

Lavena gazed into her teacup. "Sounds like the devil has hold of your husband and is fighting to keep him in his grasp."

"I never thought of that. Of course. I've made the devil angry. That's why my husband's getting worse." She took another sip of tea. "Why haven't you been to any more of our protests? We could use more of your articles about what we're doing."

Lavena pressed her lips together. "I... I can't go there again."

"Come to think of it, you didn't ask me to watch Penelope during the suffrage meeting last week. What's wrong? Did you take her with you?"

Lavena glanced toward the door, and her face turned ashen.

Betsy placed her hand on Lavena's. "It's all right. You know I'll keep your confidence."

Lavena wiped her face with her hand. "At first, this dread would come over me, but it only happened occasionally. Cage suggested I memorize Proverbs three, five and six and quote it when I felt fear."

"'Trust in the Lord with all thine heart; and lean not unto thine own

understanding. In all thy ways acknowledge him, and he shall direct thy paths.' I also have quoted those verses. They are a great comfort to me."

"To me as well at first." Lavena sipped some tea. "Then, at the suffrage march when that man stabbed me, my heart started racing so fast, I was sure I was having a heart attack. I couldn't breathe. I thought I might die."

"It must have been a fearful moment, but you survived, and your arm is fine."

Lavena pulled at the collar of her dress. "I know. But you were there when it happened again, when Cage faced those men who robbed the bank."

"I remember. You were breathing so heavy you fainted."

"I talked to Dr. Clark about it. He says I'm suffering from hysteria caused by a wandering womb, but I can't seem to get over it. Anyway, it happened again when I was at the protest in front of the saloon. Since then, I've lived in fear. Every time Cage leaves for work, a knot forms in my stomach, and it doesn't go away until he's safely back home."

Betsy took a sip of tea. "I can understand you being afraid considering your husband is the marshal of a village that's plagued with crime. And it makes sense to be afraid at the protests when you were stabbed."

"It's more than that." Her gaze darted around the room as if she were afraid someone might be listening. "When Penelope wants to walk ahead of me to the store, I run to her and insist she hold my hand. When I think about going anywhere other than church, I feel like I can't breathe. I've tried to go to the newspaper office to get a story assigned, but my heart beats so fast, I rush back to the house where I'm safe and close the door. When I have to go to the store, perspiration covers my forehead, and I barely manage. I've convinced Cage to pick up groceries a few times, but I can't avoid it forever. And I don't think I can ever face another meeting, let alone a march or a protest, again. I never thought I would be one of those shrinking violets afraid of my own shadow, let alone someone who would swoon, but I am."

Betsy stood and went to Lavena's side of the table. She sat beside her friend and embraced her in a long hug. Lavena sobbed on her shoulder. When she calmed, Betsy backed out of the hug and gave her the handkerchief she always carried, green this time to match her green day dress.

Lavena wiped her face and blew her nose. "I feel better talking about it. Until now, only Cage knew, and I never told him I was afraid when he went to work. I didn't want to place that burden on him."

"You can always talk with me. I've shared enough of my troubles with you." Betsy stood. "I'll get us another cup of tea. Then we'll try to find a solution to this."

Lavena nodded, and Betsy poured some more hot water into the tea pot along with some more tea leaves. She sat across from her friend who had replaced her tears with a look of determination.

Betsy grabbed the Bible on the table and looked up Proverbs three, verses four and five. "The first part says, '*Trust in the Lord with all thine heart.*' Isn't there another verse that says to give your cares to God for He cares for you?"

"Yes, I believe so, but how do I do that?"

"I suppose every time you're worried, tell God why you're afraid and that you trust Him to take care of it."

Lavena grunted. "What if I don't trust Him with it?"

"Then I suppose you tell Him that too and ask Him to take it from you."

She bit her lower lip. "Lord, I trust You with all my heart. At least I want to."

Betsy poured the tea into their cups. "The next part might be harder. At least it is for me. '*Lean not unto thine own understanding,*'" She took a sip of tea. "I know I'm always trying to figure things out."

"Me too," Lavena said. "Cage says I'm the one who always thinks she has the answers, but people would be better off if they just listened to me."

Betsy giggled. "That does sound like you, but it sounds a little like me too. I have no idea what God is doing in my husband's life. Maybe we need to ask God to help us with that one too."

"Maybe." For the first time in this conversation, Lavena's stiff shoulders relaxed. "I'll read the next verse. '*In all thy ways acknowledge him, and he shall direct thy paths.*' I suppose that means if we keep taking our problems to God and trusting in Him to fix them, He'll let us know what to do."

"That's what He's done for me. I had no idea how to help Nate, but God showed me what to do. Besides my efforts with the temperance society, I'm supposed to pray for him every day, quote the verses God showed me, and anoint his pillow with lard."

Lavena laughed. "You anoint his pillow with lard? You should have borrowed a little of Rev. Fowler olive oil."

"I'm supposed to anoint his pillow every day," Betsy said. "I can't ask him for that much oil. It costs too dearly."

"You could, at least, use butter. Wouldn't lard stain his pillow?"

Betsy shrugged. "Lard was all I had on hand at the time. I'd run out of butter. Once I used the lard, the pillow was stained anyway, so even after I churned butter, I kept using the lard."

"Didn't he notice?"

Betsy chuckled. "He asked what stained his pillow before he went to bed the first morning he worked nights. I told him lard, and he hasn't asked since."

"Wow." Lavena took another sip of tea. "If you can stain your husband's pillow with lard, then I can ask God to tell me what to do to get over this fear. Let's pray now."

Betsy and Lavena held hands and prayed together, but considering how much worse Nate got every time she prayed like this, she wondered how bad it would get before God answered her prayer.

Chapter Twenty-One

On Sunday morning, Nate came home from work exhausted. He couldn't imagine working another week of this shift. At least, he would have tonight off work. When he walked in the door, Betsy wore her Sunday dress and dished him out his plate for breakfast. He could barely keep his eyes open, but he was hungry enough to manage to eat every bite. He kissed her on the cheek and headed toward the bedroom.

"Today is Sunday. You need to get ready for church."

He stopped at the doorway. Heat flushed the back of his neck, but he tried to keep his tone even. "I told you I'm not going to church again. I'm going to get some sleep."

"Nate, I can understand today since you've been working nights, but you aren't really going to stop going to church, are you?"

He strode toward her until he was inches from her face. He took a breath and let it out slowly. "I already told you this. I'm not going to church today or ever again. You can go to church if you want, and you can take the children with you. I want nothing to do with it. I'm tired of feeling like a hypocrite. Now, I don't want to hear about church again. You understand me?" He was proud of the way he'd remained calm, but when she nodded, her lips trembled.

Good. Maybe she wouldn't bother him about it again. He went to the bedroom. The cross-shaped stain was still on his pillow. It had been a week. Why hadn't she washed it for him, and how did lard get on his pillow anyway? He was too tired to worry about it now. He switched pillows with her and went to sleep.

~~~~~

Betsy swallowed the lump in her throat and prayed. *Lord, I'm trusting in You even though I don't understand. Please, help me.*

She prayed it silently over and over as she fed the children breakfast and got them ready for church. She prayed it again as they drove to church in the wagon. The sun was shining even though there was a crisp chill in the air. Autumn might come early this year.

After walking into the church building, she settled the children in their Sunday School class.

"Good morning, children." As they entered the class, Mrs. Mueller, the Sunday School teacher turned to Betsy. She was a plump woman with a pleasant smile. "Where's your husband today? He normally drops off the children."

"He's not here today." Betsy hoped the woman wouldn't say anything more about it.

"Oh, dear, I hope he hasn't gotten that nasty influenza that's going around."

"No, he's fine. I must get to the sanctuary before service begins." She hurried off before the woman could ask another question.

When she passed Rev. Fowler in the hallway, he stopped. "Mrs. Teagan, just the person I wanted to see."

She let out a sigh then covered her irritation with a smile. "Hello, Rev. Fowler. What can I do for you?"

Rev. Fowler motioned her aside where those who passed couldn't hear and lowered his voice. "Is Mr. Teagan here today?"

Her cheeks grew hot. "No, he stayed home today."

"I see." He gazed into her eyes with a look that showed, what? Concern? Pity? It was obvious he knew. "I've heard about your troubles. While I must talk to your husband about his behavior, I want you to know, we consider you a godly Christian woman and will stand by you. If you need anything... Mrs. Fowler and I are here for you and your family."

Betsy swallowed. "Thank you."

He nodded and walked on.

She almost got to the doorway when Mrs. Colson, a member of the Wellington Temperance Society since its founding, hurried toward her. The woman was in her late fifties and always dressed impeccably. Her husband owned a mill in town and was wealthy, so she had a number of fine dresses and hats. Today she had on a yellow satin dress with a bustle and a beaded neckline, and a matching hat.

"Mrs. Teagan, where is your husband today?"

Biting the inside of her cheek to keep from saying something rude, she turned and glared at the woman. "He's not here, today."

"Oh, you poor thing." Mrs. Colson took her hand and patted it. "It's all over town that he's been drinking. I know you must be devastated."

Every muscle in her body tightened. Did everybody know? "Church is about to begin. If you'll excuse me." She turned and walked away briskly before Mrs. Colson could say anything more.

Betsy perused the pews trying to find Cage and Lavena. She didn't want to sit alone and have more busy bodies ask where her husband was. She found them and scooted in to sit beside her friend.

Cage leaned across his wife. "Where's Nate?"

"Not you too." Betsy blinked to hold the tears back. "He's decided not to come to church."

Lavena put an arm around her and glared at Cage.

"I'm sorry." Cage held his hands in the air. "I didn't know."

Betsy swallowed. "Apparently, you're the only one in the church who didn't."

The singing began, and even though she wanted to crawl off somewhere, she raised her voice with the others to sing one of her new favorites.

> *What a friend we have in Jesus*
> *All our sins and griefs to bear*
> *What a privilege to carry*
> *Everything to God in prayer*

As she sang on, a peace swept over her. The words echoed deep inside.

After a couple more hymns, Rev. Fowler delivered a sermon about the power of praying God's Word. He began with Proverbs three, five and six. "*Trust in the Lord with all thine heart; and lean not unto thine own understanding. In all thy ways knowledge him, and he shall direct thy paths.*"

She was surprised he quoted the verse Lavena and she had just talked about the day before and showed how it related to prayer. What a confirmation. She glanced over at her friend who was listening just as intently as she was.

Betsy was even more surprised when he ended with the verse she had recently memorized.

"John five, fourteen and fifteen says, '*And this is the confidence that we have in him, that, if we ask any thing according to his will, he heareth us: And if we know that he hears us, whatsoever we ask, we know that we have the petitions that we desired of him.*' If you have a prayer need, I invite you to come to the anxiety bench and pray."

Betsy paused for a moment, knowing everyone in the church would know why she was up there, but did it matter? They knew anyway, and she needed the prayer. She stood and made her way out into the aisle. She got as close to the anxiety bench as she could manage. The front of the church was too crowded with people answering the call to get any nearer. Instead, she knelt where she was and lifted her hands toward Heaven. A peace came over her, and everything around her faded away.

She saw herself standing in front of the saloon carrying a sign. Nate came to her with tears in his eyes. "I'm so sorry." He had a light about him, and she knew he'd repented and come back to God. She dropped the sign and laid her head on his shoulder. His heart beat against her.

Then, the vision faded, and she was on her knees in the church. What was that? She'd read in the Bible about dreams and visions from God, but she'd never experienced it before. Yet, she knew it was real. God had given her a vision about the future. Nate would be saved and would come back to her.

~~~~~

Lavena couldn't believe what had happened when she came to the anxiety bench. God directed her path. She knew what to do to help her anxious thoughts. She would memorize a verse about trusting God or about not fearing every week. Whenever she felt fear overtake her, she would quote the verses she'd learned and give the fear to God. Then she would write down the fear on a piece of paper and throw it into the stove. There would be nothing left of the fear but ashes.

After Penelope was tucked into bed that evening, she sat beside her husband in the rockers by the stove and told him what the Lord had shown her. "I never admitted it to you before, but the hysteria attacks have gotten worse."

"I know." Cage stroked his face. "I've never known you to go this long without writing a story to make a group of people in town angry, or march in a protest, or even go to a meeting. I've been praying for you."

"You knew."

Cage smiled and leaned toward her. "Sweetheart, you can't hide anything from me. Not only haven't you been going out except for the store and church, your chin quivers every time I head out to make rounds."

She touched her parted lips with her fingers. "You never said anything."

He took her hands in his. "I didn't believe chiding you for it would help. It would only make you feel worse. I knew you and God would work it out. Nothing can keep you down for long, not even fear."

She drew her chair closer to him and touched his cheek. A warmth settled over her like a warm blanket on a crisp autumn evening. She loved this man so much.

"Which passage will you memorize first? I'd like to learn them with you."

"Philippians four, six and seven."

He grabbed his Bible and read it out loud. "*Be careful for nothing; but in every thing by prayer and supplication with thanksgiving let your requests be made known unto God. And the peace of God, which passeth all understanding, shall keep your hearts and minds through Christ Jesus.*" He set the Bible down. "That's a good one, but don't expect all your worries to disappear overnight. It will take time."

She raised her eyebrow. "And what makes you think I would expect that?"

"Because I know you too well. When it comes to changing things, you're a bit impatient." He chuckled. Then his forehead furrowed. "I need to ask you something. Betsy was alone at church, and she was acting odd.

Is Nate drinking again?"

Lavena glanced down. "Yes, she was here yesterday with the children. His boss made him work nights for two weeks because he came to work late and half-drunk from a hangover. He didn't take it well." She filled Cage in on everything that happened.

He pulled on his ear. "So, I need to have a talk with that man, maybe shake some sense into him."

"I'd wait until next week. Betsy says he's a bear since he's been on nights."

Cage scowled. "I can out bear him any day of the week."

Lavena snorted. "Yes, you can."

~~~~~

The next day, as Nate slept the day away, Betsy went to the barn to try to round up the string he kept with his tools. All his tools were in a wooden crate in the corner against the wall. She grabbed the string and looked through the other tools. There was a hammer, a saw, and a shovel, everything she needed to build the fence. At least she thought it was everything. She'd need some long nails. Mr. Baldwin had mentioned that. The only nails she found would be too short.

She left the barn and headed to the corner of the house. If she could measure from the corner of the house to the edge of the railroad tracks, then measure along the tracks to the end of her yard where the neighbor's fence sat, that should be enough to keep the children away from the tracks.

Malachi ran up to her. "What are you doing, Mama?"

"I'm measuring where I'm going to build a fence."

"Can I help," the boy asked.

"Yes, hold this string against the corner of the house."

He did so. By then, Naomi came over to see what they were doing.

"Mama, I help," Naomi said.

"You help. Come with me." Betsy lined the yard to a few feet before the railroad track. She gave Naomi the string. "Can you hold the string here? Don't let it move."

Naomi nodded.

She started lining the string along the railroad tracks, but when she ran out of string around ten feet away from where she wanted the fence to end, she stopped. She didn't know what to do now.

Then she had an idea. "Malachi, Naomi, bring your string over here." The children ran to her. "Malachi, I want you to hold your end of the string on the spot where I'm standing."

"Yes, Mama."

She took Naomi's hand. "You come with me."

Naomi walked with her until she reached her destination. She turned to her daughter. "Now, hold this string right here while I get some scissors."

The girl took the string, and Betsy ran into the barn to find something to mark it with. She couldn't find anything, but maybe she could tie a knot in it. That would mark it well enough. When she stepped out of the barn, a train whistle blew in the distance. Both children dropped their string and ran to her.

She let out a sigh. How could she be angry when she'd warned them about being near the railroad tracks? When they heard the train, they did what they should do. They ran away from the tracks and toward her. She tucked a stray hair into her bonnet. This was going to be harder than she thought.

Chapter Twenty-Two

Nate sat in front of the telegraph machine that hadn't sent a message in over two hours. He tried to stay awake, but the headache he'd had for two weeks now wouldn't go away. He was glad to be working days again, but the last two nights, he'd slept fitfully when he slept at all.

Maybe it was the pillows. Now, both of them had cross-shaped stains. When he confronted Betsy that the pillows needed washed, she was evasive. She'd never shirked her housekeeping duties before. And she'd never disobeyed him, but she'd changed. Every chance she got, she was still going to those temperance meetings or protesting outside saloons. Maybe that was why she was behind on her laundry. It was too much for a woman being with child to take care of the home and decide to be a crusader. He'd have to talk to her about it.

Still, when he asked her about the stain, she said it was lard. How did lard get on his pillow, and why was it on both pillows now?

He rubbed his temples then took a sip of coffee. He'd hold off on that conversation for now. He needed a good night's sleep first. When he got off work today, he'd make his way to the saloon. He never had a problem sleeping after a few drinks. Maybe it would get rid of the headache too.

When James entered the office, Nate nodded to him and headed out the door into the warm August day.

"Hello, friend."

Nate groaned and turned back. Cage was leaning against the wall outside the telegraph office with his arms crossed.

"What do you want?" Nate growled.

Cage stepped toward him. "Do I need a reason to visit you?"

Heat rushed to his face. "No, it's just... I'm in a hurry."

"This is important. I need a few minutes of your time."

He thought about making an excuse so he could head to the saloon, but he couldn't do that. Cage was the best friend he ever had, and if he needed something, Nate would do his best to help. "What is it?"

"Come to my office. We'll talk there."

Nate followed Cage out of the jail. When they got there, Cage sat behind his desk, and Nate sank into the chair in front of him.

"A woman came to me today. Her husband hit her."

The muscle in Nate's cheek twitched. "Oh, no, you don't. I'm not getting caught up on another case like Mrs. Hanson's."

"But this woman is willing to testify. All she needs is a lawyer to stand up for her."

"She's going to have to find someone else."

"Nate, she needs help. Nobody else will take this case. You know that."

"Miss Johnson needed help too, but I failed her. I won't do that again."

Cage pressed his lips together. "I didn't see you at church Sunday."

Nate stood. "That's another thing I'm not going to do again. I'll tell you what I told Betsy. If you want to be friends with me, you'll have to accept that I like to drink, and I'm not going to stop. And I'm not going to go to church and be a hypocrite anymore." He started toward the door, tripped over an uneven floorboard, and fell onto the floor.

Cage strode toward him. "Are you all right?" He held his hand out.

Nate pushed it away. "I'm fine." He'd bumped his cheek when he fell, but he wasn't about to touch it in front of Cage. He scooted to the door and used the doorjamb and crutches to help himself up. This time, he made it through the door without falling.

"Nate, wait."

It was the last thing he heard before he slammed the door.

~~~~~

As soon as Mr. Baldwin and Johnnie piled the supplies for the fence in the barn, Betsy hitched the wagon, got the children inside, and headed for the church to drop them off where Mrs. Fowler would watch them during the protests. She was late, but she had to wait for that delivery.

She'd decided not to mention the fence to her husband. With the mood Nate had been in over the last couple of weeks, she didn't know how he'd react to her buying those supplies, especially since he kept telling her they didn't need a fence. He'd find out eventually, but she wanted to make some progress first. Mr. Baldwin was kind enough to give her step-by-step instructions.

After dropping off the children, she turned the wagon toward the saloon. When she got there, the other women were already holding their signs and protesting, so she tied the horse and wagon to the hitch post and joined them. She wasn't there long before Nate passed by. He didn't even look in her direction. Her chin trembled. It was bad enough putting up with his moodiness for the last couple of weeks. As soon as he got back on days, he went to the saloon. Now, he didn't even have the decency to look in her direction.

A lump formed in the back of her throat. *Lord, I don't know how much more I can take. I trust You no matter what, but give me the strength to be the kind of wife You want me to be because right now, I want to be a shrew.*

One of the ladies started singing a hymn, and she and the others joined in.

> There is a fountain filled with blood,
> Drawn from Immanuel's veins,
> And sinners plunged beneath that flood
> Lose all their guilty stains:

They carried signs and sang hymns for a couple of hours before shouting grew loud from inside the saloon and drowned out their voices, so they did the only thing they could. They sang louder.

> Amazing grace, how sweet the sound...

A deafening gunshot sounded, and someone screamed. Ladies ran and hid behind the temperance wagon, but Betsy's feet wouldn't move to follow them. What if Nate was hurt?

She pulled up her skirts and ran into the saloon then stood by the door. It took her a moment to adjust to the darkness in this den of iniquity.

Chaos had erupted. One man was lying on the floor, blood oozing from his gut. Thank God it wasn't Nate. Another man, big and brawny, was in the corner by the bar with a gun pointing toward three men trying to confront him.

"Get the marshal," someone shouted, and a thin man brushed by her on his way out.

Her gaze darted around the room trying to find her husband. There he was. He was so drunk the incident hadn't even fazed him. He sat at a table in another corner with an empty bottle in front of him and glazed eyes looking at who knew what. She strode toward him. "Nate." She shook him. "Nate, we have to get out of here."

~~~~~

Lavena knew something was wrong when Cage came home from work. He pulled on his ear and didn't even give her a kiss. A knot formed in her stomach, and her heart raced. Had another outlaw gang been spotted?

She took his jacket from him. "What's wrong?"

He walked over to his rocker and sank into it. "Nate."

She stepped behind him and massaged his shoulders. "What happened this time?"

Standing, he took her in his arms, and this time, he did kiss her. "I tried to get him involved in bringing another abuse case to court. Not only did he turn me down, he was moody and irritable, and I don't know..." He burrowed his face in her shoulder. "He wouldn't even listen to me. I asked him about church, and he said he wasn't going there again and stormed out of my office. He's probably headed to the saloon now."

"Betsy says the same thing. He's moody toward her and finds fault in everything she does, but he hasn't been drinking since he went on nights."

Cage pulled back. "If I'm not mistaken, now that he's on days again, that's going to change. He couldn't wait to get out of my office. I don't know how to help him anymore. I don't even know if I should try."

"At this point, all we can do is pray."

He nodded. "I know."

"I'll get dinner on the table." She served the biggest meal of the day at around three or four when Cage got home from work since he always went back out to do rounds in the evening. This way, they would have a couple of hours at home as a family, at least most of the time. She went to the stove and started dishing out smoked ham, roasted potatoes, and green beans. She called Penelope to supper, and they all sat to eat.

"This looks good." Cage ate a bite of ham.

Someone knocked on the door, and Lavena rose to answer it. It was George, Cage's young deputy who looked like a horse could ride him. She let out a sigh. "Come in. He was just eating his supper."

Cage stood. "What's wrong?"

"A fight at the Bonny and Sons Saloon. Marshal, one of the men involved is dead."

Cage quickly slipped on his jacket, kissed her on the cheek, and headed toward the door.

"I'll keep your supper warm."

"Thanks."

"Be careful," she said as he slipped out the door.

Then he was gone. Her chest tightened, and her heart pounded as if it were a drum.

"Where's Papa going?" Penelope asked.

She placed her hand on her heart and sank to the bench beside her daughter. "Work. Now, eat." She tried to take a bite but couldn't manage it. Her eyes burned with unshed tears. She set the fork down on the table. If a man murdered someone, he probably wouldn't just surrender. He'd shoot at Cage.

Grabbing her Bible, she turned to the Philippians four, six and seven. She'd been working on memorizing it, but today, she needed to read it out loud. *"Be careful for nothing; but in everything by prayer and supplication with thanksgiving let your requests be made known unto God. And the peace of God, which passeth all understanding, shall keep your hearts and minds through Christ Jesus."*

"Mama, are you all right?"

For a moment, she thought about lying but decided to use this moment to teach her daughter what to do in the face of fear. "I'm scared. I know your papa will be fine, but I want to pray for him."

"Can I pray too?"

Lavena pulled Penelope onto her lap. "I would like that. Could you pray that I won't be scared too?"

Penelope nodded.

"Lord, I give this to You. Protect my husband."

"And Lord, help Mama not be scared."

Lavena grabbed a piece of paper and pen and wrote, *I am afraid for Cage's safety as he faces a murderer*. Then she threw the paper into the stove and watched it burn into ashes until there was nothing left of it. The pounding of her heart slowed, and she was able to catch her breath. Peace swept over her. "Thank You, Lord."

Then she turned to Penelope. "Now, let's finish our supper, and I'll read you a story about a brave man named Daniel who was thrown in a lion's den."

"Mama, is Papa brave like Daniel?"

"Yes, he is. And just like Daniel, God protects your father."

A nudging doubt crept in. There were men in the Bible God didn't protect. *Lord, I believe. Help me not to doubt.*

Chapter Twenty-Three

Betsy tried to get Nate to stand up, but he kept plopping back into the chair. When she couldn't get him to move, she grabbed the whiskey bottle, took it outside, and filled it with water from the horse trough where the women were still hiding behind the wagon. She strode back into the saloon and poured the bottle of water over Nate's head.

He immediately reacted. "What in the blazes are you doing?"

"In case you hadn't noticed, there's a man lying dead on the saloon floor, and that man over there," she pointed, "shot him and is threatening to shoot someone else. We need to get out of here."

His glazed eyes cleared a bit, and he grabbed his crutches and stood although he looked like he might fall. "You need to get out of here." His speech was slurred. "Cage should be here any minute, and I... I... should help him. Get me a gun."

Betsy spoke through gritted teeth. "You're in no condition to help anyone."

His cheek twitched, and she could tell by the look on his face that she'd hurt him, but she didn't have a choice. If he got involved while he was this drunk, he might end up dead on the floor beside the other man.

"Come on," she said. "Let's get out of here."

Before he could respond, Cage came through the door, gun drawn, and shoulders taut. His deputy stood beside him.

Nate started to stagger toward him.

"Sit back down." She grabbed his arm and led him back to the table. "He doesn't need your help."

He collapsed into the chair, placed his face in his hands, and moaned.

Cage stepped toward the man with the gun and spoke in a calm manner as if he were talking to a scared child. "I need you to give me your gun."

"But I killed him," the man shouted.

"I can tell you didn't mean to do it."

"No" The man looked terrified.

Cage motioned for the other men to back up, then he glanced toward his deputy and nodded slightly. "Why don't you give me the gun? We can talk about what happened."

"No." The killer pulled back the hammer. "I don't want to hang," he said with a whimper.

"Who said anything about hanging? You can explain what happened to the judge. I'm sure he'll understand."

While Cage was talking, the deputy slowly inched behind the man. The deputy grabbed the killer's arms as Cage snatched his gun away.

"Take him in." Cage stepped over to the man on the floor and felt his pulse. "Then get the undertaker to take this man away."

The deputy nodded and dragged the killer out of the saloon.

Betsy let out a sigh of relief. She'd never seen Cage in a situation like that before, and she was impressed. He reminded her of who her husband used to be. "Come on," she said to the shell of the man he was now. "Let's go home."

Cage turned. "Nobody leaves until you all tell me what you saw." He directed his gaze to her and Nate.

She sat down beside her husband and waited even though neither of them saw the shooting. This wasn't the time to challenge him. He was the marshal right now, not their friend.

He began with the men who were surrounding the killer before he came in. Betsy couldn't help but look at the dead man lying on the floor. She wanted to go to him, but he was beyond her nursing skills. Why didn't Cage at least cover him up? She looked around the room. A horse blanket lay on the floor near one of the tables. She stepped over to it, grabbed it, then went toward the dead man.

Cage turned toward her. "I told you to stay put." His glower toward her was intimidating.

She held up the blanket. "I was going to cover him up."

"Go ahead." Cage went back to talking to the men.

She covered the corpse and went back to her seat.

By the time the undertaker arrived with a couple of other men, Cage had talked to almost all the men. The interviews stopped while they carried out the man. Apparently, he was saving Nate and Betsy for last.

Finally, he got to them. He directed the first question toward her. "What are you doing in here?"

"When the shooting began, I was worried about Nate. I ran in to see if he was all right," she tilted her head toward him, "and found him so drunk he didn't even notice what happened."

"You shouldn't have come in here. You could have been shot."

Betsy shrugged. That hadn't occurred to her. She was too worried about her husband.

Cage pulled out a chair and sat at the table. "Did he see anything?"

Nate glowered at him. "I'm sitting here too. I can answer for myself."

"Well," Cage said.

"No, I didn't see anything until my wife came in here and started dumping water on my head."

Cage stood, his mouth half curled in disgust. "Your wife was trying to get you out of a dangerous situation that you put yourself in when you crawled into a bottle of whiskey. She risked peril because she was concerned about you." He stepped away, tapped his fist against his mouth, and turned back. "I'll send a wagon for both of you." He pointed a finger in Nate's face. "Go home and sleep it off."

~~~~~

When Lavena heard Cage come home, she ran to greet him. He looked defeated. She gave him a hug. "What's wrong?"

He made his way to the rocker and sank into it with a loud sigh. "Where's Penelope?"

"She's in bed. Cage, it's almost midnight."

"I didn't mean to worry you. I should have sent word everything was all right."

Lavena sat in the chair beside him. "You didn't answer my question. What happened, and why are you so late?"

He lifted his eyebrow. "That's two questions, three if you count the first one."

She shrugged. "Now that I know you heard me, I expect you to answer all three."

"We can talk about it in the morning. It's late."

"We can talk about it now." She set her hand on Cage's arm. "I won't be able to sleep anyway if I don't know what's going on."

He set his hand on hers. "If you insist. When George and I got to the saloon, a man had been killed. The murderer surrendered without a fight. George took him into custody."

"And."

"Nate and Betsy were there."

"Betsy was in the saloon?"

"She was protesting outside and when she heard the shots, she ran in to see if Nate was all right."

Lavena smiled. "Not too many people know how fearless and determined she is. They see a pretty face with stylish clothes, and they expect a frail little woman."

"I gained new respect for her," Cage said. "She even found a horse blanket to cover up the corpse with."

She leaned back. "If everything went so well, why are you so late?"

"That wasn't the only crime going on tonight. I did my rounds and caught three burglars breaking into homes and stores." He kneaded the back of his neck. "That doesn't include burglaries where I didn't get there in time to catch the thief. I don't know how to stop all of this crime, and the city council won't let me hire more deputies."

"There's more to the story or you wouldn't be rubbing your face.

You only do that when you're worried."

Cage huffed then moved his hand to his lap. "It's Nate. I knew he drank, but I've never seen him like that. He didn't even know what happened, and he acted like he didn't care that he put his wife in danger. He's not the same man I became friends with during the war. I don't know how to help him."

"Maybe you're not supposed to. Maybe it's time to leave him in God's hands."

Cage gave her a sideways look. "Like that verse you've memorized."

"Yes." She let out a gusty sigh. "I have to admit I was so overcome with fear when you went out to confront that murderer, but I quoted the verse God gave me, prayed, and wrote my fears on a piece of paper that I burned up in the stove. It really helped."

"I'm glad." Cage reached out and held her hand. "I was worried about how you would react to this."

"I want you to stop thinking about me when you're out there. You need to concentrate on the job so you can come home safe." She pressed her lips together for a moment. "I'm going to do my best to venture out of this house, and not let this fear get the better of me. Maybe I'll stop by the newspaper office tomorrow."

Cage yawned. "I'm glad you're waiting until tomorrow. It's late. We need to get some sleep."

She smiled and headed to the bedroom. The idea of leaving the safety of the house tomorrow made her stomach tighten, but she had to try. She had to do her best to trust God and regain her courage. She just hoped she resisted the temptation to stay at home and hide under the bed.

~~~~~

The next morning, Nate woke with Betsy shaking him. He looked at the clock and let out a sigh of relief. He was afraid he'd overslept again. He got up, wiped his eyes, and began getting dressed. He was a little surprised that she rose and dressed as well. She'd stopped getting up to make his breakfast when he drank the night before. He wanted to talk with her.

After he dressed and made his way into the kitchen, Betsy placed ham, eggs, and biscuits on his plate. He devoured them. Most of the time, after a bender, he didn't feel like eating. His stomach would be too queasy, but not today. The whiskey had helped him sleep soundly, and that sleep had given him a healthy appetite.

Betsy sat beside him with her plate of breakfast. "I got up to make you breakfast because I want to talk with you before the children rise."

"Good." Nate took a sip of coffee. "I want to talk to you also. Last night, you could see how dangerous it is for you to go on those protests. I'll allow you to continue with the Wellington Temperance Society against my better judgement, but you must stop those protests. You're with child, and you might get hurt."

She placed her hand on her growing stomach. She was glad she made her skirts large enough to accommodate pregnancy. "I agree last night was dangerous, so I'll stop protesting in front of the saloon…"

He smiled. That was easy.

"As soon as you stop going to the saloon."

His smile slipped. "I'm a man. I can handle the danger."

"Like you did last night. You were in a drunken state in the corner of the room. You didn't even see what happened when a gun went off." A tear fell down her cheek. "What if the killer had turned his gun on you?"

He stood. "How dare you give me an ultimatum like that?" His neck corded. "You're my wife. The Bible says I'm the head of this home, not you. I forbid you to go to that saloon again."

She stood to face him. "Not unless you quit going there."

Heat rushed through him. "I'll do whatever the blazes I want to!" He grabbed her arms, squeezed hard, and shook her.

"You're hurting me."

He let go, and she sank into a puddle on the floor.

"See what you made me do," he yelled. "You almost drove me to do something I'd regret."

He heard the children upstairs start crying.

Heat rushed through him, and he knocked over the table. Dishes and food flew everywhere, and one of the plates broke. He couldn't stay there another minute, afraid of what he might do. He slammed the door on the way out.

Chapter Twenty-Four

Betsy sat there on the floor, sobbing. She had never thought her sweet, loving husband would ever do anything like that, but he wasn't the man she married, and she couldn't stay with a man who hurt her. She unbuttoned her blouse to look at her arms where he had grabbed her. Both arms had red handprints that looked like they might turn into bruises.

Lord, what do I do?

Cage and Lavena might be willing to have her and the children for a few days. At least, she hoped so. She'd send a telegram to her parents. They would send money for her to take the train home to Philadelphia. She hated running home to her parents, but she couldn't see any other way.

During the war, when Nate lost his leg, she'd promised him she'd never leave him again, but she couldn't stay with a man who abused her.

She wiped her eyes, grabbed a carpetbag off the shelf, and packed her clothes. Then she made the children breakfast and woke them a little earlier than she normally would. While they ate breakfast, she packed their belongings in another carpetbag including the toys Mrs. Adams had given them. When they were done, she took them outside, and they started walking.

Malachi asked, "Mama, are we taking a trip?"

"We're going to Miss Lavena's house. It will be an adventure."

That seemed to satisfy them. After walking a few blocks, she stopped and set the carpetbags down.

"Why are we stopping?" Malachi asked.

"I need to rest for a moment."

Those bags were heavier than they looked. It was hard to carry them that far in her condition, but she wasn't about to take the horse and wagon. It was only a couple miles, not a long walk.

She didn't want anything her husband owned, not his horse and wagon or his house or the money in the bank. It would only give him an excuse to chase after her. He could have the house too. She didn't want to live in a place he could so easily find a way into. Besides, too many bad memories there.

The children were getting antsy, so she took a deep breath, picked up the carpetbags, and carried on.

When she got there, she set the bags down and knocked on the door.

Lavena answered but looked surprised, probably because it was so early in the morning. She was still in her nightgown and robe.

"Can we come in?" Betsy asked.

Lavena motioned her and the children in. Cage, who was dressed, sat at the table with Penelope eating breakfast.

When he saw her, he stood. "What's wrong?"

She placed her finger on her lips. "Let's wait until Penelope finishes her breakfast. Then the children can play in the other room together."

Cage nodded, and she sat at the table and waited.

"Have you had breakfast?" Lavena asked.

"Thank you, but we ate before we came here."

They didn't say anything more. It seemed to take forever until Penelope finished.

"Children," Lavena said. "You can go in Penelope's room and play."

They all scurried out of the room and closed the door.

"Now." Lavena sat beside her. "What happened? Why are you here so early in the morning, and why have you been crying?"

Betsy tried to not show how upset she was, but when she spoke, it came out in a strangled sob. "I'm... I'm leaving Nate."

Cage grabbed hold of his ear. "What did he do now?"

She started crying again despite herself, and she wasn't able to say another word for a long time. Lavena sat beside her and held her. Cage slacked his hip and waited quietly.

Finally, Betsy was able to quit crying. She wiped her eyes, blew her nose, and told them everything that happened.

Cage gasped. "He laid his hands on you?"

Betsy rolled up her sleeves and showed them where the bruises were forming. "Could we stay here? Only for a few days. I'll send a telegram to my mother and father. They'll send us money to take the train to Philadelphia."

"Of course you can," Lavena said.

"Don't send that telegram yet." Cage's Adam's apple bulged. "I'm going to have a little talk with your husband." He cracked his knuckles.

Betsy let out a sigh. "It won't do any good. Unless he stops drinking, the children and I are in danger, and after what happened to my sister, I won't allow that."

Cage's jaw set. "You're staying here for as long as it takes. I'll make sure he never lays hands on you again."

"I don't want to move back with my parents." She looked at the floor. "But I don't know what else to do. I can't stay here forever."

Lavena stood up beside her husband. "Cage, you talk to Nate and see what he says. Betsy, can you give it a week to see what God directs you to do?"

"Then, if you feel you must leave town," Cage said, "we'll loan you the money. You won't have to wait for your parents."

Betsy nodded, but inside, she felt a heaviness sweep over her. She had given up hope that anything would change.

~~~~~

Nate leaned back in his chair. It was a slow day, and there hadn't been any telegrams for the last hour. He didn't understand why he got so angry with Betsy, but he was ashamed of the way he had acted. He'd actually caused her pain.

His chest tightened. At least he stopped before he did any real damage, although he did knock over the table and break a plate or two. Her parents gave them those plates as a wedding gift. He'd find a way to make it up to her. Maybe he could replace the plates.

Tonight, he wouldn't stop at the saloon. He might even spend three or four days away, and he'd stop at the General Store on the way home to pick up some toffee for her and the children and order the replacement plates. Toffee was Betsy's favorite treat, and she'd been craving it since the pregnancy started.

He swallowed the lump in his throat. He hurt the woman carrying his child. He took some solace in the knowledge that at least he didn't hit her.

There were some wildflowers in a field near the railroad tracks. He'd pick some of those for her too. She'd forgive him. He shut his eyes. He didn't think he could live with what he'd done if she didn't.

The door slammed open with a burst of cool air, and Cage stormed in, his dark eyes cold and hard and his jaw firm. He shut the door and strode behind the counter where Nate was.

"You put your hands on her!" He grabbed hold of the front of Nate's shirt.

Nate put his palms in the air in surrender. Cage looked like he was about to punch him, and to tell the truth, he didn't blame him.

Cage let go of Nate's shirt and kneaded the back of his neck. "What's wrong with you?"

"She made me angry. I told her how dangerous it is to protest in front of the saloon. Look what happened last night. She refused to listen to me. I was worried she might get hurt."

Cage sneered at him. "So, you hurt her instead. I saw the bruises."

"Bruises?" Nate shook his head. He hadn't realized he'd squeezed hard enough to make bruises. "I didn't mean to hurt her. I didn't know what I was doing."

Cage leaned against the counter and crossed his arms. "It had nothing to do with you being drunk and your wife embarrassing you by coming into the saloon to save you last night?"

He saw the truth in what Cage said and nodded. "I plan to apologize when I get home, and I'm buying her flowers and candy. I know how wrong I was. I promise it won't happen again."

"She's not at home. You scared her so much she packed her belongings, and she and the children moved in with us."

Nate couldn't move, couldn't speak. The heaviness in his chest became a boulder, crushing him and holding him in place. She couldn't leave him. When he lost his leg, she promised she'd never leave him again. "I need to talk to her. I... I need to tell her how sorry I am. Please, Cage, help me."

Cage rested his hand on Nate's shoulder then pulled it back. "I can't help you. Until you get right with God and stop drinking, Betsy and the children aren't safe with you."

Heat shot through Nate. He tried to keep his tone calm. "I've tried to stop drinking. I'm done trying. If you and my wife can't accept me for who I am, then I don't know what to do about it."

Cage grabbed his ear. "Betsy is not going to accept you threatening to hit her or yelling at her or knocking around the furniture. It scares her and it scares the children. And I won't remain friends with any man who gets drunk and abuses his wife and children."

He stood and pointed his finger in Cage's chest. "It. Only. Happened. Once. And I didn't hit her. I just grabbed her a little too tightly. If she'd do what I say..." He took a deep breath and let it out. "I'll be by to apologize after work."

Cage narrowed his eyes. "You won't be allowed in. I'm not letting you near her or the children until I believe it's safe."

He glowered at Cage. "I think you'd better leave."

"I was just going anyway." Cage walked toward the door. "I thought I could reason with my old friend, but you're not that man anymore." He closed the door behind him.

Nate sank into his chair. His heart ached, and he was surprised it kept beating. She left him, and she wasn't coming back.

He spent the rest of the day trying to focus on his job instead of how his life was falling apart, but it didn't help that it was a slow day, and there weren't many messages. Most of them involved train schedules.

Near the end of his workday, Johnnie stopped by to pick up the messages. "Mr. Teagan, are you all right? You look like you lost your best friend."

Nate let out a snort. His best friend, his wife, and his children. "I'll be fine."

"Would you like me to pray for you?"

He almost said no, but somewhere inside he knew he needed it. His voice thickened. "I'd appreciate that."

Johnnie laid his hand on Nate's shoulder. "Lord, I don't know what's going on, but Mr. Teagan needs You right now. Help him to lean on You for help. In Jesus' name, Amen."

"Th... Thank you."

"Well, I'd better get these telegrams delivered." Johnnie walked out the door.

The telegraph machine sounded a series of dashes signaling a new message. Nate turned and tried to focus on writing it out.

> Marshal Macajah Jones
> Billy Horton escaped penitentiary.
> Stop.
> May be headed your way.
> Warden Raymond Burr, Ohio Penitentiary

He let out a sigh. That's just what he needed, a reason to visit Cage so soon. But he had no choice. Cage needed this telegram as soon as possible. Horton was known to seek revenge on those he believed harmed him, and since he'd already been sentenced to hang, he didn't have a reason to hold back.

James, the telegraph operator, walked in the door. Nate nodded to him and left, telegram in hand. He walked straight to the jail and entered Cage's office, but he wasn't there.

"Can I help you?" the deputy guarding the door to the cells said.

"I need to talk to the marshal."

"He went home, but he'll be back in a few hours if you want to leave a message."

Nate glanced down at the telegram. It was tempting to leave it on Cage's desk, but this message was too important. He waved a hand and headed to Cage's house. When he got there, he paused before knocking on the door.

It didn't take long for Cage to come outside and close the door behind him. His brow furrowed. "What are you doing here? I told you not to come."

Nate held up the telegram. "I'm delivering this."

Cage read the paper, went back in the house, and closed the door without even saying thank you.

Nate wiped his hand over his mouth. There was no reason to go home now. Nobody would be waiting for him. He headed to the saloon.

~~~~~

"What did he want?" Lavena said as soon as her husband came in the door.

"He wasn't trying to cause trouble." He held up a piece of paper.

"He delivered a telegram."

Betsy bit her bottom lip. "Then he didn't want to talk to me."

"He did," Cage said. "But I made it clear he wasn't going to get through the door."

Betsy nodded and slipped into the other room.

As soon as the door closed, Lavena asked, "What did the telegram say?" She tried to hide the concern she felt, but when her voice cracked, she knew she'd failed.

"Not much." He placed the telegram in his jacket pocket. "Just police business."

Lavena crossed her arms and glared at him. "I told you it only makes me worry more when you hide things from me. If it wasn't important, he would have waited until tomorrow when Johnnie made deliveries."

With a heavy sign, he pulled the telegram out of his pocket and handed it to her.

She read it, and her pulse quickened. "You need to be careful."

"I will be." Cage took the telegram and tucked it back in his pocket.

Her eyes grew hot with unshed tears, and she touched his arm. "I mean it. He's a killer. He wouldn't hesitate to turn his gun on you."

Cage rubbed his scar. "He'd be foolish to come back here."

A tear rolled down her face, and she turned toward the stove and swiped it away.

He walked in front of her and took her in his arms. "I know this frightens you, but it's my job. What's the verse we've memorized this week?"

She laid her head on his shoulder. "I'll be fine, but you have to allow me to worry a little when you're in danger."

He lifted her chin and kissed her.

Chapter Twenty-Five

Nate ordered another bottle, but no matter how much he drank, he couldn't numb the pain. She wouldn't even come out to talk to him. It was right for her to leave him. He tapped his stump. He was worthless as a husband and as a man.

Before he could pour another drink, Doug Hanson sat across from him.

He let out a moan. "What do you want?"

Doug's voice slurred, or maybe it was Nate's hearing. "What do I want? How about you be a man and tell your wife to stop going to those temperance meetings and stop singing hymns in front of the saloon? She shouldn't be leaving the house with a young'un making her belly swell, let alone going to my boss to get him to pay me less."

Heat flushed through his body. "You shut your mouth. You have no right to talk about her like that. My wife is a saint."

"My woman would never do something like that. Takes a man to get his woman to obey. Shouldn't have expected a cripple to manage it. If you can't get your wife under control, maybe I'll do something about it. A woman needs to be shown who's boss." He hit his fist into his hand.

Nate's neck corded, and he stood to his feet. "Are you threatening my wife?"

"I'm just telling you to be a man and stop your wife or I will."

His heart pounded in his ears. "If you touch my wife, I'll kill you!"

Doug turned away, but Nate went after him and punched him in the jaw. Doug fought back. Voices shouted, and glass broke. Arms reached for him, but he couldn't stop hitting the man. Then a pain shot through his head, and he passed out.

~~~~~

Betsy sat in the rocking chair in Lavena's kitchen reading her Bible. She'd tried to sleep on the tick mattress in the corner of the room the children slept on, but it was no use. Since Cage left, all she could do was think about what Nate might do now that she'd left. He was probably drowning himself in a bottle.

Pray.

The voice of the Holy Spirit was so loud she almost heard it audibly. She dropped to her knees and prayed fervently for her husband. She heard footsteps, then Lavena knelt beside her.

When she'd finished and stood to her feet, Cage walked into the house. He'd been called away earlier, and now, concern etched his brow.

He made his way toward her. "Nate will be all right."

Her heart sank into her stomach. "What's wrong?"

"He's in jail."

Betsy placed her hand over her mouth. Of all the things her mind had conjured up, she never expected that.

"What did he do?" Lavena asked.

"Got drunk, started a fight, broke a chair, some glasses, and a couple of bottles of whiskey. He made a mess of the saloon."

"Nate?" What was wrong with him? Until recently, he'd never raised a hand to anyone. "Who'd he hit?"

"Doug Hanson."

Betsy sighed. If he hit anyone, it would be Hanson.

Lavena placed her hand on Betsy's shoulder. "The children will be fine. Go."

She placed her head in her hands. "What am I going to do?"

"We'll talk about that later," Lavena said. "For now, you need to go to the jail."

Betsy followed Cage out the door. She wasn't sure she'd do anything to get him out, that was if Cage let her take him home, but she needed to see him. She needed to tell him it was over between them.

~~~~~

Nate's head throbbed. He sat up on the bunk and took a moment to figure out where he was. A small room with stone walls. Only a cot and a chamber pot. A glimmer of moonlit shone through the bars on the windows. A heavy barred door with no handle or latch on this side of it. He was in jail.

Why was he here? He remembered Betsy took the children and left him. She wouldn't even talk to him, and Cage wouldn't let him in the house. He went to the saloon, but getting drunk wouldn't land him here. Cage would more likely take him home than to jail. He groaned. Doug Hanson. Doug had threatened his wife, and he'd lost it.

He felt the lump on the back of his head about the size of a half-dollar. Was he hit from behind? No. Doug wasn't landing any real punches. He rubbed his temples trying to recall what had happened. He'd punched the man repeatedly, then broke a chair over his head. Then he hit the man with a whiskey bottle and wrestled him to the ground. Men were grabbing at his arms as he kept punching him. That was when someone hit him from behind. Considering where he now found himself, it must have been Cage.

He shook his head, but all that did was cause it to throb worse. He groaned. Betsy would be livid. If she even bothered to come here. He wouldn't blame her if she left him to rot in this place. His stomach churned, and he lay back on his bunk.

Hopefully he didn't cause too much damage. If Cage kept him longer than overnight, he might lose his job. He'd be all right as long as his boss didn't find out he been drinking, had a bar fight, and landed in jail. No use worrying about it. He'd find out how long he'd be in here soon enough.

Shouting came from beyond the door.

"I want to see him!" It was Betsy's voice.

Excitement stirred within him. She came.

"Now, Betsy." Cage's voice. "I don't think you should. It won't hurt for him to spend the night in jail. Might do him some good."

"You can keep him in there as long as you want, but I need to see him."

Nate sat up, wide awake now. Cage wouldn't prevail. Betsy was stubborn when she wanted to be.

More conversation and mumbling, but he couldn't make it out. A scraping noise outside the door made his head ache, then it swung open. He rose to his feet and grabbed onto the iron bars to steady himself.

When he looked up, Betsy stood there, her arms crossed, and her lips pressed together, with tears forming in her eyes. "This is the end. You hear me, Nate? It's over between us."

Cage unlocked the cell and stood by the door as she walked into the cell and jabbed a finger into his chest.

"I am not going to raise our children alone." She placed her hand on her growing stomach. "And I won't let them know they have a father who's a drunkard. I won't abide it."

His stomach churned. "Betsy, I'm so sorry." The dizziness swirled until his stomach threatened to empty its contents.

She wiped her face with the yellow embroidered handkerchief she'd made last year to match the yellow skirt she was now wearing. "I'm sending a telegram to my parents. As soon as they wire money for train tickets, the children and I are going to Philadelphia for good." She stormed out of the cell.

He started to follow her, but when he got to the door, Cage blocked his way.

"No, Nate. I can't let you out. You need to pay for the damages you made to the saloon, and Doug Hanson says he's going to charge you with assault. I told him to go home and sleep it off, but if he goes through with it... well, you might not get out of here until your trial."

"But I can't stay in here that long." He couldn't help the pleading in his voice. "Betsy will be gone by then. I might not ever see her again."

"You should have considered that before." Cage glared at him in a way that let him know there was no point in arguing.

The more Cage talked, the more his stomach churned. "You know I'm good for it. I'll pay him as soon as I get out of work tomorrow. Let me out of here."

Cage talked through gritted teeth. "You're. Not. Getting. Out."

"What about my job?"

"Don't have to worry about that." He pushed his fist against his mouth and puffed out a breath. "How does it feel to have your God-fearing wife lie to your boss for you?" He closed and bolted the door.

Nate grabbed the chamber pot and emptied his stomach.

~~~~~

Betsy dreaded the walk to the home of Nate's boss, Mr. Wilson. She didn't want to disturb him this late at night, but her husband left her no choice. It also bothered her that she was going to lie to him. She'd told Nate she wouldn't defend him or lie for him if he got drunk. Cage told her she should leave it alone, but she had no choice. Her husband would lose his job if she didn't do this. If that happened, he might crawl in a whiskey bottle and have no reason to get out. She knocked on the door.

Mrs. Wilson, a plump woman with gray hair tucked into a night cap and a long blue robe tied around her waist answered. "Mrs. Teagan? What are you doing here at this hour?"

"I'm sorry to disturb you, but my husband has the grip."

"Oh dear. Thank you for letting us know. Will he be all right? Has the doctor been called?"

Her stomach had a sinking feeling, and she felt terrible they were concerned when she was lying through her teeth. "I'm sure he'll be fine. If he isn't better by tomorrow afternoon, I'll call for the doctor and let you know."

"Thank you, my dear. We'll pray for him."

The woman couldn't have said anything else that would have made her feel worse. She headed back to Lavena and Cage's house, praying and repenting the whole way.

When she got there, she still didn't know what God wanted her to do, but she was certain He hadn't wanted her to lie.

She stood at the door of Lavena's house, turned around, and walked a few steps toward the Wilsons to admit she lied, and Nate was really in jail. She got as far as the railroad tracks before she stopped. She couldn't do it. Her husband always stayed sober when he had to work. Even when he was drinking, he'd remember to wind the alarm clock and set it so he wouldn't be late. If he lost this job, he might never stay sober again.

After heading back to the house, she went inside. Her friend sat at the table waiting for her with two cups of tea.

Sinking into her chair, she took a sip. Lavender tea this time with a touch of chamomile. Just what she needed to calm her apprehension. "It's been a long day."

"Did Cage keep Nate in jail?"

"He won't release him until he sobers up and agrees to pay the saloon damages." She blinked back the tears welling up in her eyes. "Cage said if Mr. Hanson files charges for assault tomorrow, Nate will rot in that jail maybe for months. Then he will lose his job." The tears found their way down her cheeks despite her resolve to hold them back. "What am I going to do?"

Lavena poured some tea into her saucer and drank a sip. "I know you're hurting, and I wish I could make this go away. I do know you can trust the Lord through all of this. At least, that's what God is teaching me."

Tears flowed down her cheeks. There was nothing she could do to stop them. "I'm trying." Her voice cracked, and she pulled out her handkerchief and wiped the tears off her face. "I don't know what I can do to stop him from throwing his life away." She took another sip of tea, but no amount of lavender was going to calm these fears.

"When I made my wedding vows, I meant them, and when I promised I wouldn't leave him again after he lost his leg, I meant that too. I'll never divorce him, but I will not allow him to abuse me or take a chance of him hurting the children. That means I have to get away from him, at least for now. Maybe forever."

Chapter Twenty-Six

The next morning, Nate woke with a pounding headache. The light shone brightly through the small, barred window, and he gingerly got to his crutches and looked outside. The sun had risen and was nearing the high point in the sky. He couldn't believe he'd slept until noon. He plopped back on the cot and faced the wall. What was the point of getting up? It wasn't like he had anywhere to be and anything to do. He was in jail.

He'd been in jail once before a little over ten years ago, and it took six months before he was released. That was when he'd helped a slave escape the slave catchers during the Oberlin-Wellington slave rescue before the war, a noble cause. This time, he wasn't here because he was noble.

Sounds came from the other room. He heard Hanson's voice, but he couldn't hear what the man was saying. So, now it was over. Doug Hanson would love nothing more than to make sure he was in jail for a long time. He groaned.

He no longer tried to listen to what was being said. His head hurt too much. An eternity passed as he dozed back to sleep. The sound of the scraping door woke him. Cage stood there with his lips pursed. "You can go, but you better pay the saloon keeper by this time tomorrow or you'll end up back here."

Nate tried to focus, but his thoughts scrambled. "Why would... why would Hanson drop the charges?"

"He thought he had no choice." Cage walked away leaving the door open.

Nate followed him to his desk, his vision and speech still a little slurred. "Why would he have no choice?"

Cage sat on the edge of his desk. His eyes narrowed into a cold glare, his eyebrows drew together, and his tightly pressed lips curled up slightly on one side. "I told him I would harass him with disturbing the peace charges and put him in jail every time he got drunk and beat his wife. The man is too stupid to know there's no disturbing the peace law in this county."

Nate slid into the wooden Shaker chair in front of the desk and shook his head. He'd only seen this look on his friend's face once before, when a soldier in the Seventh Regiment tried to assault Lavena. He didn't like it directed toward him. "Thank you. You're a good friend."

"Get this straight. We're no longer friends. I didn't do it for you. I did it for Betsy. As far as I'm concerned, you could rot in my jail forever."

Nate's throat thickened. Had he gone so far that his best friend in the world had turned on him? "I don't know what to say."

"Just leave. I don't want to hear how sorry you are or how you're going to change. Go tell it to your wife. She'll forgive you, but I'm done."

Nate walked out the door and ran into the one person he didn't want to see outside the jail. Mr. Wilson.

"Nate." His eyes narrowed.

"Mr. Wilson."

"Did you think having your wife lie to me would keep me from hearing you ended up in jail? It's all over town what happened. Have any charges been filed against you?"

"No." Nate inwardly groaned. "I'm sorry, sir. Am I fired?"

"You're a good employee, but I can't keep you on under the circumstances. I need someone I can count on. I'm sorry."

"I understand. I brought this on myself."

Mr. Wilson put his hands in his pockets and looked toward his feet. "If it helps, I'll keep you on for a week or two while I train someone else. That'll give you a chance to find another position." He looked Nate in the eyes. "But if I find out you've been drinking during that time, you're done. I can train someone myself if I have to."

"Yes, sir. Thank you, sir."

Mr. Wilson walked on without another word, and Nate started toward the bank. He was grateful he at least had his job for another week. He expected his boss to not allow him on the premises again. That was what he expected. That was what he deserved.

When he entered the bank and asked the Dewey, the bank clerk, for a twenty dollar withdraw, the clerk started chuckling. "Is that all it will take to get you right with the saloon? I saw the damage. I figured it be at least fifty."

He let out a sigh. "I only need twenty."

He received the twenty dollars and headed toward the saloon. It was still early, maybe two o'clock, so he wouldn't run into the protesters. The last thing he needed was to have Betsy see him walking into the saloon right after he left the jail. She wouldn't believe he was only there to pay off the debt he owed.

When he got to the saloon, he headed inside and stopped. A knot formed in his stomach. He couldn't believe he'd done this much damage. Glass and wood from a broken chair were all over the floor, and a table was knocked over. The owner hadn't done anything to clean up the mess.

He walked to the bar. "Gus, I have the money to pay for damages." He laid twenty dollars on the counter.

Gus took the money and placed it in the money bag he kept behind the bar and glared at him. "I didn't sweep up 'cause I wanted you to see what you did to the place."

Nate glanced around the bar again. "I'm sorry. Do you want me to help clean up?"

"Don't bother." Gus pointed a finger in his face. "I don't tolerate violence in my place. Between the murder a few days ago and the fight you started with a steady customer, some men have stopped coming in here. I can't afford that. Sorry doesn't help."

Nate didn't say anything.

The owner grabbed a shotgun and placed it on the bar. "Now, get out of my saloon and don't come back unless you want some of this."

Nate held out his palms and backed away. "I'm leaving." He headed toward the turned over table and put it upright then left.

A heavy wind whipped around him, and he glanced up at the storm clouds in the distance. That was when the truth blew over him. He'd pushed away his wife and friends, caused a good boss to fire him, lost his reputation, and ended up in jail. Even the saloon owner pointed a gun at him and told him to get out. He couldn't get any lower.

Have You given up on me too? No, he felt God wooing him just as He had for years now. He was the one who gave up on God. He knew what he needed to do. He strode toward Wellington First Church.

By now, Rev. Fowler had heard what he'd done, and that gave him a sense of relief. He didn't want to hide anything or explain what he'd done. He entered the church and looked around. Rev. Fowler wasn't there, so he sat in a pew.

He couldn't help but rehearse to God everything he'd done while he waited. The first sin was turning away from the Lord when he lost his leg in the war. That led to everything else. He became a drunk, and a louse. He'd treated his wonderful wife and children with disdain. He laid his hands on Betsy and hurt her. It didn't matter that he hadn't hit her. If she hadn't left him, he was headed in that direction. Then he got into a fight and ended up in jail. That didn't even include all the lies he told.

He'd gone too far to expect Betsy or Cage to ever forgive him, but God was still convicting him, drawing him back. Now, that was what he longed for the most. *Lord, I'm done with all of it.*

Nate heard a noise behind him and looked back. Rev. Fowler had walked in. He glanced toward Heaven, knowing God was in this. He stood and strode toward him.

The preacher extended his hand for Nate to shake it. "I didn't expect to see you here. I thought you were in jail."

Heat flushed his face. "I was. I just got out."

"Sit down."

Nate sat, but he didn't say anything. He wasn't sure he could if he tried. The lump in his throat threatened to choke him.

"So, why are you here?"

He cleared his throat, and the truth rolled out of him. He told Rev. Fowler everything he'd done to destroy his family and his friendships, and then told him what happened over the last few days. He didn't justify it like he had so many times in the past. He'd hurt so many people through his self-pity and sinful behavior, and he needed to face it all no matter how painful.

The preacher placed his hand on Nate's shoulder. "So, have you finally given up running away from God?"

A sob escaped him, and he fell face down onto the floor. "Lord, I surrender. I'm so sorry. Please forgive me." Tears poured out of him, and he couldn't seem to stop them. He stayed there sobbing for what seemed like eternity as the heaviness lifted and a blanket of peace covered him that he hadn't felt since before the war. He felt constrained to the floor under the presence of the Lord, and he wouldn't have been able to move if he wanted to. But he didn't want to. The Spirit of God moved through him like a balm, forgiving him and healing him of the agony gripping him for so long.

He didn't know how long he'd been on the floor, but when he could manage it, he grabbed the pew and raised himself up to sit in it. He wiped the tears off his face.

"Now, son, I believe you've really repented, and I'd be happy to restore you to membership in the church."

"No, not yet. That's not why I'm here."

"What do you mean not yet?"

Nate tried to get his thoughts together to explain what he meant. "I've hurt a lot of people, and I have a lot of fence-mending to do. My wife has left me, my friend has disowned me, and everyone in town has heard about my escapades last night."

"That doesn't matter right now. God has forgiven you."

"Maybe so, but I need to try to make things right with them before I stand in front of the church and become a member. I don't know if I can stop drinking even though the thought of it now makes me sick. I need to prove, at least to myself, that I can stop."

"You'll still be tempted to drink sometimes. It's giving in to the temptation that makes it a sin."

Nate nodded.

"So, what are your plans?"

"First, I need to be baptized again, then I need somebody who will help me through all this. Somebody I have to answer to if I fail."

Rev. Fowler smiled. "So, you're asking for discipleship."

"I guess so. Would you be willing to do that? I understand if you won't. I know you're busy, and I—"

"I'll do it, but I won't make it easy. When do you get off work tomorrow?"

"Two in the afternoon."

"Meet me after work, and we'll get started."

"Could I ask another favor?"

Rev. Fowler raised his eyebrow. "What is it?"

"I want to give the house to Betsy and the children. I don't know if she'll ever forgive me and accept me back into her life, but even if she doesn't, she deserves to be the one to stay there. I need a place to live, at least until I make other arrangements. Do you know of a room that's cheap?"

"You'll stay with my wife and me. I have a guest room for visiting missionaries and preachers."

"I can't do that. After what I've done, your wife won't want me there."

"You don't understand," Rev. Fowler said. "I'm requiring you to move into my house. How else will I know if you go back to drinking? If you live in my house for a few weeks, you won't be able to hide it."

"In that case, I'll gather my things and bring them over before supper." Nate glanced at the clock. He couldn't believe he'd been there over an hour. "What time do you normally eat?"

"Around five."

Nate nodded. "I'll be back before then."

He said his good-byes and headed toward his house. When he got there, he packed up his belongings. Betsy had used both carpet bags, so he wrapped everything up in a sheet. Then he sat on the bed he might never sleep in again. The pillows sat there with the cross-shaped stains on them. Such a petty thing to get angry about. He took her pillow and buried his face in it. It still had her scent on it.

Lord, I love her so much. I want her back in the worst way, but I don't want to hurt her again. I leave our marriage in Your hands.

He looked around the room focusing on how she kept things so tidy. There was nothing left of her clothes. She'd taken them all with her. He saw his wooden leg sitting in the corner. She'd tried so many times to get him to wear it, but he wouldn't budge. He took off his trousers and attached the leg. The stubbornness he'd put her through stopped now, even if it was too late to win her back.

After gathering his belongings, including his pillow, he paused one last time, then made his way outside and into the barn. Wood beams, pickets for fencing, nails, and everything he needed to make that fence out back was piled neatly against the wall.

Had she planned to hire someone to put up the fence? He stroked his beard. She shouldn't have had to buy all this stuff. He should have built it a long time ago. Even if he was never invited back here to stay, he would build that fence to protect his children.

He threw his bundle in the back of the wagon and hitched up the horse. Later this evening, after supper, he would take the wagon to Betsy and tell her the house was hers.

He'd let her know he repented and surrendered to God, but he expected a huge amount of skepticism. He'd lied and made empty promises that he would stop drinking so often.

This time he'd need time to show her he'd changed if he had any hope of winning her back. If he'd used up all those chances, well... He wiped his hand through the horse's hair. At least, the Lord gave him another chance.

Chapter Twenty-Seven

Betsy paced the floor.

"Sit down," Lavena said. "If you're going to the protest tonight, you need to stay off your feet for a while."

Betsy saw the sense in what she said and sat in the rocker, but she couldn't sit still. She promised to wait to send a telegram to her husband, but now, she doubted herself. Maybe she should have sent it right away, but some kernel of hope inside her wouldn't let her do it.

Another thing that caused her to wait was she didn't want her parents to know the situation she'd gotten herself into. It was bad enough that Helen married a drunk who abused her and killed her. They were still heartbroken over it. She didn't want to add to their burden.

She remembered God's promise to her and the vision she'd seen at church. Nate would come to her while she was protesting in front of the saloon and tell her he'd repented. And he would mean it this time.

It was so hard to hold onto that promise after everything that had happened. The baby kicked, and she wiped a tear from her cheek. This baby might never meet its father. She had to stop giving into the weeping. It wasn't doing any good, and it upset the children. Thank God they were in Penelope's room playing.

One week. She had told God she would wait one week to see if He worked a miracle. She had five days left. It wouldn't do any good, but she'd wait those five days and then send that telegram. Somehow, she had to accept that her marriage was over.

She went over in her mind everything that had happened since she'd married. Two days after their wedding, Nate was involved in a slave rescue. They'd put him in jail in Cleveland for six months. She was proud of what he'd done and had moved to Cleveland and rented an apartment to be near him. She wanted to be a supportive and dutiful wife.

But since then, he had never regarded her feelings. The first two years of their marriage, he was always gone on slave rescues almost the whole time, and he wouldn't consider staying home or allowing her to come with him.

Finally, when he came back home, he'd apologized and promised her he wouldn't leave again. But when the war broke out, he was among the first to enlist, again without telling her. She almost ended their marriage then.

Over the last six years, he'd become a self-pitying drunk who never thought about how anything he did affected her, but now that she thought back on it, he'd never asked what she thought or wanted her advice. They'd never had a good marriage because he didn't really care for her. He did his own thing and expected her to go along with it. They'd never become one flesh in any way but physically. She placed her hand over her belly. Now they never would.

~~~~~

After supper, Nate climbed into the wagon and headed toward Cage's house. This would be the hardest part, apologizing to Betsy and hoping she'd know he really meant it this time. That was if Cage or Lavena would let him talk to his wife at all.

A wind blew around him, and he glanced up. The storm clouds were coming in fast. Maybe an hour before the rain began. He reached over to grab his jacket and put it on.

When he got to the house, he climbed off the wagon, grabbed his crutches, and walked to the door. He was amazed how easily he was walking with the wooden leg. He still needed crutches, but he suspected after a couple of weeks of this, he would be able to walk without them. It humbled him to know he could have been doing this all along if he hadn't been so bitter and stubborn, if he'd listened to his wife.

Thank You, Lord, for showing me that.

He raised his hand to knock on the door then paused and swallowed back the lump in his throat. Would she even see him? He knocked twice.

Lavena answered. "She doesn't want to see you."

"I understand that, but can you tell her something for me?"

She leaned against the doorframe, blocking his entrance. "What?"

He wiped his hand through his hair. "I went to the church earlier today."

"Good for you," Lavena said with a sarcastic tone.

Heat rushed to his face. "I mean... I... I surrendered my life to God and repented." He glanced at his feet. "I don't expect her to forgive me. I've lied about changing my ways so many times, but I wanted her to know."

"I'll tell her, but as you say, you've lied about this before." An impatience was in her tone, but he didn't leave. "Anything else?"

"I arranged to stay somewhere else. She can move back into the house, and I'll leave her alone unless she wants to see me. I'm leaving the horse and wagon for her."

Lavena's gaze softened. "She really isn't here. She's protesting at the saloon."

"Thank you."

"If you hurt her, you'll answer to me."

Nate nodded and headed toward the saloon, he hoped for the last time.

~~~~~

Lavena closed the door and leaned against it. She hoped she did the right thing telling Nate where Betsy was. She probably shouldn't have, but when he said he was moving out of the house, she thought her friend should know.

Cage walked over to her and wrapped his arms around her. "I was listening at the door."

She shrugged. "I hope I did the right thing."

"You did," Cage said. "Betsy deserves to know about the house, but I don't believe he's repented. It's a ploy to get her back."

"He was your best friend during the war." She laid her hand on his shoulder. "He saved your life. Shouldn't you give him the benefit of the doubt?"

Cage pulled back from her. "He's a different man now." He grabbed his earlobe. "He's a liar and a drunk who abused his wife. He would do anything to win her back, but he won't change. I can never forgive him for what he's become."

Her husband was right. She shouldn't have told Nate where Betsy was. "Do you think I should ride to the saloon and warn her?"

He nodded. "Do you want me to go with you?"

"No need." Lavena's stomach tightened and her breathing became heavy. She tried to calm herself, but she was afraid to go to the saloon alone. She collapsed into Cage's arms. "I can't. I'm afraid." She was ashamed of the way she was acting but she couldn't help it.

Cage held her for a moment. "Shh, it's all right. I'll go. I can get there faster on my horse anyway."

"Thank you," she squeaked out.

He kissed her one more time, led her to her rocker to sit, and rushed out the door.

She took a few calming breaths. She thought she had conquered this fear when she managed to get an assignment at the newspaper and carry it out. She placed her face in her hands. *Why can't I get over this?*

~~~~~

Betsy pulled her coat tighter around her and gazed at the storm clouds overhead. They needed to leave and take shelter soon, but she believed they had time to sing one more hymn. After all, the men coming into the saloon didn't let the threat of a storm deter them.

At least Nate wasn't here tonight. She didn't know what she would say or do if he showed up.

Cage rode up on his horse, dismounted, and rushed to her side. "Could we talk?"

"I'll be back," she said to the ladies. "Go ahead and sing *Amazing Grace*." She followed him away from the others as she heard the women sing.

*Amazing Grace, how sweet the sound,
that saved a wretch like me.*

"Lavena told Nate where you are," Cage said.

*I once was lost but now am found,
was blind but now I see.*

Betsy gasped. "Why would she do that?"

"Nate said he was moving out and leaving the house to you. She was trying to help."

She wiped her hand over her face. She couldn't imagine him doing that. He never considered her and the children's needs before his own. "Thank you for the warning, but I'll be fine. If he comes here, he's more likely to visit the saloon and get drunk than to give me the house."

Cage set his jaw. "I'm not leaving. If he wants to talk to you, he'll have to do it with me standing guard. I won't let him hurt you again."

"He won't hurt me." She wanted to believe that. "But I do appreciate you being here."

Nate pulled up to the saloon in the wagon. He climbed down, but he looked different. He was wearing his artificial leg, and the scowl he normally wore was gone.

Cage and Betsy walked over to him.

The ladies continued to sing.

*Was grace that taught my heart to fear,
and grace my fears relieved.*

"Could we talk for a moment?" Nate tilted his head toward Cage. "Alone?"

*How precious did that grace appear
the hour I first believed.*

"I'm not leaving." Cage crossed his arms. "Whatever you have to say, you can say in front of me."

He nodded.

They moved toward the wagon as the ladies continued to sing.

"So, say what you have to say," Betsy said, her sign still propped on her shoulder.

Nate head lowered, but he kept his eyes focused on her. "I'm so sorry for what I put you through. I don't expect you to forgive me."

She suddenly felt nauseous and placed her hand over her stomach. So that was why he came. To try to win her back? Was the house a ruse? "You're right. I don't forgive you."

A pained expression covered his face for a moment, then it was gone. "I didn't come for that."

She didn't believe him, but she had to admit there was something different about him. His voice even sounder softer. It didn't have that edge to it that had been there since the war."

"I came to tell you I've surrender my life to God and repented of my sin."

Her heart leapt despite her resolve to remain strong.

"Sure, you did," Cage said with a sarcastic tone. "And I bet you've decided to stop drinking."

Nate ignored him and kept his focus on Betsy. "I've moved in with Rev. Fowler for a time. I want you and the children to go back to living in the house. Even if you do go to live with your parents, it will be more comfortable for the time being. I'll stay away."

Her resolve crumbled, and she dropped the sign and began sobbing. He embraced her, and she didn't pull back.

When she calmed, he stepped back. "I love you so much, but I have some work to do to earn back your trust. That is if I can earn it back." He glanced at Cage then wiped his hand over his face. "And I need some time to prove to myself that I won't go back to drinking no matter what happens."

"I want to believe you, but…"

Nate nodded. "If you allow me to, in a week or two, I'll call on you and the children. We'll see how things go."

A tear escaped Betsy's eyes despite her trying to keep them at bay. "Don't bother coming unless you stay sober."

Rain started to sprinkle, and the women stopped singing and headed toward their temperance wagon.

Nate grabbed an oil cloth from the back of the wagon and draped it over her. "I'll drive you back to the church to collect the children, then I'll stay at the parsonage while you go the rest of the way to Cage and Lavena's house."

"I'll follow on horseback," Cage said.

Betsy followed Nate to the wagon and climbed aboard. "Lavena's taking care of the children. I don't need to stop at the church."

He flicked the reins. "I'll take you there, then walk to the church. You can use the wagon to move back into our house."

"How will I get it back to you?"

"The wagon is yours. I'm used to walking anyway, and I need to get used to this new leg." He tapped his wooden leg.

It appeared God had done that miracle, and what just happened was what she saw in her vision, but she couldn't let her heart go unprotected until she was sure. Even then, God had shown her there was a lot wrong with their marriage even from the beginning before he started drinking. She needed to be cautious, but she couldn't help the hope flowing back into her heart.

Nate stopped in front of Cage's house and climbed down. He reached out his hand to help her down. That was new. He'd usually had her get out of the wagon by herself. Maybe the wooden leg made him steadier on his feet. She took his hand and made her way to the ground.

He pressed his lips together a moment. "If you want, I'll call on you in a couple of weeks, but that's your decision. I won't push it. I'll wait until you're ready." He glanced up at Cage, still sitting on his horse, hovering over her. "If you decide you want nothing to do with me, I'll abide by that."

She nodded and watched him walk down the street toward the church without the oilcloth in the pouring rain. She hurried to the house and shook the oilcloth before stepping inside.

Cage dismounted and followed her in, and Lavena stood from her rocking chair and turned to Betsy as soon as she closed the door.

"I'm sorry I told him where you were," Lavena said. "When he said you could move in the house without him, I believed him."

"It's all right," Betsy said. "Are the children in bed?"

Lavena nodded. "What happened?"

"Let's sit at the table, and I'll tell you all about it."

Her friends followed her to the table, and they all sat down.

"Nate did show up at the saloon, but he didn't go inside. Instead, he came over to talk to me. I believe he surrendered his life to the Lord."

Cage rubbed the scar on his face. "He's only doing that to get you back. He said he would stop drinking before. Don't believe him so easily."

"This time is different." The baby kicked, and she placed a hand on her stomach. "It happened just like my vision."

"Your vision?" Lavena asked.

Betsy told them about the vision she had at the church service a couple of weeks ago. "It was just like in the vision. His voice and face are softer, the way they used to be, and he's wearing his leg."

"That doesn't mean anything." Cage pulled on his ear.

Lavena touched his arm. "But he moved out of the house so she can have it."

He stood and paced to the sink. "He wants you in the house so you won't leave town. Wait and see. He'll be by every day to check on you."

"He said he wouldn't come around unless I asked him to." Betsy bit her bottom lip. "And he's living at the parsonage."

He let out a snort. "The first time he goes out and gets drunk while living there, the good reverend will throw him out into the street."

"That's one reason I trust he means what he says," Betsy said. "If he intended to drink, he would have never moved into the parsonage."

"That's true," Lavena said. "Either way, Betsy is a grown woman who should make up her own mind."

"I know." Cage gazed into Betsy's eyes. "I just don't want you to be hurt. I don't trust him, and I'm not sure I ever will."

Lavena raised her eyebrow. "What if he is telling the truth? What if he did repent? Are you planning to throw away your friendship with a man who saved your life."

"He was a different man then." He let out a heavy sigh. "I don't believe this sudden change."

"I didn't say I was going to let him back in the house tomorrow." Betsy said it a little louder than she meant to. She really believed that her husband had surrendered his life to Christ and had stopped drinking, but they still had a lot of things to work out. She wasn't stupid. She would wait to see if this was real. "I'm moving back home tomorrow."

"If he causes you any problems, promise you'll come to us," Cage said.

"I will." She silently prayed that wouldn't be needed.

Chapter Twenty-Eight

The next day after work, Nate headed to the church. It surprised him that he wasn't looking forward to having a drink, wasn't craving it, didn't even want it. The other times he quit, he would have bad headaches, become nauseous, and sometimes, his hands would shake. The worst part was his nightmares about the war and the irritation he couldn't shake. Every morning, he would think about drinking, and every day, when he passed the road leading to the saloon, a longing for alcohol would go through him.

No headaches, sour stomach, or nightmares so far. He would accept whatever ailment he had to suffer to get rid of this evil and follow Christ, but he didn't even want a drink. What he did constantly think about was what Rev. Fowler had in mind for him today.

When he arrived, Rev. Fowler was waiting for him outside by his wagon that he'd already hitched to a horse.

"Where are we going?" Nate asked.

"Do you remember me asking for donations of food and money for the needy?"

Nate nodded as he noticed a few boxes and barrels in the back of the wagon.

"Let's go." Rev. Fowler climbed in the wagon.

Nate climbed in beside him.

As they rode, Rev. Fowler explained that he went to the poor side of town once a week to distribute everything that was collected. "Mr. Baldwin always donates some food as well. We'll stop by his store on the way."

"Mr. Baldwin from the general store?"

Rev. Fowler nodded.

"When I went there to pay for some items one of those poor women stole, he acted like he didn't care. He said he couldn't afford to give free food away to everyone who comes in there."

The preacher chuckled. "That's Mr. Baldwin for you. He doesn't want anyone to know, but he gives away more than all the others combined. He gives all he can, so he can't afford to have people steal from him. I can understand why he feels that way, can't you?"

Nate nodded. He felt a little ashamed about judging the man when he didn't know the situation. He had no right to judge anyone after the way he behaved.

Rev. Fowler pulled the wagon up behind the store.

Mr. Baldwin came out. "I already have it stacked and ready to go."

"Thank you. Mr. Teagan will help you load it in the back."

"I can't do that," Nate said. "Not with these crutches."

The preacher grinned. "You'll find a way."

Nate climbed off the wagon and went to where the storekeeper stood.

"You load the wagon," Mr. Baldwin said. "I'll bring the supplies to you."

Nate propped the crutches against the back of the wagon. With his fake leg on and leaning on his hip against the wagon, he felt steady. Why had he taken so long to wear that leg? He loaded the bags. The grocer helped him with the heavy barrels.

When they had finished, the grocer said, "That's the lot."

Nate climbed into the wagon.

Before they headed out, Mr. Baldwin said, "So, Rev. Fowler, is this your new project?"

The reverend smiled. "It appears so." He flicked the reins and headed out.

"What did he mean by that?" Nate asked.

"We'll talk about it when we get back to the parsonage."

They spent the next couple of hours handing out food to families in need. Most of the families didn't have their men with them. On the way back to the parsonage, Nate asked about it.

"Some of these women are young widows who rely on us to feed them and their children. They have no other means. But most of these women have husbands who work at the mill or the cheese factories in town. When they get paid, they spend all of their money drinking and gambling. There isn't any left for food."

Nate thought about that for a while. He didn't gamble and had a good paycheck every week, but if he worked at one of the cheese factories, would he have drunk away the money for food and left his wife and children in dire straits like this? It shamed him to know he probably would have.

When they returned to the parsonage, Mrs. Fowler had supper waiting for them. Afterwards, she excused herself and went to another room.

"She's giving us time to talk." Rev. Fowler poured them both a cup of coffee, then sat at the table with his Bible. "Do you remember Mr. Baldwin say that you were my next project?"

"I remember." Nate wrapped his hands around the coffee cup. "I wondered what he meant by that."

"From time to time, God shows me someone He wants me to disciple.

The Aftermath

When I first pastored this church, Joshua Baldwin was the first man I discipled."

"And God showed you I was next."

"It appears so." Rev. Fowler took a sip of coffee. "But that's only if you agree to it. For at least the next week or two, everywhere I go to minister, you'll be right beside me. I'll require you to be available for Bible study and prayer every night at first and to follow any godly advice I give you. After that, I'll need to meet with you once or twice a week even if you aren't living here. But there's a catch."

"So far, it sounds like everything I need and want. What's the catch?"

"Honesty. This won't work unless you're upfront with me about everything you're struggling with. If you're being tempted, you tell me. If you decide to go ahead and have a drink, you come to me and tell me before I find out about it. Do you agree to all of this?"

"I agree to it."

"Good, because if you don't, you're going to have to find another place to stay."

Nate's voice thickened. "I've destroyed my marriage, my friendships, and my self-respect. I've been justifying it and outright lying, but I'm done. When I surrendered to God, I meant it. I might never win back the trust of my wife or my friends, but even if it's too late for that, I belong to the Lord, and I appreciate Him allowing someone like you to help me though this."

"Good," Rev. Fowler said. "Tonight, we'll begin with how a godly husband should treat his wife."

"I assume that would be a short lesson. I need to show love to Betsy and stop drinking."

Rev. Fowler chuckled. "You have a lot to learn."

~~~~~

Lavena couldn't believe the way she had acted the day before. She was living in fear so much that she couldn't even bring herself to warn her best friend about Nate. She had to get control of herself, and she knew what the first step would be. She needed to get out of the house and not give into the fear.

She would try to do it gradually. Today, she and Penelope would walk over to the newspaper office. The last time she was there, she panicked and ran home to safety. She hoped she could manage to stay calm this time.

When she and Penelope stepped into the office, she was surprised at how calm she felt. She felt foolish about it now.

Mr. Guthrie met her eyes and strode toward her. "I'm glad you decided to come around again. When you turned in those stories last week, you left before I could give you another assignment. Where have you been?"

Lavena couldn't think of what to say. She certainly didn't want to tell him she'd been overcome with hysteria.

He waved his hand. "Doesn't matter. You're here now. I have a story I want you to cover. The city council is meeting on Monday to discuss the issue of banning alcohol in Wellington. Of course, Jake Nelson, the town prosecutor is against it, but the mayor and other two councilmen are considering it. If they decide for the ban, they'll override Nelson. So, are you taking the story on?"

"Absolutely." It was the story she'd been waiting for. She was so relieved she'd been able to make it to the office today.

"I knew you would." Mr. Guthrie took a puff of his cigar. "Since you've written all those stories on the temperance movement and how alcohol is affecting the crime wave, I wanted you to be the one to write it. I was worried I'd have to give the story to Thomson."

Lavena's mouth grew dry. Thomson was against banning alcohol and was known to visit the saloon from time to time. Maybe the Lord had urged her to come to the office today. She would be at that council meeting on Monday even if she had a hysteria attack on the way there. She couldn't wait to tell Cage.

After leaving the office, she and Penelope visited Cage at his office. She was relieved to see him at his desk. She was afraid he'd be out on a call.

Cage stood. "What a nice surprise." He kissed her on the cheek and picked up Penelope. "To what do I owe this visit?"

"I have some news." Lavena smiled. She was so proud of herself for facing her fear. "I went to the newspaper office today, and they assigned me a story."

He raised an eyebrow. "That's wonderful. I'm so proud of you. Did you have any adverse symptoms?"

"Not one. In fact, I accepted an assignment to write a story on the council meeting Monday."

"That is good news." He set Penelope down. "I assume you're covering the vote to end alcohol consumption in Wellington?"

"That's right."

"I'll be there too," Cage said. "I'll be speaking about how liquor is increasing the crime rate."

She let out a breath of relief. She wasn't really as sure of herself as she was trying to appear. It would help if her husband were there sitting beside her. "I was thinking about asking Nate to come to the meeting."

The muscle in Cage's cheek twitched. "I wouldn't do that."

"I just thought since he struggled so much with drinking, he might be willing to offer his thoughts to the council, or at least in the article."

Cage pulled on his ear. "I'm sure Nate doesn't want the consumption of alcohol to end any time soon. He only stopped drinking to win his wife back. He'll be back to it as soon as he can convince her to let him come back home."

Lavena crossed her arms. "You of all people should know that repentance goes a long way."

When they met during the war, Cage had been keeping a shameful secret from everyone, including her, but when he repented, he confessed to everyone. That was the only reason she gave him another chance.

"That's not fair."

"Maybe not." Lavena placed her arms around him. "I'm sorry."

He embraced her. "I forgive you."

She laid her head on his shoulder. "I'm going to do what I need to for this article." She pulled back and looked in his eyes. "You know I can't consider your feelings when it comes to a newspaper article. I'm going to ask Nate to come to the meeting and to allow me to interview him afterward."

Cage gazed at her a moment too long. "I hope he doesn't disappoint you."

Chapter Twenty-Nine

That Sunday, Betsy couldn't believe her eyes. Nate not only came to church, but Rev. Fowler invited everyone to Findley Lake after church to see him get baptized. That wasn't her biggest surprise.

Her husband stood in front of the whole church and spoke. "You all know me, but if you're new, my name in Nathaniel Teagan. I used to be a man who loved God, but since the war, I've been angry with the Lord about losing my leg." His Adam's apple bulged. "I've become a drunk and..." his voice thickened. "And I've mistreated my family and friends. I'm not proud of that, but this week, I gave my life back to the Lord."

The congregation cheered. Everyone in the congregation but Cage. Betsy glared at him, hoping her disappointment showed.

"If any of you have aught against me," Nate gazed Betsy, then at Cage, "I'm sorry, and I'll do my best to become a man you can trust again. That's about all I have to say. I've hurt so many people that I thought it best to say this in public." He sat down on the front pew.

The reverend came to the pulpit. "That wasn't easy for him to say. I hope you appreciate that."

The service continued. Betsy wasn't sure what to do, but she was so impressed with his confession and obvious repentance that she felt she should invite him back to live in the house. It would be easier to work out their differences there, and if he meant what he said, it would show. If he didn't mean it, that would show too.

After church, she headed toward him. "Hi, Nate."

"Hi, Betsy," he said with a catch in his voice.

"I was thinking that maybe you'd want to come back to the house and well... I'm inviting you to come home."

He swallowed hard. "As much as I want that, I can't. At least not yet."

Heat rose to her face. "Oh. I'm... I thought you'd want to... live with me again."

"I do." He gazed at the floor. "I want that more than anything, but the reverend has agreed to disciple me, and I..." He gazed into her eyes. "I need that, at least for now. I want to come back to you knowing I won't fall back into my old ways. Do you understand?"

"I think so." She hadn't felt this awkward around him since they were first courting at Oberlin College.

"It's not only the drinking. I realize now that I've never shown you the love you deserve from a husband. I've always insisted on going my own way instead of considering your needs and wants. When I come home, I want to make sure I'm ready to do that."

The tightness that had been in her chest for years now loosened, and she felt as if she'd just removed a corset. "Maybe you could come to supper one day this week. I know the children would love to see you."

"I would love that." Nate reached out his hand and touched her cheek. "Let me talk to Rev. Fowler about it first, and I'll let you know."

"Okay." Betsy was confused. Did this discipleship mean he needed Rev. Fowler's permission to visit his wife? "Hopefully, it will be soon. I need to get the children, so..."

"Of course," Nate said. "Will I see you at the baptism?"

"I'll be there."

After she gathered the children, she went to talk to Cage and Lavena. "Would you like to ride to Findley Lake together?"

Cage grabbed hold of his ear. "Lavena and I were just talking about that. She and the children will go with you. I have work to do."

"Surely the work can wait," Lavena said.

"No, it can't." He wiped his hand over the scar on his face. He walked toward his office. Lavena and the children followed Betsy to the wagon.

After the children were all settled, Lavena climbed in and sat next to her. "I'm sorry. He doesn't believe this is real. He thinks Nate is doing this for your benefit."

Betsy blinked to keep any stray tears from being shed. "And what do you think?"

"I don't know. I hope this is real, for your sake, but we'll see if it lasts."

Betsy swallowed. Maybe she was moving too quickly. If Nate really was right with God, it would show in time. And if he was lying, it was too late to protect her heart. She'd already started letting her guard down. Only this time, if he went back to drinking, it would crush her.

The children were about to climb into the wagon when Nate approached.

"Papa." Naomi threw herself into his arms.

He held her for a moment then put her down to give Malachi a hug.

"When are you coming home, Papa? Malachi asked.

"Soon, I hope," Nate gave her a hopeful gaze. "I love you both. You mind your ma. You hear?"

"We will," Malachi said.

Nate charmed her with the smile he'd used on her many times before, the one that always made her heart melt, the grin she was no longer sure she should trust. "I talked to Rev. Fowler. He says it would be all right to take an evening off to visit you and have supper."

She tugged on the collar of her blouse. "I've been thinking about that. Maybe we should wait another week or two."

His shoulders slumped, and disappointment covered his face, but a moment later he recovered and plastered on a sad smile. "If you think we should wait, we'll wait."

"I do." Betsy hated to disappoint him like this, but she needed to make sure he'd changed before she gave him the slightest chance.

"Then I'll see you at the baptism."

"We'll be there."

He stuck his hands in his pockets and walked away slowly.

~~~~~

Nate was surprised Lavena had asked him to the council meeting, but after talking with Rev. Fowler about it, he was ready to do whatever he could to convince them to ban alcohol. He couldn't help wondering if living in a dry village would have stopped him from becoming a drunk. He wasn't sure, but it might help some of the men.

When he entered the chamber with Rev. Fowler, he nodded to Lavena. Cage sat beside her but wouldn't look at him. He was afraid he had destroyed their friendship for good.

Mayor J.B. Lang opened the hearing. "On the agenda tonight is whether or not to have a ban on alcohol in Wellington. I'm in favor of this ban, but as you know, we must have a majority vote on the council to enact it." He introduced the council members as Jake Nelson, Benjamin Walters, and Gregory McCormick."

He explained that he would allow people to speak in an orderly fashion, and many got in line. Cage stepped to the front of the line.

Nate headed toward the back of the line hoping that he wouldn't need to speak. It was one thing to get up in front of the church and tell them he had been a drunk, but he didn't look forward to telling the whole town.

He chuckled to himself. As far as he could tell, the whole town already knew, so why was he so apprehensive?

It took an hour before they got to Nate. He introduced himself.

"I object," Mr. Nelson said. "This man is a known drunk and was in jail recently for starting a fight at a local saloon."

The crowd murmured, and heat rushed to Nate's face. He wanted to go somewhere and hide. Instead, he waited until the crowd died down.

The mayor banged his gavel. "Is this true, Mr. Teagan?"

"Yes, sir. Recently, I gave my life to the Lord, and I'm here to talk about the evils of drink."

"Go on," Mayor Lang said.

Nate did go on. He spoke on how drink had ruined his marriage, his friendships, and his reputation, and had cost him his job. When he was done, he felt as low as a bug, but he hoped he'd helped.

Jake Nelson asked to be heard. "We've listened to all these men speak, but before we vote, let's not forget the revenue the saloons bring to this town. Yes, some weak men..." Jake looked at Nate. "... will allow alcohol to get hold of them, but should all of us have the freedom to decide taken away from us because of a few weak men? Some in this room drink wine or even whiskey from time to time without any ill effects. And we all know alcohol can be used for medicinal purposes. As far as the crime in this city, it only makes sense that we need more revenue to hire more deputies, not less."

Everyone started talking with each other, and the mayor banged his gavel. "It's time for the vote."

The vote was three to one against the change in the statute. Nate realized he hadn't influenced anyone. Only the mayor voted for it.

As the meeting was adjourned and men began to leave the chamber, Lavena came over to him. "Are you ready to do an interview with me?"

"Why not?" Nate sat realizing he wouldn't be leaving any time soon. "If anyone in town didn't know all of my sins and depravity before, they do now."

~~~~~

Nate spent the rest of the week training a new man for the telegraph office in the morning, then in the afternoons, following Rev. Fowler around and helping however he could. He would spend his evenings reading the Bible and praying or discussing a biblical principle with the preacher. It kept him busy which helped keep his mind off how much he missed Betsy and the children. Whenever he did feel sorry for himself about not being with them, he'd ask God to help him stay on the right path no matter what happened in the future, and he reminded himself that he had brought this on his own head.

On Tuesday, Rev. Fowler preached to a large crowd in a field beside one of the cheese factories. Johnnie Hanson was there as well as many men, women, and children. On Wednesday afternoon, they met with a group of young men in that same field and had a Bible study. Again, Johnnie was in the group.

Both times, the reverend had Nate give his testimony about how drink had brought him to ruin. At the council meeting, he'd been embarrassed to admit what he'd been. The looks he received were filled with scorn. But now, it felt good to get it out there and let God's cleansing light shine on it. One good thing that came out of it was he could never sneak off to have a drink now without everyone, including Betsy and Cage knowing about it. That helped keep temptation at bay.

Wednesday night, people met for prayer and Bible study at church. Nate and Betsy had never gone to it before. Betsy had to get the children to bed, and Nate was never interested. Now he saw what he was missing out on. He was learning to experience the Lord in a whole new way and to be led by the Holy Spirit. If he was ever allowed to be a husband and father again, he would insist they go to church on Wednesday nights.

Friday was the hardest test. They went to the saloon where Betsy and the other women were protesting and singing hymns. Rev. Fowler preached to the men going into the place, and again, had Nate tell his story.

He'd drunk with these men. They all knew him and what he'd been like. He doubted they would listen to him. Between that and being distracted by Betsy being so close and yet not even looking his direction, he stumbled through his story.

It surprised him that some of the men stood outside and listened. When he'd finished, the men wandered back through the saloon doors, all but one. Josh Brunner, a man who drank with him on most weekdays and brought his family to church every Sunday, wandered over to him.

"Do you miss it?" Josh asked. "The drinking I mean. I know you miss your family."

"No, I don't." It was an honest answer. Since he'd surrendered to the Lord, he had no desire for whiskey. God had not only taken away his craving for it, he didn't even suffer the effects he normally did when he'd tried to stop before. No headaches or irritability. Even his nightmares had gone away.

"I've tried to stop lots of times, but I missed it too much to stay away for long." Jake wiped his hand across the back of his neck. "Thing is, I want to stop. I know it's hurting my family, but I just can't."

"I couldn't either," Nate said. "I finally came to the place where I wanted to be right with God more than I wanted anything else. When I surrendered to Him, He delivered me from it."

"It was that easy, huh?"

Nate snorted. "Easy? Not at all. I've lost my family. My wife doesn't trust me, and I don't blame her. My closest friend won't speak to me. Again, I don't blame him. And I've lost my job. I'm not sure things will ever be easy again, but it's worth it. Why don't you come over to the wagon with me? Rev. Fowler can pray with you."

When Nate looked up, the preacher had been leaning on the wagon listening to the conversation. He strode toward them.

"I don't know what to do," Josh said.

"I didn't either," Nate said. "I just bowed down and surrendered to God. I told Him I was done trying to do it on my own. I was giving it to Him. And I told Him I was sorry."

Josh bowed on his knees on the hard ground next to the wagon and poured his heart out to God.

When he was finished, Nate turned to the preacher. "Looks like you have another project."

He felt a soft hand fold into his and he turned. Betsy was holding his hand and smiling at him. How did this happen? *Lord, don't let it stop.*

"I heard everything you said."

He wasn't sure if she was explaining why she decided to hold his hand, but as long as her hand was in his, he didn't want to say anything to ruin it.

"Rev. Fowler," Betsy said. "Is it all right if I take Nate home?"

"Do you... mean... now?" Nate stuttered. "I promise I won't stay late."

"No, I mean for you to move back home." She turned to the reverend. "I'll make sure he comes back for your meetings any time you want, but I don't want to interfere with what you're doing in his life."

Nate didn't say anything, couldn't say anything. His words caught in his throat.

"Nate, I want you at my house after supper at least once or twice a week." The preacher turned to the other man. "Josh, I expect you at the church right after work tomorrow."

"My wife's never going to believe I'm meeting with the parson tomorrow night," Josh said. "I'll see you then." He walked toward his house, the opposite direction of the saloon.

"I have the wagon," Betsy said. "When we pick up the children at the church, you can gather your belongings."

"I'll do that." Nate knew he had a stupid grin on his face, but he couldn't stop smiling. He prayed his wife wouldn't change her mind.

Chapter Thirty

When Nate told his story and led Josh to the Lord, Betsy's heart melted. The hurt and doubts she'd had about him dried up and blew away like the aftermath of a storm. All that was left were twigs and leaves to clean away. She wasn't foolish enough to believe everything would be perfect now. Too much had happened between them. But she'd trust God to show them the way forward.

When they got to the church, the children were so excited to see their father that she had a hard time getting them to sleep that night. But finally, they were settled, and she next to Nate in the rocker in the kitchen.

"I think we need to talk about a few things." Nate took her hand in his.

"I agree," she said. "I have some things to say as well."

"If you don't mind, I'll start."

She nodded.

"I've rehearsed everything I want to say to you, so let me say it all." He cleared his throat. "The way I've treated you over the last few years is shameful. I want you to know that I understand all the grief I put you through, and I'm truly sorry." A sob escaped him. "I thought I'd lost you."

He paused for a moment and wiped his hand over his face. "I don't deserve another chance. I know that. Thank you for forgiving me and taking me back. I'll do everything I can to do right by you and the children, but if I fail, I'll admit it, and ..." His voice thickened. "I haven't even wanted to drink since I surrendered my life to God. He's delivered me from it, but Rev. Fowler's warned me I may be tempted at some point. If I am, I'll tell you and Rev. Fowler the truth about it. I just wanted you to know that."

"That's some speech." She squeezed his hand. "You sound like a lawyer making his closing argument."

He let out a snort. "Tomorrow is my last day at the telegraph office. I've been considering opening a law office in town."

"You'll make a fine lawyer."

"I need a little time though. I want to spend a couple more weeks being discipled by Rev. Fowler, and I have a fence to build out back."

Betsy smiled. "You saw the supplies in the barn."

"I did. I'm sorry I didn't build it before. We need that fence to keep the children safe."

"So, how will you know when you're ready to start your law practice?"

"I don't know. The whole town knows what I did." He stroked his beard. "When Cage forgives me, I figure the town might be ready to give me a chance."

Betsy gazed into her husband's eyes. "He has good reason to not trust you."

Nate lowered his eyes. "Yes, he does. So do you."

"With everything in me, I believe you've changed. I forgive you, and I love you."

Another sob escaped him, and he pulled her hand to his face.

As much as she wanted to leave it at that, she had more to say. She pulled her hand away. "As much as I love you, I don't completely trust you. That will take time."

He nodded. "I'll do whatever it takes for as long as it takes. I'll spend a lifetime showing you the love you deserve."

"Good. One thing I need from you is not just to say you love me but to care about me and the children. You've always gone off on your own and did whatever you wanted, not just after the war, but from the day we married. You didn't consider me at all when you went on those slave rescues or when you joined the army."

"I've been talking to Rev. Fowler about that, and you're right. I need to love you as Christ loved the church and gave Himself for it. I've spent our marriage taking, not giving."

A warmth filled her. He must have had some conversations with Rev. Fowler. "I just want to feel like I'm important to you."

"You are." His voice cracked. "I never realized how important until all of this happened, and I almost lost you."

She stood. "Let's get some sleep. You wouldn't want to be late your last day of work." By the disappointment on his face, she knew that had hurt him, but she wasn't ready to be a wife to him in every way.

She wrapped her arms around him, and he embraced her and kissed her as if he was afraid it would be their last kiss. When the kiss finally ended, she took hold of his hand. "I need time."

He nodded. "I'll give you all the time you need."

~~~~~

Nate spent most of his last day at work watching Elias Moore, a former slave who'd educated himself. He was there to answer questions, but Elias had caught on quickly and didn't have any problems. Since there was barely enough room for both of them behind the counter, when a message came in, Nate stood and watched from in front of the counter. The rest of the time, he leaned back in the wooden chair by the window and watched the people pass by.

Shortly before closing, he saw someone he never expected to see. At least, he thought it was him. "You go ahead and close up. I have something I need to do."

He darted out onto the road and watched. A man hid in the shadows of a building on the corner of Clark Street and Kelley, across from the telegraph office. It was Billy Horton, probably trying not to be noticed until there were fewer people around.

Nate tried to act like he hadn't seen him and made his way to the marshal's office. When he entered, Cage wasn't there. "Where is he?"

Deputy George glanced up. "You mean Cage? He went home."

Nate didn't wait for the man to say any more. Instead, he rushed out of the office and headed for Cage's house. He pounded on the door. Nobody answered, so he pounded louder.

Cage opened the door. "You're not welcome here." He started to close the door.

Nate wedged his crutch in it. "Billy Horton's here."

Cage inched the door a little wider. "What do you mean here? In town?"

"He's on the corner of Clark and Kelley. He looks like he's waiting for something."

Lavena rushed to Cage's side. "He means to kill you. Why don't you send your deputies? You don't need to go."

Cage grabbed his gun belt.

"I need a gun too," Nate said.

"No," Cage said. "You stay here."

"I'm going with you." Nate crossed his arms, hoping his jutted jaw made his friend realize he wasn't taking no for an answer.

Cage went back inside and came out with a rifle. "Go get George and meet me at the train depot. I'm keeping an eye on him until you get there."

Lavena placed a hand on Cage's chest. "Don't go. George will handle it."

He touched her face. "I have to." He headed to the depot.

Nate headed to the office.

~~~~~

Lavena collapsed on the floor crying. She shouldn't have let him go. She blew her nose and let out a snort. How could she stop him? Her husband was a stubborn man. She was relieved Penelope was taking a nap and didn't see her mother falling apart like this.

She quoted every verse she'd memorized about fear, but none of them helped. *Please, Lord, keep him safe.*

Grabbing a paper and pen from her lap desk, she wrote, *I'm afraid Billy Horton will kill Cage.* She threw the paper into the stove and watched it burn into ash until nothing was left of it.

A peace she couldn't explain washed over her, and her breathing and heart rate slowed, almost to normal. She couldn't do anything to keep her husband out of danger, but the Lord would protect him.

She did the only thing she could do. She prayed and gave Cage's safety into God's hands.

~~~~~

Nate rushed into the marshal's office.

George stood. "What's wrong?"

"Billy Horton is in town. Cage wants us to meet him at the depot."

George grabbed a rifle. "Let's go."

Nate looked at his crutches. Every day, he'd gone longer without them than the day before. Today, they would only get in the way. He propped them against the wall, clutched his rifle, and followed George out the door.

When they reached the depot, Cage stood inside looking out the window. He nodded to them. "George, you head to the right. Nate, go to the left. Have your rifles ready. I'll call him out." He stepped out the door before anyone could argue.

Nate cocked his rifle and headed toward the left. Once he was in position, he glanced over to see George was on the other side aiming his gun.

Horton didn't seem to know they were there. He was preoccupied with rolling a cigarette.

Cage called out. "Horton, come out of the shadows, and let's face each other like men. Or were you planning to shoot me in the back like the coward you are?"

Nate swallowed hard and focused his sights on Billy, but the man didn't come out of the shadows. He stayed in the doorway of the building where the barbershop was located.

He let up a prayer of thanks that the shop was closed on Saturday, or the men inside might have been in harm's way.

Horton broke a window and rushed into the door of the shop.

Cage took a few steps closer, but Nate was sure he couldn't see Horton. Nate had a clear view, but the sun was low in the sky and shining in Cage's eyes. Horton aimed his gun at the marshal's head, and Nate fired. The outlaw dropped the gun and cried out. Cage ran to the store with Nate and George following him.

Billy lay moaning on the floor beside the door, blood rushing out of his arm.

Cage picked up his revolver. "Thanks, George. I knew I could count on you."

"It wasn't me," George said. "I couldn't get a clear shot."

Cage stared at Nate, and Nate couldn't think of anything to say. He just shrugged. "I got lucky."

"That shot wasn't luck," George said. "Shooting him through the window like that."

"George, get the doctor before this man bleeds to death," Cage said.

The deputy nodded and rushed off.

Cage's gaze never left the outlaw. "Nate, thanks for saving my life... again."

"No need for thanks. You'd do the same for me."

"This doesn't change anything between us."

Heat rushed to Nate's face, and he knew. There would be no reconciliation between him and Cage. He had ruined their friendship, and there was nothing he could do to fix it. "Understood."

"I don't need you here anymore. Why don't you tell my wife I'm all right before you head to the saloon?"

That couldn't have hurt Nate more if he'd punched him. "I'm not headed to the saloon. I stopped drinking. Remember?"

Cage didn't say anything.

"I will stop by and tell Lavena you're all right." He headed toward Cage's house. When he got there, he knocked on the door.

Lavena answered before he could knock twice. "Is he all right?"

"Yes, he's fine." Nate said. "Billy Horton's been shot, so Cage won't be home for a while."

"Is Horton dead?" Lavena asked a little too hopeful.

"He'll live long enough to hang, but he won't cause any more trouble."

She let out a heavy sigh. "Thank you."

Nate nodded then headed home.

As he walked along the railroad tracks, Doug Hanson crossed his path, probably on the way home from the saloon since he already had a bottle of whiskey in his hand. He smelled like it might have been his second bottle.

"Well, well." Doug laughed, but not in a friendly way. "What do we have here?"

"Leave me be." Nate walked past him.

Doug caught his shoulder and spun him around.

He tightened his shoulders and fisted his hands, ready to protect himself if need be.

"So, the little woman got you to stop drinking, did she? Maybe she ought to sew you up a skirt to wear."

He knew the man was trying to goad him, but this time, he was sober and wouldn't let his good sense get the better of him. "Go home. Go sleep it off."

Doug held up his bottle. "Come on, Teagan. Don't let her tell you what to do. Just one drink. You can use my bottle."

Nate felt his skin crawl. Was this what he was like all those times he'd had too much to drink. "I didn't stop drinking because of my wife. I surrendered my life to God. You could do the same."

"Don't go Bible thumping me. I know you want this." He uncorked the bottle and flung the liquid toward Nate.

He tried to step back in time, but the whiskey got all over his shirt and trousers.

"See how your wife likes you coming home reeking of this whiskey." Doug laughed like he'd told the funniest joke he'd ever heard. Then he staggered back toward the saloon.

Nate wiped his shirt, but it didn't help. He looked up. "Lord, what do I do now? Betsy will never believe what happened. She'll think I was drinking again."

He had no choice. He headed for home to tell her the truth.

Chapter Thirty-One

Betsy couldn't wait to talk to Nate about what she'd found. When he came home from his last day of work, she knew he'd be a little sad about it. Hopefully what she had to say would help. She heard Nate's footsteps on the porch and wiped her hands on her apron then went to the door to greet him.

When he opened the door, her heart fell to her stomach. The smell of whiskey was all over him. His clothes were wet with it. She made her way to the table and sank onto the bench, afraid her weak knees wouldn't hold her up. She couldn't catch her breath.

"It's not what you think," Nate wet a cloth and placed it behind her neck. "Now, breathe."

She took a deep breath and let it out. Her head spun, and she was so dizzy she thought she might faint.

He got her a cup of water and patted her hand while she drank it. "Are you all right?"

She calmed her breathing and gazed at him. He wasn't staggering, and he seemed in control of himself, but his clothes smelled of liquor.

"I didn't have anything to drink, Betsy. You have to believe me. I saw Hanson on the way home, and he poured liquor on me. I promise I'm telling the truth."

The desperation in his voice and his pleading eyes broke through her fog. Everything he said made sense. She stood, moved close to him, and smelled his breath. No alcohol, and no peppermint that he'd sometimes use to disguise the smell.

"Walk over to the door and back in a straight line." That was something he could never do when he was drinking and used crutches. She was sure he wouldn't be able to manage it with his artificial leg if he had been drinking.

He did as she said and never staggered from the straight line. He gazed at her, willing her to believe him.

Despite the whiskey all over him, she did believe him. In every way, he acted sober. "You need to wash up and get out of those clothes." She put her finger to her nose. "You smell like a saloon."

This time, he was the one who collapsed. He sank onto the bench beside her. "You believe me?" He leaned toward her.

She backed away. "Uh uh. I believe you, but I'm not kissing you until you clean up. Then I have some news for you."

"What?"

"I'll tell you at supper. Now go."

He went into the bedroom while she finished cooking supper. By the time it was ready to put on the table, he'd washed up and changed his clothes. He came into the room, swung her around, and kissed her passionately. She leaned into the kiss then stepped back. She wanted it to continue, but supper was ready, and the children would come to eat any time.

"Children," she called. "Supper."

During supper, the children chattered away about their blocks and what they did that day. Malachi said he saw a train, but he didn't go near it. Naomi told how she took a nap with the sock monkey Betsy had made her from some scraps. Betsy smiled to hear how Nate listened to them and asked questions. There was no impatience in his manner like there used to be. He truly seemed interested in what they were saying. He was a changed man. It surprised her how sure she was that he told her the truth even when he reeked of whiskey.

After supper, Nate offered to put the children to bed while she did the dishes. That was new, but she appreciated it. The days were getting more tiring as the time for her delivery grew closer. She figured the baby would come in around four more months.

She glanced out the window. Even with him working all week, he'd made great progress with the picket fence. It should be finished in a week or two.

Nate came back to the kitchen as she was putting away the last of the dishes. "Are you about done, or would you like some help?"

"I'm done," she said.

He wrapped his arms around her and kissed her, leaving her breathless. This time she didn't pull away.

As the kiss intensified, she whispered, "I want to be a wife to you tonight. Let's go to bed."

He pulled back and chuckled. "No, you don't. First, tell me the surprise. Then bed." He led her to their rocking chairs. "So, what did you want to tell me?"

She grinned. "Don't you want to tell me about your day first?"

A scowl crossed his face. "I suppose I should."

She furrowed her brow. Her mind raced back to the smell of alcohol on him when he came home. "What's wrong?"

He told her about saving Cage's life by shooting Billy Horton, and how Cage reacted afterward. "I don't believe he'll ever forgive me. I don't really blame him after what I've done."

"Stop that. You repented before God and man, and you've done everything you needed to prove you've changed and that your repentance is genuine. God has forgiven you, and I'll not have you living in shame. Whether Cage ever forgives you or not is his decision, not yours."

He took hold of her hand. "I suppose you're right. Rev. Fowler told me pretty much the same thing when I met with him last night."

"Do you have another meeting tonight?" She tried not to show her disappointment. He'd met with the preacher at least twice a week, and tonight, she wanted him to herself.

"No. No more nighttime meetings. I'm going to help him with his ministry during the day, a couple days a week. I also want to finish that fence, so we don't have to worry about the children." He chuckled. "At least I have all the supplies I need."

She shrugged. "I wasn't going to wait for you any longer."

He glanced down. "I'm sorry I didn't build it sooner."

She touched his hand. "Remember, no shame. You're building it now. That is what's important."

He pulled her hand to his face and kissed it. "I've decided to get a law office up and running. No reason to wait for Cage's blessing since…" He wiped his hand across the back of his neck. "Now, what's your news?"

She smiled. "I made some progress in that direction. I had a meeting at the temperance society today, and the husband of one of the members is selling his office building. I went to look at it, and it's perfect. It's located on the corner of Main Street and Taylor, so not too far from the town hall, and the price is right. You have to come and see it for yourself."

"I do, huh?"

"Yes, you do."

Nate chuckled. "We'll go tomorrow."

She stood. "Time for bed."

He stood and took her in his arms in a way he never could when he was on crutches. She never felt more loved.

~~~~~

When Cage came home that night, Lavena was waiting for him. After Penelope greeted him, she told her to go into her room to play.

"I need to talk to you, Cage."

He sat in his rocker and motioned for her to sit beside him. "I know what you're going to say. Honey, it's my job to confront dangerous criminals, and I'm good at it."

"You're probably the best marshal this town has ever had."

A confused look crossed his face. "Then, please don't ask me to quit."

Lavena chuckled. "Of course, I don't want you to quit. This town needs you."

Cage scratched his head. "But I thought… What do you want to tell me?"

She patted his hand. "I was so scared when you confronted Billy Horton, but I prayed. I really prayed, and God gave me peace."

"I'm glad to hear that," he said.

She swallowed a lump in her throat. "I realize what a burden I put on you, and I'm sorry."

"No need to apologize. We'll get through this."

"Cage, you don't understand. The hysteria still grips my thoughts sometimes, but I'm not going to let my fear control me anymore. I've already gone to the newspaper office twice, and I did that story at the council meeting. Tonight was the real test. Even though you were facing a killer, and I was afraid, I prayed and gave it to God."

"I'm sorry I scared you."

She blew out a heavy breath. He didn't see where she was going with this. "My point is I might still have these attacks, but with God's help, I'll get through them. I'm not going to stop living anymore, and I'm never again going to beg you to not do your job. I know God will protect you because I'll be at home praying for you."

He took her hand and squeezed. "Do you really mean that?"

She nodded. "Next week, I'm going to the suffrage meeting in Oberlin."

"Do you want me to go with you?"

"No, I'll be safe, especially now that Billy Horton is in jail." Everything in her wanted her to ask him to come along, but she had to do this on her own. Not really on her own. The Lord would always be with her to help her overcome her fear.

Chapter Thirty-Two

A couple months later, Betsy helped Nate sweep out his new office while Lavena watched the children. Lavena had agreed with Betsy that Cage was being unreasonable, but even she couldn't convince him to change his mind. Thanksgiving was in three weeks, and it would be the first time since moving to Wellington the two families wouldn't be spending the holiday together. That made her a little sad.

She was relieved Lavena seemed to have her confidence back. Betsy was back to babysitting Penelope a couple of times a week while her friend reported on stories or attended women's suffrage meetings. The hysteria her friend had been suffering with appeared to be gone.

Nate, however, wasn't back to his old self. He was better than he'd ever been. Since they'd been married, he'd never considered her opinions or feelings about anything.

Before the war, he would take off at a moment's notice without even asking her. Now, he was back to his old self about wanting to help other people, but he listened to her advice and considered her in everything he did. They were a team now, not two people going off on their own. One flesh.

The office was ready to open. The window had been painted with the words, Nathaniel Teagan, Attorney at Law. The furniture had been delivered the day before, including an oak desk, matching chair and filing cabinet, a bookshelf, and a couple of cushioned chairs for clients to sit in.

She was relieved she'd never told her family what Nate had done. When her father heard he was opening a law office, he'd insisted on sending the furniture by train. They'd spent all morning arranging it. All that was left was hanging his law certificate and Oberlin college degree, sweeping up, and putting his law books on the shelves.

She finished sweeping and clutched her stomach.

Nate ran to her side and pulled over a chair for her to sit in. "Are you all right?"

"I'm fine." She sat. "The baby's kicking my side to let me know I'm overdoing it."

He chuckled. "No doubt about it. Only a boy can kick that hard."

"I don't know. Naomi kicked pretty hard too."

"You rest. I'll finish up." He placed the books on the shelf. "Tomorrow, I'll be ready for business."

Someone knocked on the door, and when Betsy looked up, she was surprised to see Nate letting Cage in.

"What's wrong?" Nate asked.

"I need your help."

Her husband motioned for him to sit down.

"Johnnie Hanson is in my jail. He killed his father."

Betsy placed a hand over her mouth.

"I don't believe it," Nate said.

"He confessed. Hanson came home drunk, grabbed a fireplace poker and was about to stab his wife. Johnnie picked up a piece of log cut for kindling and hit him over the head to stop him, but he killed him instead." Cage wiped his hand over the scar on his face. "He doesn't have money for a lawyer, but he needs one. The prosecutor is planning to get him hanged."

Betsy gasped. "But he's just a boy."

"That's not the way the law sees it," Cage said.

"I'll go to him now," Nate said.

~~~~~

When Nate arrived at the jail cell where Johnnie was being kept, he found the boy on his knees praying. Not exactly what a hardened murderer would do.

"Johnnie," he said.

The boy stood and shook his hand through the bars. "Mr. Teagan. Are you the man God sent to be my lawyer? I prayed he'd send someone to help me."

Nate backed up a step and looked up. If God had sent him to help this boy, he'd do everything he could. "I'm the man. You need to tell me everything that happened, Johnnie. Don't leave anything out."

"I got home from work, and Pa was drunk. He'd already punched Ma a few times with his fists. Her cheek was red, and her mouth was bleeding. She was huddled in the corner. My brothers and sisters were under the table crying. I didn't see if he hit them or not, but that's where they normally hid to get away from his wrath.

"He hit her again, and I ran over to him and told him to stop, but he didn't even hear me. At least, he acted like he didn't. He picked up the poker we used for the fireplace and pulled his arm back to stab her. I didn't know what to do. He's a lot stronger than I am. I knew if I grabbed his arm, he would just push me away and stab her anyway. He was going to kill her. So, I saw a piece of a log on the floor and picked it up. I swung as hard as I could."

"Johnnie," Nate said, "did you mean to kill your pa?"

"No, never. I just wanted to protect my ma."

"Your brothers and sisters all saw this."

"I guess so. The way they were bundled up together, I'm not sure what they saw."

"But your ma saw."

"She sure did. She started crying that I killed him and ran out into the street yelling for help. I don't know why she said that. I was trying to help her. I stood in the middle of the room, not knowing what I should do."

"Did you think about running?"

Johnnie gaped at him. "Of course not. A few minutes later, a deputy came by and asked me what happened. I told him the truth, and he arrested me."

"Don't worry," Nate said. "It sounds like you had no choice. Self-defense or the defense of another is allowed under the law."

After telling Johnnie he'd come see him again the next day, he walked back to the office.

Cage was sitting at his desk. "Well?"

"He was defending his mother from a murderous drunk, and there are witnesses. When do we go to court?"

"Day after tomorrow," Cage said.

"Not much time, but I'll manage."

After leaving the office, Nate went directly to the prosecutor's office. He shook Jake Nelson's hand, and Nelson motioned for him to have a seat in front of the desk.

"I'm representing Johnnie Hanson."

"Ah, yes," Nelson said. "The man who murdered his father."

"The boy who killed his father to protect his mother from being murdered."

Mr. Nelson chuckled, and Nate instantly remembered why he disliked him. "I suppose we can make a gentleman's agreement. If you have your boy plead guilty, I'll ask for leniency, maybe life in prison."

"You can save your breath. He's pleading not guilty by reason of defense of another's life."

"Oh, come now, Mr. Teagan. These cheese factory workers and their families are a violent bunch, the riff raff of society. They're always getting into some scrape. The jury will side with me. Unless we make a deal, he's going to hang."

"Not this boy." Nate stood and offered his hand. "I'll see you in court."

Nelson shook it and chuckled. "It wouldn't help your new career as a lawyer to get a boy hung because you won't make a deal."

Nate pulled his hand away. His skin crawled at the callousness of the man. He turned without saying another word and left.

He spent the next day getting together witnesses to call on at the trial.

Rev. Fowler, Cage, and half a dozen men in the boy's neighborhood were happy to testify about Johnnie's character and the abuse Doug Hanson heaped on his family.

When he went to the Hanson home to ask Mrs. Hanson to testify, nobody answered the door. He knocked louder. "Anyone home?"

He heard movement inside. That was all right. If she didn't want to talk to him, he'd get a subpoena. The judge would force her to testify.

~~~~

The next day in court, Betsy sat behind her husband to give him the support he needed. Judge Murphy came in and asked Johnnie how he wanted to plead.

Nate stood. "My client pleads not guilty by reason of defense of another's life."

"Any opening arguments?" the judge said to the prosecutor.

The prosecutor stood and faced the jury. "John Hanson killed his father in cold blood by knocking him over the head with a piece of wood because he was angry about the punishments he received. He confessed to it, and there were witnesses. I'm asking the jury to find him guilty."

Betsy wasn't sure what to expect, but it worried her that the men on the jury glared at Johnnie as if he'd already been convicted. Now it was Nate's turn.

He stood, walked over to the jury, and faced them. He'd gotten so used to his wooden leg that she'd be surprised if they even noticed it was fake. The only evidence was a slight limp. "Johnnie Hanson was subject to beatings from a drunken man all his life. These weren't normal punishments a father gives, but cruel abuse no man should suffer, let alone a boy who is only fourteen years old."

An air of confidence and compassion showed in Nate's demeanor. "Even so, Johnnie tried to be an obedient son. He quit school to take extra jobs to earn money for the family since his father drank and gambled away most of what he earned. Every day, Johnnie would stock shelves at the Baldwin General Store. Before and after work at the store, he'd stop by the telegraph office to deliver telegrams around town. Even though his parents wouldn't let him attend church, he never missed a service when Rev. Fowler preached in the field on that side of town, and he attended a boy's Bible study Rev. Fowler held.

"Johnnie took the beatings his father gave him stoically and many times, would keep his father from lashing his cruelty on the younger children by getting in the way and bringing his father's wrath on himself.

"But the thing that upset him the most was the way Doug Hanson punched his wife in the face and stomach on repeated occasions. The day in question, Mr. Hanson picked up a fireplace poker and was about to stab his wife with it. Johnnie did the only thing he could do. He picked up a piece of wood and struck his father to stop him, not to kill him."

He stepped closer to the jury box and leaned in. "I ask you to remember your own mothers. Would any of you not do the same if your mother was in mortal danger? He did what any decent boy or man would do in his place, he defended his mother."

Betsy wanted to clap. It was obvious by the change of expressions on the men's faces they were sympathizing with Johnnie. Her husband was doing what he was called to do, help those in need when they were facing injustice.

The prosecutor called the deputy who testified that he found Mr. Hanson on the floor and that Johnnie confessed to the crime. The coroner said that Mr. Hanson died from a blow to the head.

Then, Mr. Nelson called Mrs. Hanson to the stand. Nate pressed his lips together but showed no other outward emotion. Betsy knew he'd been trying to talk to her about testifying. Why was she called by the prosecutor?

Nelson went through the preliminary questions, then asked what happened the day in question.

"My husband, Mr. Hanson, came in. He'd heard that Johnnie hadn't done his chores. Johnnie told him he'd do them when he was ready. My husband told him he'd whip him for sassing him, and Johnnie picked up a piece of wood and killed him. I ran outside for help, and saw the deputy come running toward us. We tried to teach that boy, but he's a mean one. I don't know who's going to support me and mine now."

Betsy placed her hand over her stomach. Why would the women say untruths like that about her own son?

"No further questions," the prosecutor said.

Nate stood and walked toward the seat where Mrs. Hanson was sitting. Then he paced back and forth a few steps. "Mrs. Hanson, how did you get that black eye?"

"I fell."

"And the split lip?"

"I told you I fell."

The muscle in Nate's jaw twitched. "I can have Dr. Clark come forward and testify about other times where you sustained injuries as well. Did you fall every one of those times?"

Mrs. Hanson glared at him. "All right. My husband drank sometimes, and when he was drunk, he hit me. But that didn't mean nothing. He wouldn't have really hurt me."

"So, was Mr. Hanson hitting you when Johnnie came to your rescue?"

"I told you. He fought with Johnnie that day 'cause he didn't do his chores. Johnnie would have never lifted a finger to help me."

Betsy looked at the jury. They believed her. It was obvious on their faces. Hanson might have been a drunk and a brute, but none of them believed a mother would turn against the son who'd saved her life.

Nate's voice wavered. "No further questions." He went back to his table and sat.

"The prosecution rests," Mr. Nelson said.

"Very well," said the judge. "Court dismissed until tomorrow at nine o'clock."

They rose as the judge left. Then the jury was dismissed, and Cage took Johnnie back to his cell.

Nate didn't move. Betsy sat beside him and held his hand.

"They're going to convict him." Nate stared at the floor. "Nobody will believe that a mother would lie about her son like that. Lie to protect him, yes, but not like that."

She didn't know what to say. It was hard to believe. "Are you sure she was lying?"

His gaze whipped to her. "Do you know what he was doing in that jail cell when I came in there? He was on his knees praying. He didn't know anyone was around, but he was praying for God to send someone to defend him."

"I'm sorry," Betsy said.

"Problem is God sent the wrong guy. I should have made Mrs. Hanson talk to me. I gave up too easily. If I'd known what she would say, I could have prepared the jury in my opening statement. Now, what do I do? They'll hang that boy, and it's my fault."

She didn't see the sense in arguing with him. He wouldn't listen to anything she had to say.

"I'm going for a walk," Nate said. "Maybe pray that God find some way to help Johnnie since I can't." He ambled out of the courtroom no longer trying to hide his limp.

Betsy didn't follow him. He needed to work this out on his own. She knew that. She went back to Lavena's. Her friend would help her pray.

As she got to Lavena's house, Cage walked in. "Where's Nate?"

Betsy shrugged. "I'm not sure. He went for a walk. He might have gone home."

He nodded and walked toward the livery.

When she entered the house, Lavena and the children all greeted her.

"How did it go?" Lavena asked.

"Not good," Betsy said. "Unless God does a miracle, Johnnie will be convicted of murder, and Nate blames himself."

Chapter Thirty-Three

Nate strode toward home, his feet making a crunching noise through the multi-colored leaves on the ground. He hadn't felt so worthless and unsure of himself since he'd given his heart to the Lord.

Johnnie was going to be convicted and hanged based on his own mother's testimony. That wasn't exactly true. If Nate had done his job properly and made sure he'd talked to the woman first, he might have had a chance to negate the testimony. Now, everyone he'd found to testify as a character witness didn't compare to Johnnie's own mother testifying against him.

Even if he called witnesses that verified the beatings, what good would it do? Mrs. Hanson admitted to them.

He got to the house, and even though it was chilly, he couldn't go it. He sat on the steps of the porch and remembered the bottle he'd stashed under the steps a long time ago. He'd forgotten it was even there.

He dug the bottle out of the dirt then sat back down and stared at the liquid inside.

Please, Lord, I've never wanted this whiskey more in my life. Help me not to go down that path again.

He didn't drink it, didn't dare open it, but he couldn't bring himself to pour it out. Once he caught a whiff of it, he wouldn't be able to resist. He didn't know how long he sat there, but his hands were beginning to burn from the cold despite the gloves he wore. He looked up, expecting God to do something.

He didn't expect what happened next. Cage rode his gray horse up the road and stopped in Nate's yard. He dismounted, wrapped the reigns around the porch rail, and sat on the steps beside him. "What do you plan to do with that?"

Nate handed it to his friend, knowing God had answered his prayer. But why did he have to send Cage in his moment of weakness? "I'd forgotten I'd hidden it away until today. Could you get rid of it for me?"

Cage started to open the bottle.

"Not now." Nate shrugged. "It's the first time since I've surrendered my life to God that I've been tempted like this." He hated to admit that, especially when Cage was the one man who hadn't been able to trust him. "If I smell it, I might not be able to resist."

"I'll pour it out later. Is there a reason we're having this conversation out here in the cold?"

Nate snorted. "I guess not. Come inside."

They walked into the house. Nate closed the door then placed some coal from the chute into the stove. Then he filled the percolator with water and coffee grounds and placed it on the stove to make some coffee.

He sat across from Cage at the table. He was glad to see his friend had left the bottle outside. Friend. Was he still his friend? Would he ever be his friend again? "You're an answer to prayer."

"How so?" Cage asked.

The sound of the water boiling and the smell of coffee almost made him forget about the whiskey. "I was so tempted to drink that bottle, and I prayed for God to do something to stop me. When you showed up, I knew that was the answer to my prayer." He let out a heavy sigh. "I suppose I've proven you right. I can't be trusted."

"We all have our temptations we battle." Cage pulled on his ear. "Mine was allowing unforgiveness to take hold of me."

A lump formed in Nate's throat. He wanted so much to settle things with his friend, but he couldn't allow himself to hope.

"A while ago, you said you were sorry," Cage said. "I've seen you meant it by your changed behavior and refused to acknowledge it." He cleared his throat. "The way you risked your reputation in front of the council to try to keep strong drink out of the town, then you risked your reputation as a lawyer to help a boy that couldn't possibly pay you, well, I'm ashamed of the way I acted toward you. You, of all people, know I have no call to judge anyone."

Nate nodded. When Cage set fire to a house to flush out enemy soldiers during the war, the fire got out of control. That was when he saw a woman and children screaming in the second story window. He ran into the house and tried to save him. That was how he got the burns on his face. But it was too late, and Nate saved him by pulling him out in time. Nate kept his secret until Cage was able to confess it to Lavena, his colonel, and his men.

"I forgive you," Cage said. "I'm sorry for the way I behaved toward you. Can you forgive me?"

"Thank you." Nate's voice thickened. "Of course I forgive you. You had every right to not believe me. I'd lied so many times before."

"Maybe at first, but this went on too long."

The coffee had stopped percolating, so Nate used that moment to pour them each a cup of coffee.

"Thanks." Cage took a sip. "This is good. Lavena won't allow coffee in the house. She insists I drink tea, and the coffee at work is so bad, I don't want it." He wrapped his hands around his cup.

They both took a sip of coffee and sat there, not saying anything for a long while.

Finally, Nate felt he had to break the silence. He needed Cage's wise council. "Unless I manage a miracle tomorrow, Johnnie is going to be convicted. They'll probably sentence him to hang. I never thought a mother would act that way toward her son. I don't know what to do."

"I don't either, but I know who does. Let's pray."

They both bowed their heads, and Cage led the prayer asking for a miracle and for wisdom for Nate. They prayed for a long time. Then Nate heard a voice in his spirit.

There were other witnesses.

When they were done, he told Cage how the Lord was directing him. "First, I'm going to the courthouse to get as many subpoenas as I can for the other witnesses to the crime."

"Other witnesses?"

"The children. The judge might not grant them for the younger children, but he can subpoena the ten-year-old twins and the twelve-year-old. After that, I'm going to the neighborhood to knock on doors. Maybe someone else saw something that will help."

"A good plan," Cage said. "But I wouldn't serve the subpoenas until tomorrow morning. You don't want Mrs. Hanson telling the children what to say."

Nate nodded. For the first time since Mrs. Hanson testified, he felt hopeful.

"I'm still wondering why the woman lied about her son."

"Who knows?" Nate drank the rest of his coffee. "It's been rumored that Nelson's bribed witnesses before. Maybe he paid her off. But for a mother to take a bribe to testify against her own son…"

"Would you like some help?" Cage asked.

"Could you serve the subpoenas before court in the morning? Oh, and get rid of that bottle."

~~~~~

Betsy sat at the breakfast table with Nate and the children the next morning. She hadn't talked to him the night before because he'd gotten home so late. She'd been worried about him. He'd been so discouraged when he left the courtroom that she was afraid he might go back to the whiskey bottle.

But this morning, she realized she had nothing to worry about. He sat at the table chattering with the children in a pleasant manner. He had that air of confidence back. She wondered what he had planned.

After breakfast, Nate turned to the children. "Your ma and I need to talk. Why don't you play upstairs until it's time to go to Aunt Lavena's?"

Malachi and Naomi went upstairs.

Nate turned toward her. "There's something I have to tell you, but I don't want to." His Adam's apple bulged.

Her stomach tightened, and the baby kicked. "Go ahead."

He held her hand and gazed into her eyes. "After the trial yesterday, I found a bottle I'd hidden months ago under the steps."

She pulled her hand away.

He gazed at her hand and continued. "After what happened in court, I was so tempted to drink it. I asked God to help me fight the temptation."

Her voice thickened. "And did He?"

"He sent Cage to our doorstep. Cage forgave me, and I asked him to get rid of the bottle. I didn't give in to the temptation, but I thought you should know."

She let out the breath she didn't realize she was holding. "Thank God." She couldn't have been prouder of her husband.

"I thought you might be angry," Nate said.

"That you were tempted? We're all tempted from time to time, but you didn't give in, and you had the courage to tell me." She reached her hand out for him to hold again.

Instead of taking her hand, he pulled her into an embrace and kissed her. "We'd better get going if we want to get to court in time."

After they hitched the wagon and headed to Lavena's, Betsy asked, "So if you weren't drinking, why were you out so late?"

"I was interviewing witnesses and doing a lot of investigating."

"And?" She asked.

"You'll find out." He smirked and gave her a kiss on the cheek.

Chapter Thirty-Four

After court began, the judge asked Nate to call his first witness.

"I call Joseph Hanson to the stand."

The jury gasped when a young boy with reddish brown hair took the oath and took his seat to the left of the judge.

Nate stood in front of him. "Could you state your name and age for the court and your relationship with the defendant?

"Joseph Hanson, age twelve. What's a defendant?"

The jury chuckled and murmured, and the judge pounded his gavel.

"The person on trial," Nate said.

"Oh, that's my brother, Johnnie."

"Could you tell us a little about Johnnie?"

"He's a hero in my book."

"How so?" Nate said.

"Well, he's always working odd jobs to earn money for us to buy groceries to eat. I offered to quit school to help, but Johnnie wouldn't hear of it. Pa never had any money. And whenever Pa got drunk and went after one of us, my big brother always got in the way. He's taken a lot of beatings in our place. And then there's what happened last week."

Nate paced toward the jury then back to make sure they were paying attention. They were. He could swear they were all holding their breaths.

"So, what happened last week?" he said.

Joseph closed his eyes for a moment. "Ma told Pa she was going to leave him. He started beating on her. Nothing unusual about that, but he was madder than I'd ever seen him. We all hid under the table 'cause we was scared. His eyes bulged out, and he was yelling that she wasn't ever going to leave him."

He looked toward his brother. "That's when Johnnie got home. He started toward them to try to help. Pa picked up a fireplace poker, and threatened to kill my ma with it, but Johnnie picked up a piece of firewood and hit him over the head. Pa fell on the floor and hit his head on the hearth. I know Johnnie didn't mean to kill him, but I ain't sorry he's dead, and that's the truth."

"No further questions." Nate walked back to his table and was seated.

Prosecutor Nelson stood and walked to Joseph. "You love your brother, don't you?"

"Sure do," Joseph said.

"Would you lie to protect him?"

"If I had to, but I'm not lying now."

The prosecutor smiled. "No further questions."

Nate glanced over at the jury. He hoped the boy's testimony helped, but the jury looked more confused than convinced. That would soon change.

Nate called Faylynn Hanson to the stand. The bailiff brought in a skinny young girl with bright red hair. Faylynn testified that she was ten years old and Johnnie's sister. She also considered her brother a hero for stopping her pa from killing her ma.

Faylynn's twin sister, Bridgette, who looked just like her sister, had a similar testimony as did Jeffrey and Thomas, two of Johnnie's younger brothers aged seven and nine. The prosecutor asked each one if they would lie for their brother, and each one said the same thing. They would lie, but they weren't lying now.

He glanced at the jury again. He wasn't sure they were convinced, but they soon would be. He called a number of character witnesses including Rev. Fowler and Mr. Baldwin, Johnnie's boss at the grocery store.

Nate looked at the clock. Almost noon. He needed to get his next witness in before court was adjourned, or she might not have as much impact.

Mr. Nelson stood. "Your honor, it's almost noon. I ask for a recess, so we can eat."

Nate approached the bench. "Your Honor, I believe I can finish with this witness before noon. If necessary, Mr. Nelson could cross-examine after the recess."

"Carry on," the judge said.

"I call Mrs. Brian Conner to the stand."

A plump woman at least in her fifties, with gray hair and spectacles, took the stand.

"State your name and how you know the defendant," Nate said.

"I'm Mrs. Nancy Conner, and I live next door to Johnnie. He's such a kind boy. He helps me with my groceries and mows my lawn every week. Hard working too. Not like his pa who's always drunk."

Jake Nelson rose. "I object. The victim is not on trial here."

Judge McCarthy nodded. "Sustained. The jury will ignore the statement that Doug Hanson was a drunk."

The jury giggled, and the judge banged his gavel.

"Mrs. Conner, when's the last time you saw Johnnie?"

"Well, I hate to admit it, but I'm a bit of a busybody. Mr. Conner is always on me about it. He says I should mind my own business. Well, I heard yelling next door, and I hurried to look inside their window in the back. I've done it before when I've heard Mr. Hanson yelling at his wife and kids, and they never saw me. I only peeked through their window because I was always worried that he'd kill his wife someday. Well, that day, he was worse than usual. Johnnie walked in the door, and Mr. Hanson picked up a fireplace poker. He said he was going to kill her."

"Did you see what happened next?" Nate asked.

"No, I didn't. I ran to get a deputy. I really thought he was going to murder her this time."

"No further questions." Nate gazed at the jury. They finally looked convinced. He took his seat.

Prosecutor Nelson let out a heavy sign. "No questions."

When the court came back into session, Nate felt he had made the case for defense of another, but he had one more witness to call that he hoped would leave no doubt. "Your honor, I would like to recall Mrs. Hanson to the stand."

"I object," Nelson said. "We've already heard from this witness."

"I don't know." Judge Murphy grinned in a way that didn't reach his eyes. "In the interest of justice, I'd like to hear from her again. Objection overruled. Mrs. Hanson, please take the stand."

The woman slowly moved to the chair and sat.

"You're still under oath to tell the truth," the judge said.

Nate gazed at the woman with what he hoped looked like compassion even thought that wasn't what he felt toward her. "Mrs. Hanson, hearing all the testimony today, some of it from your own children, would you like to change anything you said?"

Mrs. Hanson pressed her lips together and nodded.

"You must answer out loud."

She let out a sigh. "I lied before. My husband would have killed me if Johnnie hadn't hit him over the head. Johnnie has always been a good boy."

Nate paced to the jury to make sure they paid attention to the next question then walked back to her. "Why did you lie?"

Mrs. Hanson glowered at Jake Nelson and pointed. "He said he'd give me a hundred dollars if I lied. With my husband gone and Johnnie in jail, I had to do something. My children were hungry, and I didn't have any money for groceries or to pay rent for the house we're living in."

"Who gave you this money?"

"The prosecutor, Mr. Nelson. He said that if I didn't lie, he'd make sure Johnnie was hanged, but if I said what he wanted, he'd ask for a short time in jail because of Johnnie's age. I did what I did to protect my son from the hangman's noose."

Nate looked over at Nelson. He looked like he wanted to crawl under his chair. Paying witnesses for their testimony was legal, but encouraging them to perjure themselves was not, and getting a mother to lie about her son like that? Reprehensible. He glanced at the jury and saw disgust on their faces. Good. That meant a not guilty verdict for Johnnie.

With all the murmurs in the jury box and the people in the courtroom, Judge Murphy had to bang his gavel several times and shout orders before things calmed down. "Bailiff, take Mr. Nelson into custody. I intend to press charges for enticing a witness to perjury."

The bailiff walked over to where a very pale Nelson was sitting with his shoulder slumped and waited. The prosecutor stood and walked out of the courtroom. Nate couldn't help but notice that he looked like he was headed to the gallows where he wanted to send Johnnie.

After they left, Judge Murphy pounded his gavel to get everyone's attention again. "Mrs. Hanson, I'm not going to charge you with perjury because you were deceived into thinking you were helping your son, but I expect you to testify at Prosecutor Nelson's trial, and I expect you to tell the truth."

"Yes, your honor," Mrs. Hanson squeaked out.

The judge continued. "All charges are dropped. This case is dismissed. I'd like to thank the jury for your service. Court is adjourned." He left the courtroom.

Murmuring continued as people sauntered out of the courtroom. Nate almost wished Lavena was here. She would have loved to have written this story, but another reporter was assigned who he was sure would do just as good a job.

Johnnie looked stunned. He turned to Nate. "Does that mean I don't have to go to jail?"

"That's right." Nate put a hand on his shoulder. "The judge dismissed all charges against you."

"Thank you." Johnnie glanced over to where his mother was sitting. "I didn't want to kill Pa. I had no choice." He walked over to where she sat looking at the floor. "Let's go home, Ma."

She stood. "I'm so sorry." A tear ran down her cheek.

"I forgive you. You thought you were helping me." Johnnie held out his arm, and she took it. "Things are going to get better now. I can make enough to support us. You'll see."

She nodded, and they walked out of the courtroom.

~~~~~

Later that day, Nate, Betsy, Cage, and Lavena sat around Cage's table drinking Lavena's tea. She had made supper for all of them, and now the children were playing in Penelope's room.

Nate took a sip of tea. He couldn't help feeling grateful for what the

Lord had done in his life, and how He used him to help Johnnie.

"So, what are your plans now?" Cage asked.

He thought for a moment before answering, but he already knew where God was leading him. "I still have my law practice. I'm sure this case will get me plenty of paid work, but I'm still going to help those who can't pay. I do believe the Lord is leading me in another direction as well." He glanced at Betsy. "I wanted to talk to my wife about it first. Afterall, we are a team."

Betsy touched his cheek. "Thank you for that, but if the Lord is leading you, I'd like to hear now. I'll support you, and I know our friends will help if they can."

"Jake Nelson's position on the city council will probably be open now. If they have a special election for it, I'd like to run. If I were on the council, I could help make a difference in the lives of many families in this village who are being abused by their drunken husbands and fathers. There needs to be a law against it, and maybe with Betsy's help, we can get the council to see the wisdom in not allowing the sale of alcoholic beverages here."

His wife took hold of his hand. "I'll do all I can."

"So will I." Cage drank a sip of tea.

"That's not the only thing I want to do," Nate said. "Child labor laws need to be passed. Children shouldn't be working in those dangerous factories before the age of twelve. They should be in school. And we still need the vote for women."

Cage chuckled. "Now you're sounding like Lavena."

The rest of them laughed.

Nate's face flushed. He didn't need to make his first campaign speech here in his friends' kitchen.

"With my help as a reporter and your campaign manager," Lavena said, "you'll win in a landslide."

Everybody laughed at that one. Imagine, a woman campaign manager. Nate glanced at Lavena. Why not? A few years ago, nobody would have thought a woman could be a news reporter.

"So, are we invited for Thanksgiving?" Cage asked.

"Absolutely," Betsy said. "But you know you don't need to wait for an invitation. You're always welcome."

Nate gazed at each of them, and his heart felt full enough to explode. Not only had God restored him and was using him to do his part to change the world, He'd restored Nate's relationship with his family and friends.

Epilogue

Betsy had finished nursing Baby Simeon when there was a knock on the door. Nate answered it, and she was pleased to see Cage, Lavena, and Penelope walk in.

"We came with some news," Lavena said.

Betsy laughed. "I thought you wanted to see the baby again."

"That too," Lavena said. "But the count has been tallied, and we have a new councilman."

Nate crossed his arms. "I'm assuming it's good news since you're so cheerful."

Cage shook his hand. "Congratulations, Councilman Teagan. I hope this means my job is secure."

Nate laughed.

"That isn't the only news." Cage grabbed hold of his ear. "Lavena's with child."

Betsy squealed and hugged her.

Nate shook Cage's hand. "Congratulations."

"The doctor says there's no reason this pregnancy can't bring forth a healthy baby, especially since she's in her fourth month."

Lavena turned to Betsy. "Could we talk, alone?"

A knot formed in her stomach. "Of course." She handed the baby to Nate. "Let's go to the bedroom."

As soon as they got there and closed the door, she turned to Lavena. "What's wrong? Are you worried about the pregnancy?"

"No, silly." Lavena chuckled and pulled a letter from her satchel. "I received a letter from America addressed to both of us. I just thought we might want to read it together, away from the others."

America Woods was a roommate of Betsy and Lavena's when they attended Oberlin College before the war, only she was America Leighton then. The three of them formed a bond that could never be broken even though each of them was so different than the others. A couple of students joked and penned the three of them with the nickname the ladies of Oberlin. Right after graduation, America married another Oberlin graduate, William Woods, and they traveled to China as missionaries. Betsy and Lavena hadn't seen her since, but they received letters once or twice a year.

Betsy opened the letter and read aloud as Lavena read over her shoulder.

> Dear Lavena and Betsy,
>
> I received your last letter, and I'm so happy that Nate is doing so well now. We have been praying for him. By now, the new baby has arrived. I've been praying for a healthy, happy little one. When I was praying, I believe God told me it's a boy this time. You'll have to write and tell me if I'm correct.
>
> I am expecting again. This makes eight children since we've made China our home. The children love to share the Gospel with the other children in the community and speak Chinese better than they speak English.
>
> The mission church has grown so large that we've had to hold Sunday services in the field next to the church until a new, larger one is built.
>
> I love you both, and I can't believe how far the Lord has brought us in His service. But why should we be surprised? We are the Ladies of Oberlin.

The End

About the Author

Tamera Lynn Kraft has always loved adventures. She loves to write historical fiction set in the United States because there are so many stories in American history. There are strong elements of faith, romance, suspense and adventure in her stories. She has received 2nd place in the NOCW contest, 3rd place TARA writer's contest, and is a finalist in the Frasier Writing Contest.

Tamera has been married for more than forty years to the love of her life, Rick, and has two married adult children and six grandchildren. She has been a children's pastor for over twenty years. She is the leader of a ministry called Revival Fire for Kids where she mentors other children's leaders, teaches workshops, and is a children's ministry consultant and children's evangelist and has written children's church curriculum. She is a recipient of the 2007 National Children's Leaders Association Shepherd's Cup for lifetime achievement in children's ministry.

You can contact Tamera online at her website: <http://tameralynnkraft.net>

THANK YOU!

Thank you for reading this book from Mt. Zion Ridge Press.

If you enjoyed the experience, learned something, gained a new perspective, or made new friends through story, could you do us a favor and write a review on Goodreads or wherever you bought the book?

Thanks! We and our authors appreciate it.

We invite you to visit our website, *MtZionRidgePress.com*, and explore other titles in fiction and non-fiction. We always have something coming up that's new and off the beaten path.

And please check out our podcast, **Books on the Ridge**, where we chat with our authors and give them a chance to share what was in their hearts while they wrote their book, as well as fun anecdotes and glimpses into their lives and experiences and the writing process. And we always discuss a very important topic: *Tea!*

You can listen to the podcast on our website or find it at most of the usual places where podcasts are available online. Please subscribe so you don't miss a single episode!

Thanks for reading. We hope you come back soon!